WHERE DRAGONWOOFS SLEEP AND THE FADING CREEPS

A.J. Massey

For Katie

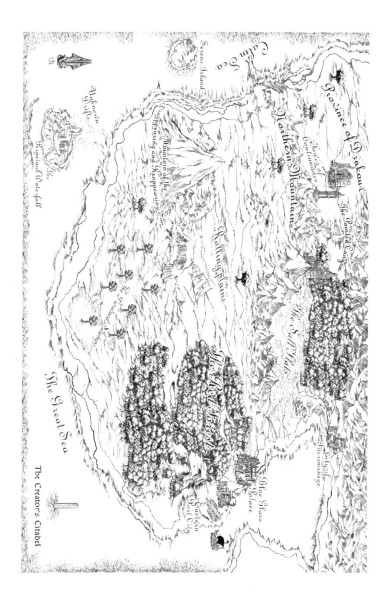

The Creator's Citadel

CHAPTER 1

The Red Forest

The snow beneath Ben's bare feet grew warmer with each step. He had never experienced snow before in his life, but from what little he knew of it, it was supposed to be cold and wet. Yet here he was, walking on snow that was as warm as a freshly baked pastry.

The black forest surrounded him, the trees grasping for the blood-red sky with gangling outstretched fingers. He could not recall where he was prior to entering these woods. In fact, the more he struggled to remember, the more he forgot.

Ben looked down to find that he was wearing matching white pajamas. A loud ticking sound came from his wrist. He pulled up the sleeve, revealing an antique metal watch with a tattered white face. But the watch was broken and the hands were stuck at midnight. Had he imagined the ticking? More importantly, why was he wearing a broken watch? Thoughts like this only caused his head to ache, so Ben turned around in hopes of leaving the forest the same way he had come, but it seemed that the trees had closed in behind him, obscuring both his entrance and exit.

Absent were the sounds of chirping birds or the scuffles of wildlife—instead, only a shrill hum that seemed to come from within the trees.

"Is anyone here?" Ben asked. "Anyone at all?"

There was no answer. Indeed, the silence would have been deafening if not for the persistent humming. But the more Ben tried to pinpoint the noise, the more it seemed to be coming from inside his head.

Ben continued walking before tripping and tumbling down a small, snow-dappled slope. He quickly stood and looked around to see if anyone had witnessed his fall. But there was still no one.

It was dark. Ben peered beyond the treetops, looking for some light—any light—from the glowing red sky. It seemed that the sprawling black branches had already grappled with the sky and won. Now only small slivers of red light seeped through, a sparkle here or a shimmer there.

Ahead, a small light glimmered faintly. The ball of white flickered as it moved between the trees from left to right.

"Hello?" Ben called out.

The orb danced playfully in and out of the trees. Ben ran toward it, but it managed to stay one step ahead of him. When it seemed like he would never catch up, it stopped moving, leading him to a small clearing in the middle of the woods.

Between the soft hues of green grass and the scarce dapples of white snow, a smattering of flowers grew in a kaleidoscope of yellows, blues, reds, purples, and oranges. It was well lit, almost as if the flowers were glowing themselves. Ben was extra careful to not step on any of them as he entered. Almost immediately, he noticed that the air here was much colder than that of the surrounding forest. In fact, it was freezing, and soon the hairs on his skinny arms and legs prickled beneath his loose pajamas.

Ben stepped deeper into the glade. Beyond the frost-covered grass, the plants, and the flowers, a hooded figure in a thick red wool cloak stooped down in the opposite end. A weird device protruded from the opening of the hood—a thin golden rod, curving upward then downward, ending with a small glowing bulb that hung freely from a squeaky metal swivel.

Was this the source of the moving light from before?

He approached the figure hesitantly.

"Hello," Ben said. "I seem to be lost."

The figure, however, remained silent. A small hand covered in a white glove emerged from the sleeve of its cloak.

"Can you help me?" Ben asked. "I'm just trying to figure out how to get home."

But the figure perpetuated the silence a moment longer before turning toward Ben and pressing a small gloved finger toward the dark opening of the hood.

"Shhh," it said.

Ben captured a brief glimpse of a face peering back at him with narrow blue eyes framed by long lashes. A girl! Unperturbed by Ben's presence, she turned her gaze back toward the ground, her fingers gently grasping the stem of a small blue flower with frosted white tips. She carefully plucked it from the ground, roots and all, and took a small glass jar with a tarnished copper lid from her pocket. She gingerly placed the flower into the jar and sealed it. The jar glowed softly with a blue pulsing light as she placed it into a red satin satchel that contained other jars of similar luminosity. Then she sealed the pouch with its intricate metallic clasp.

"That'll do nicely," she said, frost enveloping each word.

Ben cleared his throat.

The girl stood slowly, staring at him from the dark depths of her hood. Ben stared back, but he could no longer see her face.

She pulled her hood back, revealing long, shimmering black hair. Her face and high cheekbones were accentuated by soft, pale skin and dark shadows around her brilliant blue eyes.

She was beautiful.

The girl appeared to be roughly his age, give or take a year. Her eyes were cold and penetrating, but alluring; it felt as if her deep gaze was crawling under his skin. The glowing apparatus was attached to her head by a thin copper headband imprinted with intricate silver designs interlaced with green gems.

She removed the device and held it. The light emanated softly from the globe, casting shadows around them. Silence. Then, "If the weed wishes to speak, he may do so now."

"Who are you?" he asked. "What's your name?"

Her lips curled in disgust. "My name? You wish to know my *name*?"

Ben flinched.

"I find it quite presumptuous that you would ask me such a personal question, considering we have only just met," she said. "Who asks such a thing?"

Ben stared at her slack-jawed, his locks of brown hair partially covering his green eyes. "I . . . I just asked your name. You know, out of politeness."

"If you were attempting to be polite, you wouldn't ask such a thing." She flipped her long, shiny black hair behind her shoulders.

"But it's just a name."

"A name is never 'just a name,'" she said. "A name carries stories of conquest and stories of rebellion. A name contains untold tales of love and loss, prosperity and defeat. A name harbors legacy. These are not things you would simply share with a complete stranger, would you?"

Ben frowned, his gaze darting everywhere as he tried to avoid eye contact. "I guess not. I'm sorry I asked."

"As you should be."

Ben scrunched his brow. "Can you at least tell me where I am?"

The girl scoffed. "Mayhap it's my turn to ask a question. Communication, by its very definition, requires the exchange of words between more than one person, does it not?"

"I—"

"What are you doing here in my grove?"

"Your grove?"

"Are you normally this obtuse? Do you answer every question with another question?"

"What? I don't think so."

"Then you are being combative?"

Ben sighed. "Not at all. I'm not—"

The girl circled Ben, her boots leaving deep imprints in the snow. "Let's look at this from my point of view, shall we? You haven't provided an appropriate answer to any question I have asked. How would you describe that behavior, other than combative or obtuse?"

"I just want to find out where I am," Ben said.

She paused for a moment, biting her lower lip. "You're rather young to be lurking around all by yourself. That much we can agree on."

Ben laughed. "We look the same age. I'm probably older than you, if anything."

Her eyes narrowed. "You're older than thirteen?"

"I . . ." Ben tried to remember his age, but it made his head ache.

She cleared her throat. "Whatever. You're in the forest alone, you're wearing children's pajamas, and you appear to be unarmed. These facts raise more questions than answers."

Then she gasped. "Are you an assassin of the Drakour?"

Ben peered at her, dumbfounded. Meanwhile, her fingers slid toward the front pocket of her red cloak, where Ben witnessed a quick flash of steel.

"You must answer, if you are indeed an assassin of Drakour," she said. "It's the rule."

"I don't know what you're talking about."

"So, you're not?"

"No. I don't even know what that is."

"Good," she said. "Then we can continue to converse like civilized beings." Her hand slid away from the front pocket of her cloak and toward her satchel. Light poured out as she opened the flap. "This grove traps the chill just right. As you know, the prettiest flowers grow in the cold. I collect them. That is what I am doing here. Not that you bothered to ask."

She produced a small jar containing a glowing yellow flower with pulsing blue veins. "There aren't many of these left."

Ben peered inside the jar. "What are they?"

"They are all that is beautiful in the world. All that remains, anyway. Naturally, I am here to save them."

"Save them from what?"

"The Fading." She yanked the jar away from Ben's view, placing it back into her satchel.

"The Fading?" Ben asked. "What's that?"

"Can you not see it happening everywhere around us?"

Ben spun around in a circle. "See what?"

She sighed. "The Fading. We were just talking about it not one moment ago. We have not changed subjects as far as I am aware. You should learn to pay better attention to those you converse with, especially while you are here."

Ben looked up at the red sky before resting his gaze on the girl. "Yes, but where is *here*?"

As Ben asked the question, two tall, hooded figures in heavy red cloaks entered the clearing, mounted on large black stallions.

The muscular horses were almost indistinguishable from one another with coarse, dark manes that had been combed to perfection. Yet, it was the riderless white stallion between them, with his flowing silver mane and feathered legs, that caught Ben's attention. The white stallion sported long, muscular legs with pronounced veins that pressed against his skin. Ben watched in silence as the horse snorted gently, looking suspiciously in his direction. It wore a lead made of white leather and silver studs.

The hooded figures dismounted the black stallions, bowing their heads toward the girl.

"It's time for me to go," she said. "The time is past for playing questions and answers." She plopped her satchel onto the ground and began rummaging through it. "Here." she produced a small glass jar. In it, a blue flower with a black stem glowed softly. "I found two of these. Consider this one a gift."

Ben hesitated.

"Go on, take it." She smiled as she placed the jar into Ben's hands, closing his fingers over it with her gloved fingertips. "Best of luck to you, weed. Perhaps when we meet again, you will be more adept at conversation."

She clasped her satchel shut and raced toward the white stallion, mounting it in one graceful leap.

The two other figures followed silently as she trotted into the darkness of the forest. All Ben could do was watch as they disappeared.

"I'm also thirteen!" Ben's voice trailed off as he realized she couldn't hear him. "I just remembered."

He stuffed the jar into his front pajama pocket, creating a ridiculous bulge.

The humming of the forest resumed.

"This weed is lucky she didn't see the trinket," a child-like voice said from behind him.

Ben spun around, but there wasn't anyone there.

"This weed was smart to hide the trinket from her," the same voice said. Again, it came from behind him. He spun around once more, but still didn't see anyone.

"This weed would do best to find shelter before the snow falls."

A single white snowflake fell from the red heavens, dancing back and forth through the air before careening to the snowy ground. Another snowflake fell. Then another. Before long, Ben was surrounded by falling snow on all sides. He stared up at the sky and saw a rather large snowflake make a beeline straight toward his face. He shut his eyes.

Hiiiiiisssssssssss.

The snowflake burned Ben as if his skin had been splattered with boiling oil. "Ouch!"

"What did this weed expect from the snow?" the voice asked.

The flaming-hot snowflakes careened toward him in greater numbers. Ben tried to take refuge underneath a tree with thick, sprawling branches, but the snow seemed determined to find its way through to burn his hands, neck, and feet.

"This weed would do best to seek shelter immediately," a tiny faerie said as she buzzed by Ben's face.

Standing at no more than six inches high, the faerie wore a small dress reinforced at the hem with knotted twigs and straw. For a brief moment, the faerie stopped and hovered in front of Ben's face like a deranged hummingbird; her eyes glowing faintly turquoise. Ben realized the hum of the faerie was identical to the hum of the trees in the forest.

"Most avoid the burning snow," the faerie said, "but this weed seems captivated by it."

"Snow isn't supposed to burn, it's supposed to be cold!"

She laughed. "Cold snow? How absurd. It would no longer be snow if this were true."

Ben cowered beneath the branches of the tree, attempting to pull the sleeves of his pajamas over his hands to shield them from the snow. Unfortunately, when he did this, the pajamas rose from where his shirt met his pants, exposing his lower back.

"This weed defies logic by refusing to seek shelter," the faerie said.

"We're outside, how do you expect me to find shelter?" Ben asked.

"This weed need only ask the question."

"I just did, didn't I?"

"No." She buzzed in front of his face, just out of reach. "This weed asked how we would expect him to find shelter. This weed has not asked *where* the shelter is."

Snow landed on Ben's bare skin with a sharp hiss and an even sharper sting. Annoyed, Ben yanked the shirt back down, revealing his hands again. It was not long before Ben found himself trapped in a seesaw of frustration as he pulled the pajamas back and forth between his hands and torso in a futile effort to escape the snow's burn.

Attempting to dodge snowflakes, Ben ran underneath the branches of an even larger tree. "Okay, where is the shelter?"

The faerie sighed. "The shelter is where it last was. This weed does not ask the appropriate questions."

"What is the appropriate question?"

The faerie flew two laps around Ben before speaking. "Pertaining to what?"

Ben threw his arms in the air. "The shelter!"

"That is not a question," she said as she flew behind him. "This weed is not very good at this."

"Okay then, where is this shelter?" Ben asked.

"The shelter is where it last was."

"You're impossible," Ben said.

The faerie crossed her arms, snorting. "Perhaps this weed is impossible."

Another snowflake landed on Ben's neck. He yelped and jumped into the air. "I'm the one being impossible?"

"Yes," the faerie said. "This weed refuses to ask the right questions in order to receive the right answers."

Ben sighed. "What is the right question to receive the right answer?"

"Pertaining to what?"

Ben growled before speaking slowly and deliberately. "What is the right question to receive the right answer to find the shelter?"

The faerie spun in the air. "Ah, of course, the right question to receive the right answer to find the shelter would be for this weed to ask if it can follow us to the shelter."

"Can I follow you to the shelter?"

The faerie flew away from Ben and deeper into the forest. "Yes, why did this weed not ask us this before?"

Ben followed.

"Come." Her voice emanated from the darkness. "This weed would do best to see with its ears and listen with its eyes if it wishes to survive."

CHAPTER 2

Guest of Honor at the Boiling Pot Swamp

Deeper into the dark forest he traveled. The faerie whisked by an inch in front of Ben's face, and the draft from her wings made his nose itch. "This weed must follow us to the shelter," she said.

"Yes, this weed must follow," she repeated as she whipped past him, coming from the same direction as before.

There were two of them. They left two distinct trails of sparkling dust as they swooped over and under each mangled tree limb. He peered high above in hopes of seeing some remnant of light from the red sky, but it was hidden behind a rat's nest of tightly intertwined vines and leaves. Even still, the snow made its way through, stinging him. He pushed forward, ducking beneath the wet shrubbery in an attempt to dodge sharp thorns and branches.

The air smelled of wet socks. Warm, murky water pooled on the ground, and before long, the legs of his pajamas were sopping wet.

"We are close," the first faerie said.

"Yes, so close," the second faerie said.

It was difficult to tell them apart because their voices were indistinguishable. Their faces also looked identical.

His pajama pants caught on the root of a tree and Ben fell forward, landing face-first in a black puddle that smelled of rotting milk. He emerged soaked, with both his knees and ankles skinned, bleeding, and itching. The humming of the trees grew louder until the sound rose to a high-pitched frenzy. Ben staggered, moments away from collapsing.

"We are here!" the first faerie said.

The second faerie performed two flips. "Yes, we are here!"

Ben pushed through the branches and fell into a clearing, landing on all fours. The two faeries hovered overhead, waiting patiently.

The first faerie's eyes gleamed with satisfaction "The shelter is this way."

"Yes, this way," the second faerie said.

Ben propped himself up on one knee, scanning his surroundings. The clearing was small in size, covered in flat, ashy mud and surrounded by a fence of gnarled trees. The clear, red sky loomed overhead.

"It's not snowing anymore!" He rubbed the red marks on his hands in relief.

The first faerie flickered a glance at the second faerie and cleared her throat. "Yes, it is not snowing at present, but this weed must make haste to the shelter for snow will return most definitely."

"Yes, most definitely," the second faerie said.

"I am done walking through forests and swamps and bushes," Ben said.

"There is no need to walk through forests, swamps, or bushes," the first faerie said. "For we are already where we need to be."

The second faerie grinned. "Yes, where we need to be."

The faeries raced toward the other edge of the clearing, lighting it up with two trails of dust. Ben caught a glimpse of a small recess in the tree line. He barely made out the outline of a lazily placed plank of rotted wood, low to the ground, which acted as a makeshift roof. "I came all this way for this? This is the shelter?"

"Yes," the first faerie said. "This shelter will keep this weed safe from the snow."

"Yes, safe from the snow." The second faerie said.

Ben peered at the shelter doubtfully.

The first faerie glanced at the other, irritated, before turning back to Ben with a smile filled with jagged teeth. "This weed must enter the shelter. The snow will fall again any moment now." She hovered just out of arm's reach, bobbing up and down gently. Her round cheeks glowed orange under the red light of the sky. Her tiny, reedy fingers fidgeted with the twine that hung from her dress.

Ben floundered toward the shelter, his legs aching. The entrance was so low to the ground that he had to crouch on all fours to peer inside. Even then, he could not see anything. A dull hum emanated from within as a warm breeze pushed toward him from beyond the darkness.

"It's too dark to see anything!" he said.

"This weed must hurry!" the first faerie said.

"Yes, must hurry," the second faerie said.

Ben peered at the sky overhead. There was not a single snowflake in sight. "Are you sure the snow will come back?"

The first faerie's eyes narrowed. "Sure as a snake eats the meer-rabbit's eggs."

"Yes, egggsss," the second faerie said.

Ben took a long, deep breath and crawled into the entrance of the hole, mud and grime caking his clothing. As he moved through the darkness, he began to feel moist strands of rope beneath his hands and his knees, woven symmetrically into checkerboard squares about six inches long by six inches wide. He also found an assortment of loose, hard objects in many shapes and sizes: some short, some fat, and some jagged; some long, some skinny, and some smooth. They reminded him of large seashells.

He remembered the flower in the jar that the girl had given him earlier in the night. Clumsily, he pulled it from his pajama pocket, illuminating the interior of the shelter.

The hard objects were bones. Human bones. A pelvis. A leg. An arm. A skull. Fingers. They rested on top of a thick tattered net that sprawled the ground and ran up the sides of the walls like vines. Ben held his breath, cold sweat seeping through his pores. He had just crawled into a trap.

He scrambled to the exit, but it was too late. There was the deafening crack of snapping wood, and then he was airborne, trapped in the net. The dark tree trunks rushed below him as he catapulted toward the sky; there was another loud pop and he plummeted back down toward the ground.

For a brief moment, Ben was weightless inside the net, the bones floating and spinning in the air in front of his face. There was another snap and everything in the net slammed upward, then tumbled back downward before coming to a crashing halt.

It was quiet, now. The wind blew peacefully, swaying the net back and forth. A long, aching creak came from the rope above. He faced the ground, his arms and legs dangling though the holes in the net, staring at the darkness below him. He shifted his legs in an effort to free himself, but instead kicked a leg bone through one of the holes. The bone landed with a splash.

He was suspended over a body of water. A swamp.

Curiously, the swamp water rolled over itself, almost like waves in an ocean—except these waves lacked the grace and rhythm of the sea. Instead, the water swirled and bubbled at random, almost as if it there were a raging storm below. But there was no storm. The air around Ben was as calm now as it had been when he entered the shelter. Heat and steam rose from the water. He realized in horror that the swamp was boiling.

Ben pulled his arms and legs back inside the net. As he did, the jar containing the flower rolled. Ben reached out to catch it, but it was too late. The jar slipped through one of the holes, disappearing into the swamp.

The thick branch above him groaned from the weight of the net. Across from him was a tall tree with an assortment of broken branches. That tree, with its curved trunk and long, malleable branches, had been used as the catapult that sent the net flying in the first place.

The first faerie whisked by. "This weed finds itself in quite the predicament."

The second faerie followed. "Yes, quite a predicament"

Ben propped his back against the net, sitting up.

"This weed will give us the trinket," the first faerie said.

"Yes, the trinket," the second faerie said.

The faeries stared at his watch pointedly. Ben ran his fingers along the edges, feeling a strong pull to the watch. He thought about giving it to the faeries—after all, he could easily pass it to them through the net. But the more he thought about handing it over, the more his head hurt. Then the reality of his situation hit him, and he realized that the alternative to giving up the watch was slowly boiling to death in a swamp. "It's a deal," he said. "Just promise you'll let me go first."

"This weed must give us the trinket, and then we will let it go," the first faerie said.

"Yes, the trinket first," the second faerie said.

Ben stared at the boiling water below and sighed. He turned over his wrist to unbuckle the clasp on the watch—but there was no clasp to be found. Instead, the solid metal band wrapped completely around his wrist with no latches, buckles, or openings to speak of. He tugged on the band and even attempted to pull it over his wrist, but the watch was too tight and would not budge. "It won't come off!"

The first faerie peered at Ben. "The trinket commands a hefty reward from the Sovereign. Perhaps this weed hopes to keep it for himself?"

The second faerie frowned. "Yes, keep it for himself!"

"I just want to get out of here, I swear!" Ben held up his wrist. "Look, it won't come off!" He tugged at the wristband, but it would not move.

"It is of no consequence to us," the first faerie said. "We will simply remove the trinket after the feast!"

The second faerie grinned. "Yes, after the feast."

"What are you talking about?" Ben asked. "What feast?"

"This weed does not know of the feast," the first faerie said. "This weed does not know it is the guest of honor!"

"Yes, the guest of honor!" The second faerie licked her lips with her forked green tongue.

"This is crazy!" Ben said. "You aren't going to eat me, are you?"

"Of course not," the first faerie said. "We would never eat this weed raw. We will cook this weed first."

"Yes, we will cook it first!"

"Cook me?" Ben asked. "How—?"

He already knew the answer.

The first faerie flew along the rope that ran from the top of the net and around the bough of the tree. Her glimmering dust stung Ben's eyes as he looked up at her, his heart thudding in his chest. She dove straight toward the ground, following the rope, where the other end connected to a makeshift wheel and crank mounted to the base of a tree.

"This weed is scrawny," the first faerie said. "This weed will cook quickly!"

The second faerie hovered outside the net a foot away from Ben's face. "Yes, so quickly!" She tapped each of her pointed teeth with the tip of her tongue.

"Get down here and help me turn this," the first faerie said.

"Yes, help turn this." The second faerie swooped down toward the crank, dust trailing behind her.

The first faerie sang a tune as the second faerie hummed along, "Into the Boiling Pot Swamp this weed will go, this weed will go, this weed will go to cook for our grumbling tummies!"

With their combined might, the faeries turned the handle of the crank in a circular motion, feeding slack into the rope around the bough and toward the net, causing it to descend slowly toward the swamp.

"Why are you doing this?" Ben asked.

He tried to pry the net apart, but it was too thick. His gaze darted toward the top, looking for an opening, but the holes were too small for him to squeeze through. He grabbed the loose pelvis bone and attempted to saw though the side of the net, but the fibers were too strong.

The net descended toward the swamp, the water below rumbling louder and louder as the heat became hotter and hotter. Frustrated, he grabbed an arm bone from inside the net and attempted to throw it at the faeries, missing them completely. The faeries kept pushing and pulling the crank, lowering the net further, until it was only three feet above the water.

"Weeds are so gullible," the first faerie said.

The second faerie smirked. "Yes, so—"

An object pierced her chest, launching her backward, pinning her to a tree. She gasped as green blood ran from her lips. A wooden arrow, twice her length, protruded from her body.

"No!" The first faerie flew toward her companion.

Another arrow screamed past, narrowly missing her.

Panicked, the faerie scanned the forest. Another arrow whipped by, this time so close it cut the side of her face. The faerie screeched, launching herself toward the treetops. Another arrow followed her from below. Soon, both arrow and skewered faerie fell to the mud with a thud.

"Despicable faeries," a voice said from beyond the perimeter.

"You owe me five coins," another voice replied, raspier than the first.

"The hell I do. It took you three arrows to take it down!"

"It was four arrows and there were two of them. Two arrows each. Five coins."

The first voice grumbled. "You'd be lucky to get three coins for that display."

"Three coins it is."

A person emerged from the woods and made a beeline to the faerie on the ground. "I bet her name was Mathilda. These faeries are always named Mathilda."

Ben shifted inside the net to get a better look. From this distance, he could see that the person was short and thin, and his ears were long and pointed. "An elf," Ben whispered.

The elf had white hair that had been pulled tight into a topknot. He wore a tunic made of animal skins stained with dark dye, and he carried a quiver slung on his back containing arrows fletched with colorful feathers. He wore leggings, thick leather boots, and an expertly crafted leather belt hung loosely around his waist, with a dagger, a pouch, and a few other instruments secured to it with oiled twine.

"What they lack in originality, they make up for in vileness," a second elf said as he emerged from the forest into the clearing. His voice was much raspier than the first. He wore similar clothes, except his hair was long, straight down the sides of his face.

As they neared him, Ben realized he could see muscles and blood moving underneath their skin. They were translucent.

Both elves peered into the net as Ben struggled.

"What about the weed?" The long-haired elf asked.

"Must truly be a genius to fall for the oldest faerie trick in the book," the topknot elf said.

"Yeah. A real ballista scientist."

"I say we cut him down, drop him in the swamp, and be done with it."

"You won't hear any argument here."

The elf with the long hair freed a dagger from his belt and walked toward the rope tied to the wheel and crank. "Off you go then, weed."

Ben clambered up the side of the net "Wait, let's talk about this first!"

"The decision has been made." The long-haired elf placed the sharp side of the blade against the rope. "Better luck next time."

"Stop!" a voice said from the edge of the clearing. Ben watched as a boy around his age came out of the trees. He was almost the same height as the elves, but definitely not as thin. He wore similar clothing and gear around his plump body. Unlike the elves, his ears and eyes were rounded; his hair dark, short, and curly, and his skin was black. "Look," the boy said, pointing toward Ben. "He has the trinket. He's the one the elders told us to look out for."

The long-haired elf peered hard at Ben. "Impossible. This weed is too stupid."

The boy looked up at Ben. "Hey weed! Is it true that your trinket makes you immune to the Fading?"

Ben stared at the watch around his wrist and shrugged.

"Help him down, Tam," the boy said to the long-haired elf. "And I don't mean into the boiling swamp, either."

"What for?" Tam asked in his raspy voice. "He's just another useless weed!"

The boy grimaced. "Another useless weed? How many useless weeds do you know?"

"I did not mean you, Marcus."

Marcus shifted his attention from Tam toward the elf with the topknot. "Char, help your brother free the weed."

"Of course." Char climbed the trunk of the tree with his bare hands.

Tam didn't budge. "Since when are you in charge? Last I checked, weeds do not give orders to survivors of the Elven Genocide."

Marcus leaned in toward Tam. "I'm in charge because the elders put me in charge of saving our forest from the Fading. Remember?"

Tam's eyes narrowed. "I remember."

"Good."

"We have a long journey," Tam said. "He will just slow us down!"

"He won't slow us down, Marcus said. "In fact, he's going to help us."

"What if he doesn't want to?"

Marcus shifted his attention toward Ben. "Weed!"

Ben pointed at his own chest. "Me?"

"My name is Marcus. These are my colleagues, Tamerlane and Charlemagne. We will get you out of that net on one condition."

Ben stared at the boy, waiting.

Marcus stared back. "Imagine you're walking through the forest. You pass by the birds. You pass by the trees. You even pass by a small brook. But when you turn around, you find that the same birds, the same trees, and the same brook have all vanished. *What once was never was.* That is the mantra of the Fading. Everything and everyone it touches no longer exists. Worse than that, they'll never have existed at all. The Fading will consume the land and everything in it. It has already destroyed parts of the forest, our homes. It grows as we speak and we need you and your trinket if we're going to stop it. Will you help us?"

CHAPTER 3

The Yellow Mailbox

B en awoke in a cold sweat, his alarm clock beeping on the bedside table. He slammed it with his open hand, silencing it. For a very brief moment, he didn't know where he was. It felt like he had awoken from a dream, but he couldn't remember any of it. Fortunately, it didn't take long before he recognized his surroundings: an old wooden bed frame, a cheap particle wood dresser, a cluttered desk, and a closet with a sliding door that doubled as a mirror.

Was it morning already?

He couldn't tell thanks to the thick curtains that masked his tiny window. The deep chill in the room suggested that he had woken up before the sunrise again. Fortunately, he was wearing his favorite matching pajamas, which kept him relatively warm.

He checked his wrist. For some reason, he thought he had lost his watch somehow, but there it was, right where he'd left it. Although the watch was broken—and the hands were stuck on midnight—it was the last thing his father had given him. Ben had promised himself he would never lose it.

He checked the foot of his bed and found his nine-year-old cat, Finny, curled up on the blankets and snoring lightly.

Ben burrowed in the warmth of his blankets. He wished Mom would turn on the heat in the mornings. It would have made his transition from the bed to the cold floor a whole lot easier, but she couldn't afford the high electricity bills.

If it were up to Ben, he would stay in bed under the warm covers right next to his warm cat. But it was a school day. The thought crept down his spine like ice-cold water, and after a few more minutes he crawled out of bed and got dressed.

As he neared the kitchen, he heard the familiar sounds of a spoon scratching the edges of a half-empty coffee mug. His mom wore faded purple scrubs and sat at the metal circular table with the puke-green surface, reading the paper, her brown hair tied back in a limp ponytail. A box of cereal and a quart of milk sat next to an empty plastic bowl near Ben's chair.

"Mom, you're home," Ben said.

"Not for long," she said. "Ellen's sick so I'm covering her rounds in the ward today. There's no one else who can do it so—"

"Didn't you work all night?"

"Better notify the Department of Labor. Or, better yet, notify the press. They've been waiting for a breakthrough story like this."

"Har har Mom, you're so funny." Ben filled the plastic bowl full of cereal.

"Speaking of the coma ward," Mom said. "There's a kid in there. I think he went to your school. Jason something. Did you know him?"

"No." Ben poured milk into the bowl.

"I guess you wouldn't, huh?"

Ben stirred his cereal. "If we stopped changing schools every five seconds, maybe I'd get to know more people."

"It's been six months since the last time, Benjamin."

"Can you drive me to school?" Ben asked through a mouthful of cereal.

"I can't. I have to make a stop on the way in—utilities are past due. What's wrong with the bus?"

"Nothing, it`s just a long walk to the bus stop.

"Then you'd better do less talking and more walking. You don't want to be late."

"I'm never late. I just thought I could get a ride, for once."

"When you're a millionaire, you can hire a chauffeur. For now, you have to make do like the rest of us."

Finny meowed loudly and paced in front of the cupboards.

"Feed the cat before you go," she said.

A cockroach scurried out into the crevice between the cupboard and the wall when Ben opened the door containing Finny's treats.

"I have to run now," Mom said as she rushed toward the door. "Remember that I love you, okay?"

"I know, Mom. It's impossible to forget when you always remind me."

Mom smiled, then opened the door and left. Ben heard the car door open and close in the driveway. The engine in her car struggled to turn over.

Ben scattered the cat treats on the floor and left out the front door.

* * *

The bus passed the same streets and the same houses it had passed hundreds of times before. However, today, there was one distinct difference. While passing a particular house, Ben noticed that the mailbox had a coat of yellow paint. It seemed peculiar to paint a mailbox bright yellow, but it wasn't long before he forgot all about it.

* * *

First period World History was especially boring. The only light that entered the classroom came from a small, inward-opening window at the top of the high concrete wall. Mr. Perkins decided to show a film about the bubonic plague. Unfortunately, he spent half the class fumbling with the projector. He had instructed the class to read pages three hundred thirteen to three hundred twenty-seven of the textbook while he figured it out, but most of Ben's classmates just passed notes to each other instead.

Ben tried to read his book, but his eyes kept gravitating to the far corner of the room, his gaze finally landing on Taylor Bell. As far as Ben was concerned, Taylor was the most beautiful girl in school, with her long, light-brown hair and hazel eyes. As she sat there, writing notes and smiling her crooked smile, Ben wondered how he could possibly strike up a conversation with her. Suddenly, she looked up, her gaze moving in Ben's direction. Ben tried to shift his gaze away, but too late. She caught him red handed. Looking at her.

Taylor smiled. Ben wanted to smile back, but his heart began to pound. Instead, he looked down at his textbook and pretended to read about the bubonic plague. Why was it so difficult for him to maintain eye contact with her?

Mr. Perkins eventually solved the mystery of the projector. But, before playing the film, he posed a question to the class. "Who here can tell me how the Black Death was transmitted?" His gaze scoured the classroom and stopped on Ben. "Mr. Young. What did you learn from the reading?"

But Ben had not read any of the text, he had only pretended to. "Umm. I think the book mentioned that it might've come from the water?"

"No!" Mr. Perkins said. "It came from rats!" He stuck out his front teeth, moving his hands toward his mouth to mimic a rodent, and making loud squeaking noises. The rest of the class laughed. Taylor smiled at Ben. Ben looked away nervously.

"Since Mr. Young has demonstrated that some of you are incapable of reading, I hope that this film will teach you a thing or two about the Black Death, also known as the bubonic plague."

The bell finally rang.

Ben quickly gathered his belongings. He took a deep breath and walked in Taylor's direction. This was his chance to finally talk to her.

Fortunately for him, she was more deliberate with her escape, slowly and carefully placing her book and binder into her bag. Ben waited a bit in hopes that the rest of the class would clear out so he could talk to her alone. Just when he thought the coast was clear and he had finally mustered up enough courage to approach her, Summer Poppy raced between them.

"Cafeteria?" Summer asked Taylor.

"Lead the way," Taylor said.

With that, they both left the classroom.

Ben, now alone, punched himself in the arm. "Just go up to her next time!"

As Ben made his way toward his next class, he could not help but notice some jocks talking to a group of girls. Why was it so easy for them? Did they get their confidence from playing football? Ben was terrible at team sports. He had tried to play football once, but the first time he attempted to catch the ball, he caught it with the inside of his lip. The coach didn't stop laughing that day.

Ben was a nerd. He knew that because most of the kids in P.E. called him that when they weren't coming up with other names. The joke was on them because Ben did not fit in with the actual nerds either. He lacked the expertise and confidence to get into a discussion about comic book crossovers or the best Dungeons and Dragons builds. He was also terrible with homework. How could he be a nerd and be so bad at school? He was stuck in junior high purgatory: Not cool enough for the popular kids and not geeky enough for the nerds.

Woodshop. Ben hated woodshop. He stood near the drum full of lacquer, attempting to varnish his deformed block of wood.

"Hey look, it's Oscar Meyer," Trey Jones said. He always wore some variation of a soiled football jersey.

"It's Wilde," Parker Andrews said, his long black hair greased over the top of his head.

"What's the difference?" Trey asked.

"One's a hotdog," Parker said. "The other one's a queer from the eighteen hundreds."

"Like I said, what's the difference?"

Trey and Parker both laughed in unison, high-fiving each other.

"I'm not gay," Ben said.

"What?" Parker asked. "You have a problem with gay people now?"

"No."

"Hey!" Parker shouted to the rest of class. "Ben here is a homophobe. He just said he hates gay people!"

The rest of the class booed.

Mr. Anderson, oblivious to the conversation, continued cutting a rather large piece of wood with a band saw, his glasses pressed firmly against the inside of his yellowed safety goggles.

Ben ignored them, snatching a brush from a nearby coffee can, and dipping it into the large vat of clear coat. He hoped that they would lose interest and walk away.

Trey bumped into Ben from behind. "Hey, I heard you hate gays. What's it like hating yourself?"

Ben spun around to face him. He had forgotten that he still had the brush clenched in his hand. The tip hit Trey's jersey, dabbing it in lacquer.

"What the hell, dude?" Trey asked. "This jersey cost, like, two hundred dollars!"

"I'm sorry," Ben said. "I didn't do it on purpose."

"You're sorry?" Parker asked, stepping toward Ben. "Sorry ain't gonna cut it. It looks like you owe this man a new jersey!"

"Yeah," added Trey. "And tell your mom I don't accept food stamps, either."

Both Trey and Parker laughed.

"It's just clear-coat, it will wash off," Ben said.

Trey punched Ben in the face. Pain shot through his nose and out both his eyes. He grabbed his nose, and his hand came away bloody.

"It's just clear-coat, it will wash off," Trey mocked.

Ben scanned the room to see if Mr. Anderson had noticed them. But the teacher continued cutting his piece of wood, oblivious.

Trey pressed his chest up against Ben, towering over him. "You gonna do something about it?"

Parker laughed. "Oh man, if someone punched me in the nose, I'd knock him out!"

"You gonna knock me out?" Trey asked, glaring at Ben as he breathed heavily through his teeth.

Ben wanted to hit Trey back so badly, but he'd never been in a fight. What if he didn't know how to fight? Worse, what would his mom think if he were suspended for fighting?

"Just leave me alone," Ben said.

Trey pushed Ben against the vat of clear coat, splashing it all over the back of his shirt.

"What a wuss," Trey said.

"Yeah, what a wuss," Parker said.

Ben, clenching his nose, walked toward the table where his stuff was. Mr. Anderson moved toward the front of the class to show off the piece of wood he had finished cutting. He looked at Ben suspiciously. "What's wrong with you? Allergies?"

"Can I use the restroom?" Ben asked.

"I don't know. Can you?"

* * *

Ben sat on the toilet, holding his head back and collecting blood on multiple square pieces of one-ply toilet paper. There were constant interruptions from other students as they entered and exited the bathroom. One student banged on the stall with his open hand, while another pressed his face between the two-inch gap between the stall door and wall while making kissing noises. Ben sat there, miserable, pondering how his day would have gone differently if he had just asked Taylor to the dance and she said 'yes.' Maybe then he would have had the courage to stand up to Parker and Trey.

CHAPTER 4

The Glass Palace of Queen Regent Avery and Her Crystal Automatons

Avery stood atop the glass mezzanine, studying the automatons as they effortlessly cleaned the fixtures throughout the entire glass palace. Although this was a nightly routine for the fifty or so creatures, and she had seen it countless times before, she was still fascinated by their methodical dedication to cleaning every inch of every massive room and every piece of glass furniture.

Brushing a speck of dust off her white silk dress, Avery wondered once again where the automatons had originated from. Who had created them? What compelled them to enter a cleaning frenzy, without fail, each and every night?

Standing at only three feet tall, each automaton was made entirely of crystal, ball-bearing joints and all. They were portly creatures with stout torsos, short, fat legs, and long, skinny arms. The only part of them that was not made of crystal was a thin copper faceplate secured around each of their heads with copper wire. Each faceplate was crudely engraved with two eyes, a nose, and, oddly enough, a mouth that was etched into a perpetual smile. Although the automatons spoke, their facial expressions remained fixed and their words varied just as little.

Whether Avery asked a question or offered a statement, the automatons would always provide the same response: "Your desire is my imperative, Queen Regent."

When she asked, "Why do you clean the palace night in and night out?"

"Your desire is my imperative, Queen Regent," the automatons always replied.

"Why do you always give me the same answer to my questions?"

"Your desire is my imperative, Queen Regent."

In the past, this frustrated Avery to no end. But tonight, she simply marveled at their tenacity to make all things pristine. She witnessed the dexterity employed by an automaton as it skillfully maneuvered a crystalline-handled white feather duster between the nooks and crannies of each piece of glass furniture. Meanwhile, a different automaton whizzed behind the first with a floor duster comprised of similar white feathers, and in a perfectly synchronized harmony, cleaned the floor immediately to the left of the first automaton as it shifted to the right, and conversely, cleaned the floor to the immediate right of the first automaton as it shifted to the left. This waltz continued, one automaton leading while the other followed, until every square inch of the floor, walls, and furniture was clean. When they finished, the automatons turned opposite to one another and raced off to find new cleaning frontiers.

Avery stepped toward the polished glass wall until she could see her reflection. A thirteen-year-old girl stared back at her, mimicking each and every one of her movements. She turned to the side, admiring her long, golden hair as it spiraled down the back of her brilliant-white dress. She grinned, accentuating her eyes, then produced a pair of oversized glasses from her gown and watched as the world blurred around her. When she took them off, her surroundings came back into focus. She smiled and placed the glasses back into the pocket of her gown.

Avery was inundated with the sweet fragrance of crisp linen and freshly polished glass. It reminded her of Sebastian, the conductor of this cleaning orchestra.

"Sebastian!" Her voice echoed into the glass corridors. There was no response.

Avery whirled, her dress spinning half an inch above the polished glass floor, and marched into an adjacent hallway. On both sides of the glass hall hung beautiful silk tapestries that displayed a yellow tower on the blue sea, the official crest of her realm. She encountered more automatons as they cleaned the narrow glass baseboards with dusters coated in a blue-tinted concoction of their own making.

Although she distinctly remembered her first night in the palace, she could not remember much of anything that had occurred before. All of the fifty or so automatons were already present. From day one, the automatons had placed a glass crown on her head and addressed her as queen regent and led her into the royal chambers where she had changed from cotton shorts and an old, faded T-shirt into the pristine gown that she wore. It was a dream come true. She was the acting ruler of the magnificent Blue Glass Palace by the Port City.

Since then, Avery had spent most of her nights reading countless books from the massive shelves in the grand library. Indeed, the books covered as many subjects as one would expect from the royal library of Meridia, including the diverse flora and fauna throughout the land and the cities and people located near and far. Avery read about the Province of Drakour and how assassins trained there would endure complete cultural assimilation to successfully hunt their targets. She read about the

Elven Genocide and how the rulers of the time ordered the poisoning of water supplies to thin the ranks of the translucent elves.

Tonight, however she was not reading books about the Perpetual Waterfall, the Shadow Judge, the Undercurrent, or salty cats and their loyalty to their ship captains. Instead, she wandered the halls in hopes of finding Sebastian, the only automaton that could say something other than, "Your desire is my imperative, Queen Regent."

Avery eventually found Sebastian perched on an absurdly tall glass ladder cleaning the chandeliers that loomed over the grand library. He swayed back and forth, back and forth, the automaton's crystal hand whirling atop his crystal wrist as he dusted each candle holder.

Above Sebastian, the starry sky glimmered through the spotless glass ceiling. Avery often wondered why, on certain nights, the stars cast an eerie blue glow throughout the interior of the palace. This was one of those nights. As she gazed upward, a shooting star zipped across the sky.

She smiled. "Sebastian."

Sebastian's torso swiveled to face Avery. Like the other automatons, his portly body and joints were made entirely of crystal, and his faceplate was made of polished thin copper held around his head with copper wire. Even so, his faceplate was decidedly distinct from the others, for Sebastian's face was always in a state of sorrow, his eyes and mouth etched in a frown.

Yes, my Queen Regent," Sebastian said with enthusiasm, although his face remained sad. "What can I do for you, today?"

"I was wondering," Avery said. "Where do you and the other automatons come from?"

Sebastian peered at her from the ladder. "I've told you this before. From the Creator, like all living things."

"But I do not come from the Creator."

"Weeds seldom do."

Avery sighed. "I have acted as queen regent and ruler for almost a year. How much time must pass before I'm no longer considered a weed?"

"Weed refers not to the amount of time spent at a given place but instead refers to the mode of arrival. For this reason alone, you will always be a weed."

"I grow tired of that word," Avery said. "Can you please stop calling me that?"

"Of course, Queen Regent."

Avery smiled. "While we are on that topic, why queen regent? Why not just call me queen?"

Sebastian descended the ladder a few rungs at a time. He stopped about four rungs down. "You are the acting queen, hence your title. This is the way it must be."

"Where's the real queen then?" Avery asked.

"She is away."

"Where?"

"Far away."

"Who is she?"

Sebastian stared at her, his expression unchanged. "We automatons do not ever speak of Lenora, The Nightmare Queen."

A long silence.

Avery fiddled with the sleeve of her dress. "Anyway, I was wondering if you'd like to share a kettle of tea with me."

"Most certainly, my Queen Regent. I will brew one up immediately. Shall we head toward the Royal Pantry?"

"We shall."

"Race you there?"

Avery beamed. "Race you there."

Sebastian placed his stubby feet on both sides of the ladder and slid down toward the floor. He turned and raced away from Avery, exiting into an adjacent glass hallway. Avery lifted the hem of her dress off the glass floor. She shot after Sebastian, her bare feet moving clumsily across the freshly polished surface. It took a few moments to gain her balance, but once she had, she maneuvered around the glass furniture with practiced ease.

Unfortunately for her, Sebastian was already rounding the corner on the opposite side of the hallway. Avery ran, lifting her knees higher and higher. She almost crashed into a lone automaton who had made the unfortunate decision to dust that particular portion of the hallway just before tea time.

Despite Avery's efforts, Sebastian was still several paces ahead of her and her lungs burned, making her huff and puff.

Sebastian stopped and slowly rotated his upper body toward her. "My Queen Regent, is there a problem?"

Panting, Avery walked toward Sebastian. "You move so quickly, I can hardly keep up!"

"My apologies, my Queen Regent. If the law of physics allows, I will make every effort to reduce my speed to something more suitable for her majesty."

"What'd you mean 'if the law of physics allows'?"

"It is quite simple," he said. "Physics dictates that speed equals distance divided by time. However, if speed is negative, the formula is no longer viable. As such, the law of physics may prevent me from slowing down to a speed that is acceptable for the queen regent."

Avery curled her lips. "Is that sarcasm?"

"My Queen Regent," he said. "I am incapable of sarcasm, as is the fate of all automatons."

"I see. Tell me, in all the time spent cleaning the palace, when does an automaton find time to learn physics?"

"Knowledge of physics is necessary to facilitate both of our prime directives, the second of which is cleaning the palace."

Avery smirked. "What's this first prime directive? Running your mouth?"

"My Queen Regent, the first prime directive has little to do with my mouth."

"Then, what is it?"

His eyes seemed colder than usual, even though they did not physically change. "This I am unable to reveal, my Queen Regent."

"Well, there's one thing you don't know about physics," Avery said.

"I know all there is to know about physics, my Queen Regent."

"Not this."

Avery yanked a silk tapestry from the wall, covering Sebastian completely within its yellow and blue patterns. She dashed away from Sebastian down the hallway. "Speed is reduced greatly by . . . erm . . . wall rug. Race you there!"

Sebastian wrestled underneath the tapestry like a meer-rabbit trapped beneath a blanket. He finally broke free and raced after her.

Avery ran as fast as her legs could manage over the slippery glass surface, laughing giddily. Although Sebastian's running looked more like a waddle, he was gaining on her fast. She turned a corner and ran down yet another hallway, but soon her lungs started to burn again, consuming her in a coughing fit that stopped her dead in her tracks. Sebastian came to an abrupt halt right beside her and gently patted her on the back.

"There, there," he said. "As with most living beings, the desire of the captain can outpace the capacity of the sails."

Avery wheezed as she placed her hand on Sebastian's cheek— or what might be considered his cheek. "You're my best friend."

"Thank you, Queen Regent."

"Am I your best friend?"

Sebastian paused. "Your desire is my imperative, Queen Regent."

"Oh, don't start with that!" Avery laughed before being consumed by another coughing fit.

Sebastian looked up at her blankly. "You are my best friend, Queen Regent."

"It's 'Avery,'" she said, smiling.

"Yes, Queen Regent. It is."

Suddenly, a white light enveloped the glass palace. Avery shielded her eyes.

Beyond the glass corridor, beyond the ceiling, far in the distance toward the black mountains, a white column of light beamed brilliantly into the heavens.

"It's coming from the mountains." Sebastian said.

"What is it?" Avery asked.

Although he could not express emotion with his face, the tremble in his voice spoke volumes. "Change is coming."

They were both interrupted by another automaton as it approached Sebastian from behind and whispered into his ear.

"My Queen Regent," Sebastian said. "I have been informed that you have visitors in the throne room."

Avery straightened and cleared her throat. "Politely inform them that I am not of a mind to entertain visitors at the moment," she said.

"My Queen Regent, this automaton states that the visitors are comprised of two weeds and two elves."

"Impossible. Elves have been extinct since the Elven Genocide. Tell him he is mistaken."

The automaton, again, whispered into Sebastian's ear.

"He insists that he is not mistaken. Furthermore, he insists that the two weeds have invoked their right for Royal Intervention." He paused. "According to Meridian law, you cannot refuse this request."

"I am well aware of Meridian law. Royal Intervention can only be requested during times of consummate crisis. There is no such crisis in Meridia that I am aware of."

Sebastian stepped forward. "My Queen Regent, the law dictates you give audience."

"What if they invoke Royal Intervention under false pretense?"

"Then the law dictates treason and they must be dealt with accordingly."

"Fine, I will receive them in the throne room."

"Yes, my Queen Regent. I will ensure that we are accompanied by ten of our finest automatons."

"For what purpose? So they can clean over and over again until our guests pass out from dizziness?"

"No," Sebastian said. "It would be hospitable to offer our guests food and drink. I will make the necessary arrangements."

Avery turned her back to Sebastian. "I request that you personally accompany me to this meeting. Stay by my side at all times. Also, I will require my sword belt from my chambers. The one with the white blade."

"My Queen Regent, do you plan for trouble?"

"No. I plan for talk." She spun back around to face him. "My actions afterward will be dictated by theirs."

CHAPTER 5

The Royal Intervention

Ben awoke abruptly to trees towering overhead, reaching toward the black heavens and sparkling stars. He tilted his head sideways to find a translucent elf seated at the edge of a rocky cliff staring listlessly into the horizon beyond.

"Where are we?" Ben asked.

"We are beyond the edge of the Red Forest overlooking the palace," Tam said, his long white hair illuminated by the moonlight.

"Was I asleep?" Ben couldn't remember closing his eyes.

An elf with a white topknot entered the clearing from the surrounding forest.

"Indeed you were," Char said. "The dead awaken easier than you."

"How did we get here?"

"We've been traveling for days. Do you not remember?"

Ben shook his head. His thoughts were muddled and his head ached. He sat up to find Marcus snoring lightly beside him.

"He dropped off right after you did," Char said. "Don't bother trying to wake him. It is impossible to wake you weeds from your slumber."

Ben tapped Marcus's shoulder, but Marcus did not budge.

Ben sat up, the warm night breeze blowing gently on his face with the slight scents of pine and moss. He surveyed his surroundings, realizing that they were in a makeshift camp near a ridge.

He suddenly remembered the journey they had undertaken to make it this far. Through swamps, hills, and deep brush they had ventured as day disappeared into night and night disappeared into day. He had observed that, in Meridia, the sun did not set, nor did it rise. Instead it appeared, then disappeared—only to reappear again in the same exact spot in the sky. This cycle had repeated itself three and a half times since they had ventured from the depths of the Red Forest.

On the horizon, just beyond the tree line, was a brilliant palace made entirely of glass. Just beyond the palace were the twinkling white lights of a city by a port. Beyond that, the Great Sea shimmered underneath the moon.

Ben turned to Char. "What will we find in the palace?"

"Queen Regent Avery," Char said.

"Why are we looking for Queen Regent Avery?"

"To request a Royal Intervention."

Ben sat there, confused. "Will the Royal Intervention stop the Fading?"

"No, it will get us a boat."

"Why do we need a boat?"

Marcus jolted awake. "Where am I?"

"We are beyond the edge of the Red Forest overlooking the palace," Ben said.

"I remember something," Marcus said. "I was having a dream. There was a girl and I was running toward her. When I was finally close enough for her to see me, she turned around and walked away."

Ben made an attempt to recall his own dreams prior to waking, but the more he tried, the more it made his head hurt.

Tam neared Marcus, extending his translucent hand. "It's time to train."

"Now?" Marcus asked. "But, I don't need more training."

Tam's eyes narrowed. "The elders may have put you in charge of this expedition, but I am still in charge of your training."

Marcus grasped Tam's hand and pulled himself off the ground. He snatched his long bow and quiver from the ground.

Tam pointed at a distant tree.

Marcus nocked the arrow, aiming at the tree. He released it, hitting the trunk dead center.

"Good," Tam said. "Split it."

Marcus gulped. He nocked another arrow into his bow and aimed at the tree. A few moments later, he exhaled and released. The arrow took flight, splitting the previous arrow right down the middle.

"See," Marcus said. "I told you I don't need more training."

Tam reached into his own quiver, and in rapid succession, launched two arrows toward the tree. The first one split Marcus's arrow and the second one split the first.

"There's always room for more training," Tam said.

Char cleared his throat. "Perhaps we should make our way down to the palace before day appears."

"Agreed," Marcus said. "But before we go down there, you need to disguise yourself with your cloaks. Both of you."

Tam spat in the dirt. "And why should I have to hide my identity from a bunch of lowly palace dwellers?"

Marcus sighed. "We've already discussed this. You know Meridia is not ready for the return of the elves. They already tried to extinguish your kind once. For the most part, they succeeded. Last I counted, the only ones left are you, your brother, and a handful of elders." Marcus turned to Char. "Please talk some sense into your brother."

Char pulled his black, hooded cloak from his sack. "Brother, you know what must be done. We wear the cloaks every time we go near civilization. That was the agreement we made with the elders."

Tam removed his folded cloak from his satchel. "Fine."

* * *

The palace was showered in moonlight. Its size and beauty beckoned as they approached the shimmering glass walls. They ventured into the courtyard made entirely of glass, and Ben marveled at the gleaming walls as they towered above him on all sides. Mounted throughout the glass courtyard floor were tall glass statues of creatures and humans alike. Most of them wore regal attire consisting of crowns and heavy robes, leaving Ben to wonder if they were the kings and queens of days long past.

At the other end of the expansive courtyard, pressed against the base of the palace, sat an imposing red door, arching at least one story high and about three quarters of a story wide. The door was split down the middle, each half reinforced with large steel rivets around the edges. It was peculiar that there was a red door in a palace where everything else was made of glass, but Ben had seen stranger.

Every glass surface, be it a wall or floor, had been polished to sparkling perfection.

"Why is everything so clean?" Ben asked.

"A butt-load of Windex would be my guess," Marcus said.

"There are stories of slaves who clean this palace," Tam said. "Each time the stars appear in the black sky."

"The stars appear every night," Marcus said. "Why not just say every night?"

"They are not slaves, brother," Char said. "The stories say they are keepers of the palace, and we'd do best to mind ourselves while we are their guests."

Ben whispered into Marcus's ear. "How'd you meet them?"

Marcus spoke at full volume. "How'd I meet who?"

Ben shushed him. "The elves!"

"Oh, the elves," Marcus said. "They found me wandering around in the forest one night, took me in. The elders have treated me like family ever since. Trained me to become one of them."

"Do you remember anything before that?"

Again, Marcus spoke at full volume. "Before what?"

Ben shushed him again. "Before they found you in the forest."

Marcus peered into Ben's eyes. "Sometimes I think I remember. But then I forget."

"Me too," Ben said.

"That's why we must stop the Fading. If we don't, everything will be forgotten."

Ben ran his fingers across the face of his watch. "How do you plan to stop it?"

"We can't," Marcus said. "Only the Creator in the citadel at the center of the sea can. That is why we must ask the queen regent for a ship."

Ben, Marcus, Tam, and Char soon found themselves directly in front of the massive red door.

"What do we do now?" Ben asked.

"I guess we knock," Marcus said.

Tamerlane banged on the door with his fists. Charlemagne joined him, banging in tandem.

"Calm down!" Marcus said. "You keep pounding on the door like that and they'll greet us with an army!"

The right side of the double door creaked inward, revealing the round head of a creature with a copper faceplate.

"We are here to see the Queen," Marcus announced.

But the creature shook its head from side to side.

"We wish to invoke our rights for a Royal Intervention," Marcus said.

The creature, again, shook its head.

"Don't shake your big head at me. Roooyaaal Interrrvennntion! Do I need to spell it out for you? You are obligated to let us speak to the Queen!"

The creature slipped back into the doorway and slammed the massive door shut.

"Crap balls!" Marcus said. "That was supposed to work!"

Then both sides of the red door opened, revealing the interior of the palace. The creature stood before them, its long arms and short legs protruding from its rotund body. The creature was entirely made of pure crystal. The only exception was a thin copper faceplate that had been wrapped around its head with a stiff copper cord. Two eyes, a nose, and even a smile had been etched onto the faceplate. The creature beckoned them through the doorway, before shutting the heavy doors behind them with a thud.

The hall was vast, lined with tall glass walls that stretched at least three stories high toward the arched glass ceiling. At the opposite end of the hall, centered atop a raised glass platform—with small glass steps leading up to it—stood an elaborate throne made of pure glass.

High above them, on both sides of the hall, was an elevated glass mezzanine balcony that stretched from one end to the next. Each narrow balcony had four spiral glass staircases leading up to them, two near the main door and two near the far end. Colorful tapestries made of translucent silk hung from the balconies, each adorned with the image of a bright yellow tower on the blue sea. Several corridor entrances lined the walls, both on the ground floor and on the balconies. Beyond the glass walls and ceilings, the stars pulsated in the black sky, casting an ethereal blue light throughout the hall.

Tam and Char maintained a pace two steps behind Ben and Marcus, unimpressed with the decor. Ben and Marcus, on the other hand, were awestruck by the hall's sheer size and beauty.

The crystal creature stared at them intently.

Marcus cleared his throat. "Could you please let the queen regent know we are here to speak to her?"

"Your desire is my imperative," the creature said, then zipped through one of the corridors nestled between two massive glass columns.

A few moments later, a brilliant white light filled the sky, illuminating the palace from outside.

"What was that?" Ben asked.

"It came from the north!" Tam said.

Char raced toward the nearest spiral glass staircase with Tam hot on his heels.

Marcus turned toward Ben. "Do you think we can see it from up there?"

Ben nodded enthusiastically, then raced after Char and Tam up the spiral staircase. Each step was immaculately polished, allowing him to see right through. He grasped the glass handrail tightly. Fortunately, his bare feet had enough grime on them from the forest floor to maintain a bit of traction.

As they neared the top of the staircase, they saw a white beam of light shooting from the northern mountains into the dark sky above. The bright beam vanished. A few moments later, the beam reappeared directly in front of the palace, blinding them.

Ben raced toward the wall that housed the large red door. He pressed his face against the glass, the thickness warping and bending what he could see outside.

An army of at least two hundred soldiers, clad in black armor, stood in perfect formation just beyond the front gate.

Marcus motioned the others toward a large yellow and blue tapestry that hung over the balcony railing. He crawled behind the tapestry on all fours. Tam and Char moved behind him, nocking arrows into their bows. Ben, the last to arrive, peered around the side of the tapestry.

Suddenly, the main door burst open. The wood moaned as it slid heavily over the glass floor. Ben watched several soldiers enter the hall and stand in formation on both sides of the door. Each one was clad in iron armor from head to toe that had been charred black as night, their faces hidden behind large helmets with thin, vertical slits. Standing upright in each of their grips was a pike, a six-to seven-foot pole with a blackened serrated blade at the tip.

They waited silently.

A boy entered the hall and the soldiers bowed. He had long, black hair and wore matching black trousers, a tunic, and a coat made of reinforced tarred leather and charred iron clasps.

"He's a weed," Ben whispered.

CHAPTER 6

The Foreboding Visitor and His Addiction to Magic

When Avery entered the throne hall, she expected to find two weeds and two survivors of the Elven Genocide. Instead, she found a gaunt-looking weed with long black hair and pale skin. He couldn't have been older than thirteen.

Beyond the visitor, at the base of the giant red door, stood sixteen soldiers—eight on each side. They were only about three feet tall, but each one held a long pike that was twice their height.

Avery approached the solid-glass throne, but she did not sit. "The Iron Pike Army," she said.

Sebastian raced to her side. "These must be the guests that the doorkeeper spoke of."

Avery looked back at Sebastian, perplexed, "But I thought he said there were two weeds and two—."

Sebastian peered at the tapestry on the balcony, then back at the weed and his soldiers. "These *are* the guests he told us about, Queen Regent."

The weed in the all-black leather garb spoke, his voice echoing across the hall. "Do not be alarmed, Queen Regent. We are simply here to have a conversation."

Avery straightened and projected her voice across the hall. "Many who wish to have a conversation do not attempt to break down my front door."

The visitor walked the expanse of the hall toward her, his heavy boots filling the large glass hall with a clickety-clack.

"My apologies, Queen Regent," he said. "I attempted to knock on the door, but there was no answer."

"I see, and what of your entourage?" Avery asked. "Are they here to converse as well?"

"Oh, them." He twisted his body toward the entryway. "They are merely here for my protection. As you know, Meridia is not a place where one should find oneself alone."

"Yes." Avery's eyes narrowed. "Especially when one is unaware of what surprises one might find."

Sebastian cleared his throat. "Let us prepare a table for our very special guest!"

Avery glanced at Sebastian before looking back at the weed with a slight smile. "Of course. That would be proper."

Suddenly, automatons appeared on the ground floor from the surrounding corridors with various objects in their hands. One automaton placed a small circular table between Avery and the visitor while another added two glass chairs. Another draped a brilliant-white tablecloth while another placed a glass candlestick. Another lit the candle with a taper and another dropped off a glass tea set. Yet another filled the empty glass teacups with hot, fragrant mint tea.

An automaton circled back toward the other side of the table to pull the glass chair out for the visitor. He promptly took his seat.

Another automaton pulled back Avery's chair, allowing her to take the seat opposite him.

"So, with whom do I have the pleasure of speaking?" Avery asked.

"I am Christopher." The weed lowered his nose toward his teacup and inhaled deeply.

Sebastian approached Avery. "My Queen Regent, the candle bearer and kettle pourer will wait over there to serve you and your guest if more tea as required." He pointed toward the glass column nearest to the throne. "The remaining automatons will dispatch to their *other* duties."

Sebastian remained at Avery's side while the automatons dashed away from the table, disappearing into the various corridors in between the massive glass columns. Meanwhile, the candle bearer and the kettle pourer turned away from the table and began marching slowly in the direction Sebastian had indicated.

Christopher slurped down his tea and banged the empty teacup on the table before the two automatons could get three feet away. "More!" he said.

The automaton returned briskly and filled his cup.

"Don't spill any!" Christopher said. He turned back to Avery. "If only we had slaves as efficient as these back where I live."

Avery's eyes narrowed. "The automatons are not your slaves, nor are they slaves to anyone in the land of Meridia."

Christopher smirked. "Let us discuss the business at hand. I act on behalf of the Sovereign. Do you know of him?"

"I know of him. Ruler of the northern mountains and keeper of the Tower of Continuance."

Christopher drank his tea. "Yes. You are better versed than I expected, considering you haven't been queen regent for very long. At any rate, the Sovereign would like me to discuss an issue of great importance with you."

Avery scoffed. "Great importance? If it is so important, why didn't he bring me the message himself?"

"I am simply a humble servant. But I can assure you that my lord does not mean to offend."

"What does your lord intend?"

"Our lord," Christopher said before slurping the rest of his tea down with one gulp, "the Sovereign now rules the realms of Meridia from the Calm Sea, to the Red Forest, to the Port City. This includes your glass palace."

"You are mistaken," Avery said. "I am Queen of the Blue Glass Palace, Keeper of the Red Forest, and Ruler of the Eastern Realm."

Christopher leaned in. "No. It is you who are mistaken, I am afraid. You are not a queen. You are simply a queen regent; you are an acting ruler. You come into title neither through birthright nor experience. The Sovereign claims these lands, now."

"My people love me," Avery said. "They will not stand for this."

Christopher laughed. "People? I'd hardly call these simpleton robots people."

"This conversation is over," Avery said. "You can tell your lord you delivered his message. While you're at it, tell him he can eat a bag of hollow whale dung."

Avery stood from her glass chair. "Sebastian. Please escort this weed to the exit."

Sebastian bowed his head. "Your desire is my imperative, Queen Regent."

"I don't think I'll be leaving just yet," Christopher said. "We haven't finished the negotiation."

A cool breeze filled the hall, promptly extinguishing the candles on the table. Like clockwork, the candle bearer scurried from the glass column toward the table with a lit taper. But before it could get near the table, Christopher waved his fingers over the candles, reigniting them with a bright yellow flame.

Avery flinched. "Magic? No doubt, you know that the practice of magic is forbidden in Meridia."

Christopher grinned. "Is it, now? Sorry, I had not heard."

"It is an offense punishable by death. Does the Sovereign know of this?"

Christopher chuckled. "Know of it? The Sovereign instructs me in its use."

Avery glared at the boy. "You have entered my kingdom uninvited. Worse, you enter my palace with soldiers. One might think that you plan an invasion."

"One might." Christopher snatched Avery's tea and sipped it, his cold eyes penetrating. "But nothing rash needs to happen, as long as you cooperate."

"Cooperate?"

"Yes. I bring terms. The Sovereign seeks a trinket that recently appeared in the world. A special trinket that slows time. He would like you to help us find it."

Avery stood up. "I do not know of any such trinkets."

But Christopher remained seated. "Find this trinket and the Sovereign will let you keep your glass house. On top of that, he will allow you to continue ruling over the Port City. If you're lucky, he might give you back the Red Forest as well."

Avery laughed. "Even if I knew where this supposed trinket was, both you and the Sovereign are in no position to make such demands."

"Then I believe this conversation truly is over," Christopher said. "Such a pity, too. Now I have to kill everyone in the palace and shatter it to the ground."

The soldiers near the door shifted into a fighting stance, the tips of their spears pointed inward, the edges glistening in the starlight.

Sebastian stood near the table like a statue.

Avery turned toward the automaton. "Sebastian?"

"Yes, my Queen Regent?"

"I don't suppose your first directive is kicking butt in the name of the Queen?"

"Yes."

With an uncanny display of speed and momentum, Sebastian hurled himself toward Christopher, toppling him off his chair, slamming him to the ground.

"Our first directive is to protect the palace against all invaders," Sebastian said. He glanced up at the mezzanine balcony. "Archers, post!"

Two groups of automatons streamed in from both sides of the hall on the mezzanine balconies, bow and arrows drawn and aimed upon the Iron Pike Army soldiers.

"Loose," Sebastian ordered.

The twenty automaton archers fired a flurry of arrows from both sides. The arrows penetrated deep into the soldiers' blackened armor like hot knives through butter, killing all sixteen of them.

Avery walked toward Christopher as he lay on the floor, his face bloodied. But instead of cowering, he laughed.

"You should have taken my terms," he said.

"Terms, you say? You will die in a puddle of your own making for threatening me in my palace. Those are my terms."

But Christopher rose from the ground, cackling.

"Foolish Queen Regent. Do you think I only bring a small detachment of men with me? I have an entire army to bring these walls down!"

The massive red wooden door exploded inward as one hundred and eighty-four Iron Pike Army soldiers poured into the glass hall.

The automatons on the balcony released a flurry of arrows into the horde, but there were simply too many soldiers. Soon, the archers ran out of arrows, allowing the soldiers to rush the spiral staircases on both sides.

"Kill them all," Christopher said.

The Iron Pike Army soldiers overwhelmed the automatons, slamming the butt ends of their pikes into their crystal bodies. The ten or so automatons on each side fought back with their fists, but they were quickly outnumbered. After only three or four hard blows, their crystal shells cracked. One soldier inserted the bladed tip of his pike into an automaton's ball bearing joint, severing the arm completely, then bashed in its face with the blunt end.

Christopher laughed as he watched the carnage unfold. He turned back toward Avery to find Sebastian lunging toward him. But Christopher stretched out his arms, pointing his fingertips in Sebastian's direction. Christopher's veins turned pitch black, distending against the inside of his skin as if they were going to burst through.

Searing-hot flames ejected from his fingertips, enveloping Sebastian completely.

Sebastian screamed, his copper faceplate melting from the blazing heat.

"No!" Avery charged toward Christopher, drawing her white short sword from the sheath on her waist. She tackled Christopher, cracking the back of his head against the glass floor, and raised the blade above him, ready to strike.

A soldier blindsided her, toppling her to the ground. Avery spun the soldier on his back, sinking her blade through his armor. Black, oil-like blood gurgled from the wound, tainting her blade with dark streaks. The soldier howled in anguish, pulling a dagger from his belt and slamming it into Avery's thigh. Searing heat shot through her leg, and she howled in pain. She pulled her sword from the soldier's stomach and planted the blade firmly through his vented helmet.

Avery stumbled to her bare feet as blood poured from her wound.

Another soldier charged Avery, but she dropped to the ground on her back, pointing her sword upwards as the soldier impaled himself on her blade. Avery used her bare feet to kick the soldier clean off her blade.

She turned to find Christopher rising from the ground, seething with anger. "This is where you die," he said. "You and your robots!"

Avery turned her attention toward the balcony to witness the soldiers tossing the bodies of the dead automaton archers to the ground below, where they shattered. Christopher approached her as she lay on the glass floor, both his arms extended in her direction. Avery wanted to flee, but she could not even stand. His veins pulsed black and his eyes changed from a light brown to a fiery yellow.

Suddenly, an arrow impaled his shoulder from behind, the steel tip protruding all the way through. Christopher turned to find two transparent elves aiming their bows at him from the balcony. He unleashed a stream of fire in their direction. The elves rolled out of the way with ease, but the tapestry near them caught fire, revealing two weeds.

* * *

The soldiers on the balcony turned away from the dying automatons and rushed toward Ben and Marcus. But the corridors on both sides erupted as more automatons, at least thirty of them, flooded the throne room from both sides of the ground floor and the balcony, clashing into the Iron Pike Army.

Soldiers on both sides fell from the mezzanine balcony as the automatons knocked them over the glass railing. Some screamed as they fell through the air before cracking the glass floor with their helmets. Some landed on other soldiers below.

"Help the queen!" Marcus said as he fired arrows into the horde of soldiers. Ben nodded, then raced down the spiral staircase. Tam followed.

As soon as they hit the ground floor, two soldiers rushed them, their pikes extended. Tam aimed at one of the soldiers and released an arrow straight into his skull. He immediately nocked another arrow and shot another soldier clean through the neck.

The arrow pierced right through, then slammed into the face of a third soldier behind him. All three soldiers fell dead to the floor.

From the balcony, Char nocked another arrow and aimed it at Christopher.

Christopher waved in a circular motion. A transparent blue sphere surrounded him, electricity coursing throughout. Char released the arrow, but instead of hitting Christopher, it slammed into the sphere, the rear shaft protruding from the outer edge.

As Christopher moved toward Avery, both the sphere and the lodged arrow moved along with him. Blood ran down his shoulder. "You will pay for this!"

Ben raced toward Christopher just as Tam nocked another arrow. He released it, but again, the arrow lodged into the sphere like it was an electric pin cushion. Christopher turned toward Ben and Tam, his arms outstretched. For a brief moment, the sphere vanished and the arrows dropped to the ground. It was quickly replaced by searing-hot flames from his fingertips. Tam shoved Ben away from the flames, then dropped face-first to the ground. The flames shot directly over him, singeing his back.

From the balcony, Marcus launched a barrage of arrows into the horde as they climbed the spiral staircase closest to the main door. Fortunately, the steps were narrow, providing a bottleneck.

"Gotcha!" Marcus said as the arrows penetrated their helmets.

On the ground floor, five Iron Pike Army soldiers had shattered another automaton before noticing Tam. They immediately broke ranks to engage.

Upon seeing this, Christopher shifted his attention back to Avery and moved toward her.

On the balcony, Marcus launched the last of his arrows. Piled on the balcony ledge were bodies of Iron Pike Army soldiers. More and more soldiers made their way to the top of the steps. He hit one, two, three soldiers.

The automatons on the ground floor fought valiantly, but that was not enough to turn the tide. The Iron Pike Army outnumbered the automatons four to one and the automatons were dropping, despite their efforts.

Char ran down the spiral staircase, firing arrows at the Iron Pike Army soldiers as they neared Tam. Meanwhile, Tam rolled back and forth on the ground, his back smoldering from the flames, his quiver and accompanying arrows burnt to a crisp. As the soldiers approached Tam, Char unleashed several arrows in succession, killing three and wounding two.

Ben tried to tackle Christopher, but Christopher raised his hands, redeploying the large electrical sphere around him. Ben slammed into the shield and convulsed until he fell unconscious to the ground, smoke pluming up from his pajamas.

Christopher waved his hands again, dropping the shield. He strolled toward Avery, stopping just a few feet in front of her. He aimed his fingertips at her, smiling.

Avery attempted to crawl backward, blood trickling from her leg. "The magic will consume you like everyone else."

Christopher laughed. "Not before it consumes you, first."

Suddenly, an automaton grabbed Christopher from behind, its faceplate deformed, its body charred from the flames. It lifted Christopher clear off the ground. Christopher yelled, his flames shooting over Avery's head toward the arched glass ceiling above.

"Sebastian!" Avery said.

Ben raced toward Avery and helped her to stand. His eyes met hers. "We need to get out of here!"

Avery wrapped her arm around Ben's neck, using his body as support as she limped along.

"The throne," she said. "There is a secret exit underneath!"

Ben and Avery staggered toward the throne as Char pulled Tam off the ground.

Up on the balcony, Marcus, out of arrows, ran down the spiral steps.

Ben and Avery raced toward the throne. She grasped a lever on the arm, sliding it with an audible click. Suddenly, the throne rolled backward, revealing a dark passage below. The walls lining the secret passage were made of opaque stone.

Tam and Char appeared behind them.

"There," she said. "You can escape!"

"What do you mean *you*?" Ben asked. "Don't you mean *we*?"

"No. I must go back for Sebastian!"

Tam grasped Avery's face, forcing her attention toward Christopher. "You can't save him!"

She watched as Christopher rolled Sebastian onto his back. He held his open palm above Sebastian's face. Sebastian turned his head and gazed at Avery from afar. The melted faceplate made it look like he was smiling.

"*Run*," Sebastian said. Christopher engulfed Sebastian's entire head in flame, melting his face off completely.

Avery screamed at the top of her lungs, then collapsed to the floor, unconscious.

"What happened to her?" Ben asked.

"She fell asleep!" Char said. "This is what you weeds do each and every time! You collapse where you stand with zero warning beforehand!

"We have to go now!" Tam said.

Marcus and Ben grabbed Avery and pulled her through the trapdoor and into the dark passage. The elves followed.

The throne rolled back into its original position, concealing the passage, as soldiers rushed it, pounding their pikes onto the glass surface.

CHAPTER 7

The Goat

The morning sun illuminated the matte white walls through double-paned glass. Avery awoke in a pool of her own sweat, her head pounding and her skin flushed. Almost immediately, she panicked, thinking she had slept in too late, but the alarm clock on the desk read 6:50, which meant that she had a good ten minutes before she had to actually get up.

The slats creaked above her. Her roommate, Stephanie, was waking.

Avery moved her legs toward the side of the bed, but felt a fairly significant wet spot underneath her. She panicked. *Oh no! Please, not again!*

When Avery was just nine years old, she had the most embarrassing problem a person could possibly have. Nocturnal enuresis is what the doctors called it. Bedwetting is what her friends called it.

Fortunately, the problem had gone away with age. There was no way it could ever happen again. Especially now that she was thirteen!

Avery pushed the blankets away toward the foot of the bed.

Sure enough, she had wet the bed.

Avery hopped out as quietly as she could, careful to not wake Stephanie on the top bunk. She stripped her bed, bundled up the sheets and blankets, and headed toward the door, but she couldn't see anything without her glasses.

She dropped the bundle and snatched her oversized glasses from the desk. She watched as the world came into focus around her. When she took them off again, her surroundings blurred. She frowned and placed the glasses back on her face. She picked up the bundle and walked toward the door.

Then the alarm clock went off.

Avery froze, and her gaze darted toward Stephanie. Still asleep, Stephanie mumbled incoherently, her mouth guard falling out. Avery lunged toward the alarm clock and shut it off. Stephanie rolled over in the opposite direction and mashed her pillow over her ear.

Avery cracked open the door, carefully peering outside to see if anyone was in the hallway. If she was lucky, the other girls would still be asleep in their rooms. She usually set her alarm clock earlier than the others to make sure she had hot water when she used the shower. The coast was clear, so she ducked out of her room.

Her arm bumped the walls, the texture making her shudder. The halls were painted with the same dull off-white paint that had been used to paint her room. The paint had a matte, scratchy surface, and as a result, every bump with a tray or scrape with a shoe left a noticeable black mark. It was one of the chores she and other girls in the home had to do often, removing the marks with old sponges and cleaning solution.

Now Avery only had to make it to the washing machine located down the hall, down the stairs, across the living area, and past the kitchen.

She remembered her grandfather and what he would tell her back when he was still alive. He used to say, "If you find yourself in a situation where you are too scared to do something, simply tell yourself 'race you there,' and you will find the courage to do it."

"Race you there," Avery said under her breath.

Avery made her way down the hall, the sheets cradled in both her arms, careful to avoid making any noise. But a loud squeak followed each step she took as the old wooden floors in the group home moaned beneath her bare feet.

The stairs were even less forgiving. They creaked in protest as she descended, step by grueling step. She passed the living area, with its tattered sectional sofa and broken TV. She also passed the large kitchen, with its circular dining tables and stools. But as she headed toward the long hallway, she heard the familiar sound of swishing water and thumping. The washing machine was already being used!

Before she could turn around and make her escape, she heard a familiar voice.

"What are you up to so early this morning?"

Tracy stood in front of the washer and dryer, her long dark hair streaming over her shoulders. She wore a large shirt with an oversized neck that drooped around her thin arms. The outfit was much cuter on Tracy than it had any business being. Tracy was the prettiest girl in the group home, and she knew it. Avery, on the other hand, was a stick with frizzy hair.

Tracy was the last person Avery wanted to run into this morning. She rarely missed an opportunity to put Avery down. Sometimes, she ridiculed Avery's glasses or the fact that she actually read books. Most of the time, she commented on what Avery was eating. "That pudding will make you a total cow," she would say. Or, "Only trailer trash eats macaroni and cheese from a box."

Right now, her eyes penetrated Avery, her lips curled into a sneer. "Why do you have all your sheets rolled up into a ball?"

Avery didn't say a word.

Tracy smirked. "You'd better tell me. I'm going to find out anyway."

Tracy would find out anyway. She had a knack for knowing every secret about every person in the house, and she knew how to leverage that information to get what she wanted. For all intents and purposes, Tracy was the queen bee of the group home, and the rest of them were lowly drones.

"You know that pervert Samuel is going to take all of our sheets to the coin wash tomorrow, right?" Tracy asked.

"Ummm . . . Really?"

"You forgot?" Tracy asked. "He's been taking them to the cleaners every Saturday since forever."

"Yeah, I know," Avery said. "They're just dirty. I didn't want to wait until tomorrow, that's all."

"Whatever, I'm washing my bras right now. I tend to go through them pretty fast during the week. You're lucky you don't have that problem."

Avery winced, wondering if she would ever hit puberty during this lifetime. "Anyway, how long do you have left on the machine?"

Tracy snatched the bundle out of Avery's hands.

Avery lunged toward it, but Tracy yanked it away, unraveling it. Tracy reeled back from the smell.

"I had an accident," Avery said.

Tracy laughed. "Yeah, gross, no kidding!"

"I think I had a bad dream or something."

Tracy turned toward the washer, lifted the lid, and stopped the cycle. She reached down into the water and pulled out two bras: one black and one red. She dropped the sheets into the washer, dumped a cup of detergent into the machine, shut the lid, and started the machine.

"Problem solved," Tracy said.

Avery peered into Tracy's eyes. Was it really going to be this easy?

Tracy stepped toward her. "Avery. I'd like to give you some advice"

Avery shrugged. "Okay. Sure."

"You want good fosters, right?"

"Yeah, who doesn't?"

Tracy scoffed. "Not me. I told you a thousand times, my mother dances in Las Vegas. I'm just waiting for her to come back, because when she does, it's going to be maid service every day of the week."

Tracy approached the washing machine and opened the lid, stopping the machine. She peered inside. "Anyway, everyone here knows you're trying to find a good foster home. I can show you how." She closed the lid, resuming the machine.

Avery's eyes lit up. "Really?"

"Well, for starters, you need to keep this a secret between us and only us. Don't tell anyone, especially Mrs. Dewey. Do you understand?"

"Why not Mrs. Dewey?" Avery asked.

Tracy sighed. "Think about it. Mrs. Dewey has to disclose this kind of stuff to potential fosters, right? Do you think anyone's going to adopt you once they find out you wet the bed every night?"

"But it's only happened to me once since I've been here!"

Tracy touched Avery's cheek. "It doesn't matter. Look, you need to start trusting me. I'm a pro at attracting rich fosters. I lived with six families before I came here. I'll teach you."

Avery smiled. "Thank you, Tracy. For everything."

Tracy smirked. "Of course! What're friends for? Besides, I wouldn't want you to have another asthma attack over it."

* * *

There was a nervous energy in the classroom as Mrs. Dewey gave the big news. She stood at the podium in front of the chalkboard in her frumpy muumuu full of colorful patterns, the skin of her shapeless arms drooping over her elbows. "After months and months of red tape and such, we finally have approval. After today, all girls in the eighth grade and higher will attend morning classes at South Point Middle School. The semester has been in session for a week already, but I have no doubt that you smart ladies will catch up in no time."

The small classroom of eight erupted into a frenzy.

"Hold on, quiet, everyone!" Mrs. Dewey said. But her voice was drowned out by the ruckus. "Remember, this is only for the eighth graders. The rest of you have the pleasure of attending classes with me for another year."

This news was met with several moans.

There were only eight girls total in the home, and as a consequence, the class. But only three of them were old enough to be eighth graders this year. They were Avery, her roommate Stephanie, and of course, Tracy.

"Samuel will pick you girls up in the van on Monday morning," Mrs. Dewey added.

The prospect of going to school simultaneously excited and terrified Avery. On one hand, she was ecstatic to meet some friends outside of the group home. On the other, the prospect of attending a real school made her nervous. She enjoyed the classes by Mrs. Dewey and was, by far, the best student in the group home when it came to math. Avery could solve almost any equation with ease. Would she still be the top math student at an actual school?

Stephanie spun toward Avery, her braces shining in her crooked mouth. "We get to meet boys!"

Tracy chimed in from the other side. "They aren't going to know what hit them." She traced her figure with her hands. "By this time next week, I will be the most popular girl at school. Rich fosters will be lining up outside the door to adopt me. Too bad I'll have to turn them all away."

"Does it really work like that?" Avery asked. She removed her glasses and cleaned them with the bottom of her off-white shirt.

Tracy stared at her a moment. "You know, you don't look half bad without those tragic glasses." She ran her fingertips through Avery's hair. "A little conditioner and a blow dry and we could have ourselves an extreme makeover. Have you ever considered contacts?"

Avery laughed. "Contacts? Who's going to pay for that?"

Tracy scoffed. "You're right. It's no use trying to make you look good."

Avery placed her glasses back on her face.

Tracy leaned in, grinning. "Hey, how about you trade me for landscaping duty today?"

Avery shook her head "No way, I have countertops today. I never get countertops. I need a break from the hard stuff."

Tracy presented her fingers. "But I just painted my nails!"

"How about I trade you next time?"

Tracy sulked. "I thought we were friends. You know, close friends with secrets."

Avery sighed. "Fine, I'll do it."

Although Avery preferred landscaping to something like, say, wall scrubbing or bathroom detail, it was still a pain. This was mostly because of Barney, the old goat who lived in the fenced yard outside the group home. When he wasn't sleeping for ten hours at a time, he patrolled the yard in search of garbage and whatever else he could find. Like baseballs, or Frisbees, or leaves. Barney was not a connoisseur. He loved Mrs. Dewey, who fed him table scraps every night, but he hated the girls and always charged them while they worked. Many girls, Avery included, returned from landscaping duty with bruises, cuts and scrapes.

This afternoon, however, Avery had a plan.

"Here, Barney!" she said, using the highest-pitched voice she could muster. Barney emerged from the side of the house, his lips pulled back to show his yellowed teeth. His fur was coarse and streaked in silver and his beard and tail were pure white. The bell around his neck jingled softly. As usual, he approached Avery slowly. But she knew better. Despite his meandering pace, once he came within striking distance, the festival of bucking would commence.

Avery was ready. She had smuggled a muffin from her breakfast and hid it in her coat pocket. As Barney crept closer, she revealed it. Barney stopped dead in his tracks and sniffed the muffin. At first, he looked at Avery suspiciously. But then his tongue rolled out of his mouth, snatching the muffin, then swallowing it whole.

"Good boy. Eat it up!"

Barney looked up at Avery, licking his lips.

"There's no more."

Barney grunted and meandered toward the side of the house.

* * *

It was night. This was the only time that Avery and the other girls were free of chores and school. Not surprisingly, this was also Avery's favorite hour. She would nestle on the couch with a pillow, her feet curled under her while she read and reread her favorite books. She would never read one book at a time. Instead, she preferred to read multiple books at once, sometimes opting to switch between them every few pages or so. Avery could plow through three books in the time it took the other girls to read only half of one.

Tonight, Tracy, Stephanie, and the other girls played The Game of Life in the dining area. Avery pulled her stack of books from under the end table and placed them neatly on her lap. She loved the smell of books, especially the glue that held the pages together.

She grabbed a book from the top of the pile. There was a pamphlet beneath it: *House Break your Dog in Twenty Days.*

She heard a snicker from the dining room table.

Tracy held back her laughter as the other girls giggled, laughed, and pointed in Avery's direction.

Mrs. Dewey, wearing her oversized pajamas, entered the living area. "What's all the fuss about?"

The other girls composed themselves as Avery hid the pamphlet underneath her books.

"Nothing, Mrs. Dewey," Avery said.

Mrs. Dewey pulled Avery aside. "I have good news for you, young lady. A very nice young couple will be visiting you a week after tomorrow. They are really excited to meet you!"

Avery sulked. "Why do they want to meet me?"

"What do you mean? Why would anyone *not* want to meet you?"

"What if they don't like me or what if they find out things about me that they don't like?"

Mrs. Dewey smiled. "Hun, just focus on your first week of school and making new friends. Everything else will work itself out by the time Saturday comes."

Mrs. Dewey turned toward the other girls. "Lights out in fifteen minutes."

Tracy shuffled her way toward Avery as Mrs. Dewey left the room. She whispered in Avery's ear, "I overheard your conversation with the walrus. It'd be a shame if those fosters found out about your little problem. Maybe next time I ask you to switch chores with me, the first word out of your mouth will be 'yes.'"

CHAPTER 8

A Voyage to the Middle of the Sea

Avery awoke with the sun on her face and the scent of salt in the air. She sat up in a bed comprised of a lacquered wooden frame and a white down comforter with silky cream sheets. She immediately noticed that the cabin was teetering left before tottering right in a rhythmic wobble that reminded her of a rocking horse. The walls on each side of the room were constructed with large wooden logs that had been stacked and sealed tightly with a liberal amount of wax. The small port holes in the far wall were ajar, and fresh air and sunlight poured into the cabin.

As Avery stepped out of bed onto the wooden floor, she noticed that her royal dress, while mostly intact, was stained in several places.

She immediately recalled her escape through the sewers deep beneath the palace. She remembered the sandstone tunnels and the twisting turns within. Those who did not know the exact route through the labyrinth would be lost for days, weeks, months, or even years. Luckily, when she was appointed queen regent by the automatons, they had forced her to memorize a map of the tunnels and the passageways until she was able to recite the exact sequence of left turns and right turns from memory.

Just thinking about the automatons brought a tear to Avery's eyes. She missed them. Most of all, she missed Sebastian. When she had set sail with the two boys and the two elves, she had looked back toward the ocean cliffs to see her glass palace one last time before it shattered to the ground. She had vowed revenge on the weed, Christopher, who had murdered Sebastian with his illegal magic and destroyed her home.

Her dress dragged heavily as she walked toward the cabin door. The quarter-inch layer of eel's wax that covered the cabin from floor to ceiling looked smooth, but there was a stickiness to it. Her dress, with its long skirt, was better suited for the slippery glass floors of the palace and not so suited for a ship, where splintered floors and steel rivets snatched it at every turn.

Her right leg throbbed with a dull pain. She lifted the hem of her skirt to find a makeshift bandage that had been wrapped tightly around her thigh. Seeping from the wound was a putrid ointment that one of the elves had applied during their escape.

Her short sword stood against the wall, its blade looking less like metal and more like white satin. Avery had heard tales about how this particular blade would remain pure white until it was stained with blood. She wondered how red it would become before she was able to exact her revenge on the weed who had destroyed her home.

She grasped the sword by the hilt and walked toward a large oval mirror near the wooden closet. She pressed the blade against her dress and began slicing through the material just above her knees. She turned her attention to her long flowing sleeves, cutting them off at the shoulders.

She glanced at the loose pieces of silk material on the cabin floor. "This will do nicely," she said, admiring her new dress.

Avery opened the cabin door, flooding the room with sunlight. The door opened to the deck, where the sounds of waves crashing and wood creaking overwhelmed her ears. Avery had to squint tightly and rub her eyes to acclimate to the brightness.

The ship was small compared to other ships in her fleet. Made entirely of wood, it had one small cabin built upon a wooden deck, which was enclosed by three-foot wooden walls.

She looked up to find Marcus steering the ship with the large oak helm on top of the cabin.

The ship moved swiftly, high winds slammed into its large cloth sails and sprays of salt water exploding over the hull. Long lines of rope from each sail led to a peculiar-looking wooden gearbox located near the helm, where Marcus would pull the levers to change the direction of the sails.

Marcus seldom smiled. But here on this ship, with the sun overhead and the scent of salt on the breeze, he actually grinned, his cheeks as round as his stomach.

She watched as the two translucent elves disappeared below deck and reemerged with a slew of goods ranging from explosive powder to sugar canes.

The elves always seemed to be one step ahead when it came to fighting. While she did not condone the act itself, she could almost see how fear had driven the various kingdoms of Meridia to go forward with the Elven Genocide. The elves were simply too good at war. This terrified the rulers at the time, so they sent out their armies en masse in an attempt to wipe out the elves for good. Not surprisingly, their armies were slaughtered, so the rulers sent alchemists to the outer reaches of the Red Forest to poison the rivers and streams. Soon, the elven women could no longer bear children and their numbers began to wane. From what Tam and Char had told her, there were only a handful of elves left in the world, all of them male.

Tam and Char used the sharp ends of their daggers to fashion a bundle of sugar cane into arrow shafts and fit in arrowheads they'd carved from fishing weights. The fletching was no doubt plucked from the gulls that had been circling overhead soon after they left port, white with gray tips. Avery did not know how the elves had captured and de-feathered the birds, nor did she want to.

Near the bow of the ship, Avery spied Ben wearing his pajama top around his head like a bandana. Ben had hardly said a word to her while they were escaping. But as he stood there, with his eyes shut and the ocean wind in his face, she could not help but remember when their eyes had first met, when he had lifted her off the floor. Avery wanted to talk to him, but what about? Perhaps she would thank him for saving her. She had not done that yet. But then Marcus called for her from atop the wooden cabin. "Queen Avery, can we talk?"

"Of course." Avery walked around the outer edge of the cabin to the spiral wooden steps that led to the roof.

On top of the cabin, she could see that the brilliant turquoise sea surrounded the ship for miles. The water was clear, so clear that Avery could almost see to the ocean floor. As clear as it was, however, there was no sign of life within its depths.

"Where are the sea animals?" Avery asked.

"Sea animals?" Marcus asked. "Like the kind at the water zoo?"

Avery used her hand like a visor as she scanned the ocean. "Yes, the fish, the dolphins, the octopuses, the sharks, even."

"Nah. I haven't seen anything like that at all since I've been up here."

Avery ran her fingers across the top of the helm. "What did you want to talk to me about?"

Marcus turned the helm with both his arms. The large wooden gearbox near him creaked and sputtered as the ropes moved to and from the sails high above. "I just wanted to ask you how you were doing with your leg and all."

Avery presented her leg. "Thanks for asking. It's much better."

"That elf poultice is legit. It smells like horse poop, but it works wonders. Anyways, you've been asleep since we left the dock. I wanted to make sure you weren't dead or something."

Avery laughed. "I'm not dead. I'm walking around the ship!"

"Nah, you never know," Marcus said, his eyes scanning the ocean. "I've heard that the dead can walk in Meridia, depending on where you go."

"If I were dead, I'd stink. I don't stink, do I?"

Marcus laughed. "Well, you did just come out of a sewer."

"You're one to talk," Avery said. She peered ahead into the horizon. "The Creator's Citadel? Can we just sail up to it?"

Marcus shrugged. "We're going to find out. We must stop the Fading."

"In all my time ruling the Blue Glass Palace, I have never heard of this Fading you keep talking about."

Waves crashed into the sides of the boat, the crests a brilliant white froth.

"Haven't you noticed both the days and the nights getting shorter?" Marcus asked.

Avery furrowed her brow. "Now that you mention it."

"I like to think of it like a puzzle," Marcus said. "You connect all the pieces to create a picture, whether it's a painting of a wheat field, a windmill, or an ocean. As you come close to finishing it, you notice that there are pieces missing from the box. You can see what the overall image is supposed to be, but there are gaps— missing pieces. Now imagine those gaps getting bigger and bigger until you can no longer recognize the picture at all. The Fading is like those gaps in the puzzle, and those gaps are growing. Only the Creator has the power to stop it."

The wind blew through Avery's hair. "What makes you think he will?"

Marcus looked down. "He has to. I mean, he's the Creator, right?"

The sky flashed, then turned black, almost as if someone had flipped a switch. The bright blue sky was now replaced by black night. Avery blinked to adjust to the sudden darkness, only to find the sky filled with bright twinkling stars.

"See what I was saying about the days being shorter?" Marcus asked. "At least we're another day closer to the Creator's Citadel."

Marcus grabbed a thick wooden stick near the base of the helm and slid the end across the floor. It lit up like a match, the fire illuminating the wheel in front of him.

"Strike anywhere torches?" Avery asked as she stared at the flame.

Marcus's face brightened. "I found a bunch of these below deck. Cool, huh?"

But Avery stared at the stars above. "How far away is the citadel?"

Marcus stared at the horizon. "Put it to you this way, how many people have you met who have traveled to the center of the sea and returned to tell the tale?"

* * *

Ben stared up at the night sky and wondered why the sun was no longer there. The air suddenly became chilly, so he pulled the pajama top from his head and ran his arms through the sleeves. He clenched and unclenched his fists. It felt like a million ants were crawling over his skin, almost as if his hands were falling asleep. Was he getting seasick?

He moved to Char and Tam. "Why does the sun always disappear like that?"

Tam laughed in his raspy voice.

"Don't worry, weed," Char said, his translucent skin glistening in the moonlight. "The sun will reappear again tomorrow to coddle you in its loving embrace once again."

"Why doesn't it rise and set?" Ben asked.

Both Tam and Char laughed.

"Why would it do that?" Tam asked. "It disappears and reappears like it has always done."

A loud bellow came from the starboard side of the ship. Tam and Char raced toward the rail, peering over the edge into the black sea below. Ben followed.

A gigantic beast swam out from underneath the ship. It resembled a whale, but it was like no whale Ben had ever seen before. Instead of skin, its gigantic bones were wrapped in a clear gelatinous substance, like a jellyfish. The organs within glowed a deep purple, pulsating as the beast moved gracefully through the water, wailing a high-pitched moan through jagged, pointed teeth.

"A hollow whale," Char said. "Hungry, by the looks of it."

"If the hollow whales don't get you, the tea-light sharks will," Tam added.

"What are tea-light sharks?" Ben asked.

"They are exactly what they sound like," Tam said. "They are sharks with a light that extends from their head like a fishing rod. It helps them see their prey in the black water of the night."

"Do they only come out at night?" Ben asked.

"All beasts come out at night," Char said.

"When the sun decides to retire, wolfbats and other creatures of the night spread like unkempt fire," Tam said.

"A nursery rhyme told to elves when we are children," Char added. "Although there will be no more elf children to hear it."

"Hollow whales," Ben muttered. "Tea-light sharks. Can they get on the boat?"

"Of course not," Char said. "They cannot survive outside the water. Not long enough to eat you entirely, anyway."

Tam handed Ben a small dagger. "Here you go, just in case."

* * *

From atop the cabin, Avery stared at the hollow whale in shock. "Where did *that* come from?"

Marcus directed her attention to the greater sea around them. Across the expanse of the ocean were thousands, if not millions, of glowing lights in the blackened depths, each one belonging to a creature of the night sea.

"Guys!" she shouted down to the deck below. "I think you should come up here and see this!"

A deafening crash came from beneath the hull, and the ship listed sideways. Marcus, one arm hooked around the large wooden wheel, grabbed Avery's wrist with his free hand. For a moment, Avery was suspended in midair, the waves crashing into the deck far below her dangling bare feet. Before the ship capsized completely, it righted itself, hurling them in the opposite direction toward the sea.

* * *

The hull moaned as Ben, Tam, and Char slammed into the wooden deck face first, ocean waves crashing over them. The seawater stung Ben's sinuses and lungs. He lifted his head above the pooling water, turning toward the helm.

Marcus and Avery were gone. "Avery! Marcus!"

Tam pushed himself to his feet, his long, white hair dripping wet. He spun around frantically as the sea smashed into the ship on all sides. "Where's Char?"

A gigantic eel with white circles on its scaly blue skin exploded from the depths of the black ocean, slamming its thick body on top of the deck, sinking the hull below the waterline. Its beady yellow gaze landed on Ben, and it howled a high-pitched scream, revealing rows upon rows of razor-sharp teeth.

It lunged at Ben with snapping jaws. Ben dove sideways just in time to avoid its bite. He pulled out a dagger, waving it frantically in front of him to scare the eel off. But the eel lunged after Ben again, knocking the blade out of his grip and into the ocean depths.

Tam appeared beside the eel, brandishing his blade. He sliced his dagger deep into the creature, his arm submerged well into the black guts as he sawed through, severing it completely in half. The eel squealed in torment, flopping around the deck maniacally. Ben barely dodged the head, but soon the eel ran out of fight, its cold, dead eyes staring through him.

Meanwhile, the back half of the eel convulsed and slunk back into the ocean, pitch black blood spurting from its wound.

A brief moment of silence.

Ben opened his mouth to thank Tam, but multiple deafening shrieks filled the air as five more eels emerged from the black depths.

"An eel hydra!" Tam said as the creature rose from the sea, revealing that the five heads were part of a single beast. Slick, black skin wrapped tightly around a fat walrus-shaped frame and thick flippers protruded from both sides of its massive body.

The eel hydra slammed its flippers on top of the deck, tilting the starboard edge of the ship down into the water with its massive girth. Five elongated scaly blue heads—plus one decapitated neck—protruded from the creature's chest, each flailing independently from the others. The eels, with their beady eyes, breathed heavily as salt and water sprayed from their gills, creating a putrid mist in the night air.

Ben gave Tam one look before retreating below the ship's deck.

Tam shook his head in disgust. "Coward!"

* * *

Marcus surfaced next to the ship, sputtering and coughing. He looked around hopelessly before Avery popped up beside him, gasping for air.

"Aww, crap balls, we have to get back on the ship." Marcus's arms flailed in the water.

Avery grabbed him. "Calm down. Panicking won't help!"

Flashes of light moved in the water beneath them. Treading water, Avery pulled her short sword from her sheath. She held the dripping blade above the surface, waiting to strike anything that came near her or Marcus. "We need to swim around the ship until we can find a way back up," she said.

"Swim around the ship? Who am I? John Cousteau?"

"It's Jacques," Avery said. "Either way, you need to stay with me no matter what happens!"

"You think?" Marcus said, his teeth chattering.

"Are you ready?"

Marcus disappeared beneath the surface of the water.

"Marcus!" Avery took a deep breath and dove.

Below the surface, Marcus flailed about as a six-foot shark with gray and black tiger stripes pulled him deeper into the black depths below. The shark had a rod protruding from its head that emitted a glow. Avery swam toward Marcus, grabbing him by his hand. She tried to pull him to the surface, but the tea-light shark pulled Marcus back like a dog with a chew toy, its teeth clamped securely around his boot. Marcus screamed, bubbles erupting from his gaping mouth. Avery pulled Marcus with all her might. Finally, she freed him from the shark's hold. But the tea-light shark charged straight toward Avery, baring multiple rows of cookie-cutter teeth. As it neared her, Avery slammed her sword between its jaws and into its throat, clouding the water around it with black blood. The shark moved erratically, freeing itself from Avery's blade and swimming away.

Avery, making eye contact with Marcus, motioned him toward the surface with her finger. Her lungs burned mercilessly as they both swam upwards. They broke the surface, hacking and gasping for air.

* * *

Tam nocked an arrow, aimed at one of the five flailing heads of the eel hydra, and released it. A direct hit. One of the eels crashed lifeless onto the deck. The rest of the heads bellowed in agony. Tam nocked another arrow, then released it at another head. But it moved, and he missed. The middle of the creature's heads lunged at Tam, but he hopped on top of it, nocking another arrow. He released it straight into the top of the creature's head. It shrieked and crashed back down on the deck. Tam hopped off. The head convulsed, slamming repeatedly into the wood.

There were only three heads left, but Tam only had one arrow. He fitted the last remaining arrow into his bow. But the creature, seething with rage, pulled its entire body from the sea onto the ship with gigantic fat flippers. The boat teetered back and forth as the ocean rushed over the deck. Two of the hydra's lifeless heads and one severed neck dragged on the deck as the creature inched its way toward Tam, its three remaining heads flailing wildly. Tam aimed his last arrow at the beast and fired, taking out one more head. The eel howled in pain, but still inched its way closer toward him. It towered over him, sea water spurting from the gills of its two remaining eel heads. They watched Tam hungrily.

Tam pulled his dagger from his belt, but a thick, black dust covered the eel hydra from above. Tam looked up. Ben was perched atop the cabin, dumping a barrel of black powder onto the monster. Ben dropped the barrel and pulled a torch from his waistband. He struck the torch on the floor, igniting it. Tam's eyes grew wide. He spun around and dove off the side of the ship into the open sea.

Ben held the torch up, aiming at his target. But the eel hydra lunged toward him with one of its last remaining heads, knocking the torch out of his hand and onto the deck where the sea water quickly extinguished the flame. The creature wailed, its two heads positioning for the kill.

Ben clenched his eyes as he held his hands out in front of his body, bracing for the impact.

Then something happened.

A blissful feeling coursed through Ben's body. It was the warmth of the sun on a frigid day. It was a nice, cool plunge into a lake on a scorching day. The energy caressed his body, traveling though his arms and hands. A tiny spark flickered from his fingertips, followed by a scrawny flame. The tip of the flame barely touched the powder on the creature's body.

It ignited. The creature screamed in agony and exploded, taking most of the wooden deck with it.

Ben launched into the air and slammed backward into the ocean as the ship blew up into a thousand flaming pieces around him. He emerged from the water, greeted by debris from the ship.

"Ben!" Avery yelled from afar.

He turned to find Avery and Marcus floating on a large piece of wreckage. He swam toward them, hoisting himself up with the others. Engraved into the wood were the words "Her Majesty." Ben stood up on the piece of wood, scanning the ocean around them.

He found what he was looking for: a translucent elf with long white hair treading water. "Tam!" he said.

As Tam neared the raft, he asked the one question that no one knew the answer to. "Where's Char?"

CHAPTER 9

The Creator's Citadel and an Unexpected Quest to Find the Sphinx of Fact

Days had passed, or at least it felt that way. Avery, lying on her back, turned her head to the water as the makeshift raft drifted aimlessly in the middle of the sea. Unlike before, the ocean was calm now, reflecting the moon high above as it cast its cold glow upon the glasslike surface. She stared into the black sky, watching the brilliant, white stars flicker. They seemed so far away, yet their light sparkled so near. She reached out to touch one, the breeze swimming between her fingertips. She tilted her head to her left to see Ben clenching and unclenching his fist repeatedly, massaging his wrist. Had he been injured during the attack?

Tam stood at the opposite edge of the raft, scanning the surface of the empty ocean. Behind him, Marcus sat near the center of their raft. He watched Tam intently, concern in his eyes.

"I'm sorry, brother," Marcus said.

"If he is out there, I must find him," Tam said, his gaze darting over the surface of the sea.

"Maybe he found a piece of floating wood like we did," Marcus said.

Tam ignored him, scanning the ocean over and over.

Avery rolled over to face Marcus. "Marcus, do you ever get the feeling you're living a double life?"

Marcus laughed nervously. "What do you mean?"

"I mean, do you ever feel like you're living a life that isn't yours when you're not here? Like when you're asleep or whatever."

Marcus shrugged. "Like in a dream?"

"Yeah, sorta."

Marcus stared up at the night sky. "Now that you mention it, yeah."

Avery's eyes widened with interest. "Do you remember anything?"

"Bits and pieces, only."

Avery leaned in. "What do you remember?"

"I remember a girl standing in front of me. To me, she is the most beautiful thing in the world. But she doesn't think that way about me." Marcus rubbed his bulging waist. "I try to change for her, but it's never enough."

Avery shut her eyes for one, brief moment to give them a quick rest. When she opened them again, she was greeted by a sharp, white light.

Day had appeared. Had she fallen asleep?

They were shrouded in dense white mist, making it impossible to see three feet beyond the perimeter of the wood. The raft creaked and moaned. Avery peered over the edge and found white marble tile just below the surface of the water.

"We're here," Marcus said. "Look." He pointed high above their heads.

Avery stood up to get a better view.

The mist thinned high above. The Creator's Citadel towered overhead. What the tower lacked in embellishments, it made up for with size. At least ten stories high, the pure-white tower stretched into the blue sky with grace and simplicity.

Ben also stared at the tower. There was a single window located near the top. For an instant, he thought he saw a young boy peering at them from the window. But he blinked and the boy was gone.

Avery tested her footing on the marble tiles, then stepped off the raft. Marcus followed, then Ben. Tam took one final look at the ocean. He sighed heavily, then followed them.

The mist dissolved slowly around them as they walked toward the center of the platform. All except Tam marveled at its sheer size. Inches below the water, the platform spanned at least two hundred square yards.

Marcus and Tam splashed their way toward the center with their thick boots while Ben and Avery led the group barefooted. Even though the water was cool around their feet, the heat from the sun baked from above. Soon, they found themselves walking on dry tile.

Avery noticed a red door at the base of the tower. Were all the doors in Meridia red? The door appeared to shrink smaller and smaller with each step taken toward it. Upon reaching it, Avery realized the door was only half her height, forcing her to crouch. Ben, Marcus, and Tam crouched beside her and Avery knocked gently on the door. Not a moment had passed before a three-inch slot in the center of the door opened, revealing a pair of gibbous eyes.

"Who goes there?" the man shouted gruffly from behind the door.

"I am Queen Regent Avery and these are my companions."

"Sorry, we are not accepting visitors, especially queen regents!" The man slammed the slot shut in her face.

Avery looked at both Ben and Marcus in disbelief.

"Let me try," Marcus said.

Avery nodded, then shifted toward the outer edge of the small door. Marcus shuffled to the center and knocked.

Again, the man slid the slot open. "Who goes there?"

"I am Marcus of the Red Forest. I represent the last survivors of the Elven Genocide. This is my elven brother Tamerlane. We are here to stop the Fading."

"There is no such thing as the Fading!" The man slammed the slot shut.

Avery and Marcus both turned their heads toward Ben.

"Y-you want me to try?" Ben asked.

Avery and Marcus nodded.

Ben crawled to the door while Marcus shifted out of the way.

Ben knocked.

Again, the slot slid open. "Who goes there?"

"Who goes *there*?" Ben asked.

"Well, no one has ever asked me that before! I am Sir Reginald, the doorkeeper, third of my name and protector of the Creator's Citadel."

Ben leaned in. "A pleasure to meet you, Sir Reginald!"

Marcus and Avery stared at Ben in disbelief.

"And who do I have the pleasure of meeting this fine day?" Sir Reginald asked.

"I am Ben."

"Eggdens? I do not know any Eggdens."

"Eggdens? That's not even close. It's Ben. B-E-N."

"Ahhh! I do not know any Bens, either."

Ben smiled. "Well, now you do."

Sir Reginald squinted. "Yes, I suppose I do now, don't I? What brings you to our lovely citadel today?"

"I wish to help my friends."

"You wish to help your friends? And how do you wish to help them?"

"They—we would like to speak to the Creator about the Red Forest. Parts of it seem to be disappearing without a trace."

"Ah yes, the Fading!"

Marcus sighed loudly, but Sir Reginald ignored him.

"The Fading is a calamity of our time," Sir Reginald said.

"Would you allow us to speak to the Creator about stopping it?" Ben asked.

"The Creator is sick. He cannot see anyone in his condition, I'm afraid."

"There must be a way, Sir Reginald." Ben said. "We've come a long way. Certainly, someone with the title of doorkeeper would have some power over, say, who can come through the door?"

"Hmmm. As doorkeeper, I do have that power. But alas, the Creator is not here."

"But you just said he was sick!" Marcus said.

Ben shushed Marcus and turned back toward Sir Reginald. "Sir Reginald, is the Creator away or is he sick?"

Sir Reginald blinked slowly. "He is away. Away with sickness."

"I see. Is there anything we can do to help his sickness, perhaps?"

Sir Reginald's eyes widened. "There is something you can do!"

"What is it?"

"There is a sphinx who lives on the Serene Island in the Calm Sea," Sir Reginald said. "If you were to bring us its head, it would help cure the Creator's ailments. After which, I am certain that the Creator would grant you an audience!"

"You speak of the Sphinx of Fact," Tam said.

"Yes," Sir Reginald said. "The sickness can only be cured if you bring us its head! Will you take on this quest?"

"How do we find this Sphinx of Fact?" Ben asked.

"That much is easy. You use the contraption over there to beam yourselves to its lair on Serene Island!"

How did they not notice it before? To the left sat a peculiar machine made of rusted metal and stamped with multiple large rivets. The machine was gigantic, about ten feet tall and ten feet wide. Several rusty metal tubes of differing shapes and sizes protruded from the machine, burrowing into the white marble below. On the face of the machine was a large tarnished dial, five feet wide, not unlike a roulette wheel. There were seven slices in all. Each slice of the wheel was engraved with a location in Meridia:

"Red Forest"

"Blue Glass Palace"

"Pariah"

"Perpetual Falls"

"Tower of Continuance"

"Rolling Plains"

There was one final slice: "Serene Island," but it was covered by a piece of parchment that read "Out-of-Order."

"Sir Reginald, how does the machine work?" Ben asked.

"It's quite simple," Sir Reginald said. "You must turn the wheel to your desired location, hit the large red button, walk into the circle painted on the tile over there, and go."

"But the location where the sphinx lives has an out-of-order sign on it," Marcus said.

Sir Reginald did not respond. Instead, he slammed the slot shut.

Avery, Ben, Marcus, and Tam walked toward the wheel.

A fret near the top indicated the desired location. Opposite the wheel was a large circle that had been sloppily drawn onto the marble platform with yellow paint. There was even an open can of paint resting there.

Everyone stared at the circle except Avery. Something on the ocean's horizon caught her eye. "What is that?" she asked.

Marcus squinted, unable to see anything.

Tam walked two paces toward the ocean. "They are ships. Seven of them, all warship class, flying flags with a black pike on a white anvil." He paused. "They have found us."

"You can see all that?" Ben asked.

"Of course. I am an elf."

"They'll be here soon!" Avery said. "We have to use this thing to get out of here!"

"But where?" Ben asked. "The one place we need to go is out-of-order!"

Tam walked toward the wheel and turned the dial to "Rolling Plains."

"This is the closest location to the Serene Island," Tam said.

"Are you sure?" Marcus asked.

"Of course I'm sure."

"On every map I've ever seen, the Rolling Plains are four days on foot to the Calm Sea," Avery said. "On top of that, you have to scale the Mountain of the Disappearing and Reappearing Sun to even reach the coast!"

"It's still the best choice, considering our options," Tam said. "Most of these places are on the wrong side of the world. We don't want to go to the Tower of Continuance unless we want to end up at our enemy's doorstep." Tam paused for a moment as he contemplated. "The closest physical location to the Serene Island is the Rolling Plains."

"Then it's settled," Ben said. "We should go to the Rolling Plains."

"Ok Alfred Einstein," Marcus said. "There's a plot hole with your logic."

Avery sighed "It's Albert.".

"Whatever, Alfred was his brother," Marcus said. "Anyway, if we use the wheel, the Iron Pike Army will use it to follow us."

"Not if we destroy the wheel immediately afterwards," Tam said.

"How do you propose we do that?" Avery asked. "Are you suggesting one of us stays behind?"

"I think I have an idea," Marcus said. "We could start a small fire. By the time it gets big enough to burn the entire machine, we'll be long gone!"

"And how do we start this fire?" Avery asked.

Tam peered into the horizon toward the ships, shielding his forehead. "The Iron Pike Army is loading their soldiers from the main ships onto shore boats. They will soon be upon us. We must hurry."

"I know what to do," Ben said. He scurried behind the contraption. Soon, smoke began pluming from behind the machine.

Avery gasped. "How did you do that?"

"No time to explain!" Ben slammed the large red button with his open palm.

Avery raced toward the center. "Everyone in the circle!"

The rest of them ran into the circle, except Tam who walked toward it nonchalantly.

Meanwhile, several landing parties from the Iron Pike Army disembarked their shore boats at the far edge of the marble platform.

Lights embedded near the perimeter of the painted circle flashed in unison as a shrill beeping noise came from the shaking contraption.

"It's working! Avery said.

The fire spread, encompassing the machine in flames. Steam burst from the pipes. The machine shook violently. There was a loud pop and soon steam was escaping from the pipes with increasing pressure.

The wheel began to spin on its own.

"Why is it spinning?" Avery asked.

"Crap balls!" Marcus said. "Ben, you jacked it up!"

The wheel spun faster and faster.

"What do we do now?" Avery said. "It could send us anywhere!"

The lights surrounding the perimeter of the circle flashed faster and faster and the beeps were louder and louder. The Iron Pike Army was closing in on them, their charred metal boots clapping heavily on the marble tile.

From the inner edge of the circle, Tam nocked one of Marcus's arrows and aimed it toward the spinning wheel.

"What're you doing?" Marcus asked.

"Survivors of the Elven Genocide do not rely on fate," Tam said. "We make our own."

Tam watched the wheel spin round and round, breathing lightly as the fletching from the arrow touched his cheek.

He slowly inched it backward.

Then he released it.

The arrow hit the top of the wheel, superseding the fret, bringing the wheel to a complete, premature stop.

The wheel stopped on "Tower of Continuance."

But Ben, Avery, Marcus, and Tam were already gone.

CHAPTER 10

The Tower of Continuance

Avery and Marcus appeared on a large, semi-circle platform surrounded on all sides by an enormous mountain range made up entirely of black coal rocks, black coal cliffs, and black coal peaks under an ashen sky. Overhead, the clouds shot from one horizon to the next, obscuring the sky with an impenetrable layer of smog.

"Where are Ben and Tam?" Avery asked.

She peered over a deep chasm to find the opposite half of the circular platform perched upon a ridge roughly one hundred yards away. She squinted and saw two figures. One wore pajamas and the other wore a tunic. She waved her arms to get their attention. "I think I see them."

"How did they end up way over there?" Marcus asked.

"We must have gotten separated somehow. Something to do with the platforms being split in half."

Avery approached the edge of the platform. The wind whipped through her hair with a coarse black dust that stung her face.

"There's a trail here!" She pointed below the ridgeline. Her gaze followed the trail to a black castle nestled between the towering mountains.

A black clock tower loomed high above the castle. The hands spun around the face of the clock, the second hand lapping the minute hand and the minute hand lapping the hour hand as each raced clockwise in a feverish blur.

At the exact moment the hour hand completed a revolution, the clock chimed loudly. The bells within the tower clanged. It hadn't taken an hour for the bells to ring, nor even an entire minute. The bells rang every few seconds, filling the night sky with an endless clamoring of ticks, tocks, and clanging.

Avery's lips trembled. "This is the Tower of Continuance." She turned her attention to Marcus. "Why did he send us here? Why?"

"He must have, um, missed?"

"I thought elves of the Red Forest don't miss?" Out of all the places he could've sent us, this is by far the worst."

Marcus shrugged. "I'm sure there's a good reason."

Avery scoffed. "A good reason? This is where the Sovereign lives. In case you haven't been keeping track, he's the one who sent an army to kill us! There's *no* good reason for us to be here!"

Marcus sighed. "Let's try to think like an elf. Maybe he thought we'd be safe here. I dunno, because the general and his army are stuck back at the citadel."

"You do know that the Sovereign commands *three* generals, don't you?" Two of those generals have armies. Who's to say there isn't an entire army waiting for us at the bottom of this ridge?"

Marcus sighed. "Look, Tam wouldn't send us here unless there was a reason. Also, it doesn't make any sense for the generals to be here. This is the last place they'd expect us to be. They're probably out there somewhere looking for us. I mean, we'd have to be pretty stupid to come here, right?"

"You have a point," Avery said. "We'd have to be pretty stupid to come here."

"Hold on," Marcus said. "You said that only two of the generals have armies. What about the third? How is someone a general with no army?"

Avery leaned in. "The General of One Thousand Wars. He is rumored to be the most cunning of all. A brilliant general who became so bored with winning war after war, he decided to dabble in bounty hunting in order to make his conquests more personal. Without an army bogging him down, he could be anywhere. In fact, he could be standing right behind you."

Marcus spun around wildly in a panic.

Avery grinned.

"We . . . we should get going," Marcus said. "Don't want to wait around here for bounty hunters, generals, or anybody."

Marcus glanced over the edge of the ridge before sliding down on his bottom toward the trail below. Avery followed Marcus down the side of the ridge as well, the edges staining and ripping her white dress.

She peered over the chasm to her left to find Ben and Tam doing the same on the opposite ridge. She looked ahead to determine where the two trails would intersect, but her view was blocked by blackened hills and rock formations. Soon, the trail dipped deeper, making it impossible to see Ben and Tam at all.

Avery's stomach growled. "I'm so hungry."

"Me too," Marcus said.

"I feel like we haven't eaten in days."

Marcus rubbed his belly. "That's because we haven't."

Eventually, the trail dumped them into the barren plaza in front of the castle gates. The floor was made of the same black rock that covered the mountains around them, except it was sanded level and smooth. The gate at the edge of the plaza towered high above, its iron bars reaching twenty feet high or more. Chiseled coal walls just as high as the gate stretched across the mountain range on both sides.

Tam and Ben appeared from the opposite trail.

Avery turned her attention to Tam.

"Elf!" she said. "Why did you send us here?"

"Keep your voice down, Queen Regent." Tam scanned the black walls. "I have my reasons."

Avery scoffed. "Care to share those reasons with the rest of us?"

Tam's eyes narrowed. "Now is neither the time nor the place to explain. We are being watched."

"No duh we're being watched. This is the Sovereign's home! And we're here because of you!"

The gate moaned as the platform beneath them trembled. Both halves of the gate lumbered outward. A person about three feet tall and covered from head to toe in a hooded cloak made from blackened steel wool walked through the opening.

"Passersby or tourists?" the person asked as he inspected them with shrouded eyes from left to right.

"We should say 'passersby,' right?" Marcus whispered to Avery.

Avery stepped toward the hooded person. "We are travelers stuck in transition. Maybe you can help us decide if we are passersby or tourists now that we have arrived at your gates?"

"Of course m 'lady," the person said. "If you are here without an invitation from the great Sovereign himself, you are a passersby. The punishment is ten years in a dark prison cell where your meals will be served in the same bucket you use to do your business."

Avery winced. "And what if we are tourists?"

"Well, tourists are a different thing entirely. You see, some of the contraptionists got together and decided that it would be nice if we had a venue to show our inventions to citizens far and wide. Tourists, if you will. You see, we contraptionists have created many amazing things. We take great pride in our marvels and it would be a shame if no one ever got to see any of them!" The contraptionist pulled back his hood, revealing a mole-like head with wrinkled skin, gray thinning hair, and black eyes. "Now, I know what you're thinking. Why would the Sovereign allow such a thing? Well, the short answer is he wouldn't. But since he isn't here, what harm could possibly come from a little tourism?"

"So, the Sovereign's not even here?" Avery asked.

"No. I just finished saying that."

Avery sighed in relief. "We are tourists, most definitely."

The contraptionist jumped for joy. "Great! You will be the first we have had the pleasure of giving the grand tour!"

"The grand tour?" Avery asked.

"Of course! How can you be tourists without a grand tour? We give a tour of the clock tower and its inner workings, a tour of the trinket melting facility, and finally, a tour of a contraption that beams you anywhere in the world instantaneously. Unfortunately, the gift shop is under construction at the moment and will be open at a later date."

Avery flickered a glance back at Tam to find him subtly nodding his head.

"Yes," Avery said. "A grand tour would be wonderful."

"Splendid. Follow me!"

They followed the contraptionist through the gates into the castle courtyard. Not surprisingly, the courtyard was also made entirely of chiseled black rocks. The giant tower loomed over them as the clock's hands raced round and round.

"Over here, we can see the famed Tower of Continuance. Built from the ground up entirely by contraptionists like myself, it was designed to push the flow of time."

"Push the flow of time?" Avery asked. "I thought clocks only keep track of time?"

"That would make no sense at all," the contraptionist said. "If I look at, say, a trinket and it tells me it's two o'clock, and there are no other trinkets around to dispute that fact, then isn't it safe to say that it really *is* two o'clock?"

"I guess when you put it that way."

The contraptionist pointed his stubby finger toward the black mountains at the edge of the horizon. "One peak, two peak, three peak, four!"

Avery stared at the mountain range in question. Sure enough, there were four peaks in the distance. She turned her attention back toward the contraptionist. "Yes, I can count to four."

"Can you?"

Avery glanced back at the mountain range to find only three peaks. "What happened?"

"Ahhh. It's time for the tour! Follow me, please!"

They entered a large red door and were led through a long, dark corridor that had been chiseled out of coal rock. Eventually, the corridor ended at a large foyer filled with huge, interconnected gears that crawled up each massive black wall. They spun quickly, filling the air with deafening clangs and screeching metal. Each massive gear was connected to another by smaller gears or gigantic belts that had been stained black by grease and coal.

Instead of a ceiling, there was a gaping hole at the top of the room. Avery realized that they were standing at the center of the hollow clock tower.

Nearby, a huge bellow fanned a giant fire pit. Surrounding it were twenty or so contraptionists. Each one wore the same blackened steel wool cloak as the guide, and each had the same wrinkled skin, black eyes, and thinning white hair.

The contraptionists scrambled about the base of the tower checking gauges and pulling various levers. One contraptionist approached the fire pit with a large cart filled with metal pieces.

"This should be the last of them!" the contraptionist announced to cheers and applause from the others, including the tour guide.

A second contraptionist approached him. "The last in the realm?"

"That's what I just said!"

The guide leaned in toward his tour group. "That's what he said the last ten times."

As the contraptionist wheeled the cart toward the fire, a flash of metal dropped to the floor and rolled toward Avery. It almost looked like a pocket watch. But before she could grab it, a contraptionist snatched it from the floor.

"No missy! All trinkets get melted in the fire. Them's the rules."

Avery turned back toward the guide. "Why are you melting them?"

The guide pointed toward the fire. "Watch and see what happens."

The contraptionist walked toward the edge of the pit with his cart as flames billowed from below. He tilted his cart forward, dumping the shiny contents into the hungry fire. As he did, the gears on the wall clanged louder and spun faster. Bells from the top of the tower rang loudly, filling the entire room with more cheers and applause. But it was short-lived. Soon, the gears slowed down again. A collective moan filled the room.

"I guess those weren't the last trinkets after all," the guide said.

Ben tugged on his pajama sleeve to hide the watch around his wrist.

"Won't be long until we find them all," the guide said. "Follow me this way to the next part of the tour!"

The guide herded them toward the far end of the foyer through a small side door that led into another long hallway made of tunneled coal. Soon they emerged into a small room.

The room was empty with the exception of a large ornate iron table at the center. Piled high upon its surface, covering every square inch and then some, was an assortment of candies, cakes, and pastries. There were milk chocolates, dark chocolates, white chocolates, and even pink chocolates. There were donuts, strudels, puffs, éclairs, cookies, muffins, and cupcakes. There was white cake, yellow cake, black cake, brown cake, and even Bundt cake. There was butter frosting, caramel frosting, chocolate frosting, vanilla frosting, lemon frosting, and strawberry frosting.

Avery stared at the table of treats, licking her lips. Her stomach growled.

The guide turned to a small doorway at the opposite end of the dining room. "Through this passage, we will view the marvelous contraption used to beam an individual anywhere in the land instantaneously! I will run up ahead to make sure the other contraptionists are ready for the demo. In the meantime, please wait here and, under no circumstances should you eat anything on that table!"

"What are the desserts for?" Marcus asked.

"They are for celebration, of course! For the day we have a fully operational tower working at top speed!"

"You mean after you find and melt every clock—er, trinket—in the land?" Ben asked.

"Yes. And not a moment sooner. We have been waiting a long time for that day to come; the day when we can finally celebrate and eat every treat on that table!"

The guide made a beeline for the side door. He turned around one last time. "I'll be right back. Remember, do not eat anything on the table. Don't touch anything. In fact, don't even look at anything!" He exited.

Tam looked to Marcus. "This is what we have come for!"

Marcus stared at Tam. "What? A table full of treats?"

"No, of course not! The contraption! There are only two known contraptions in the land. One located at the Creator's Citadel and the one located here at the Tower of Continuance. We've already destroyed the one at the citadel. We need to destroy this one also!"

"This was your plan all along?" Marcus asked. "Why?"

"So that we can continue our quest to stop the Fading, of course! Stopping the Fading is our top priority. We can't do that with armies beaming after us everywhere we go!"

"But if we break the contraption, doesn't that mean we'll be stuck here?"

As Tam and Marcus conversed, Avery crept closer and closer to the table full of desserts.

"Not if we do the same thing we did with the last one." Tam turned to Ben. "Whatever you did to break the contraption last time—can you do that again?"

"Wha—what do you mean?" Ben asked.

"Setting the contraption on fire! What else would I mean?"

"Oh yeah. Su—sure. I'll cross the wires in the back of the machine like I did before. Start a fire. Yeah."

Marcus peered at Ben suspiciously.

"So, it's decided," Tam said. "When these little mongrels show us the contraption, we'll distract them while Ben starts the fire. Then we'll all run toward the circle and beam to the Rolling Plains like we originally planned."

"Who will provide the distraction?" Marcus asked.

"Avery will—"

Tam spun around, but Avery was nowhere to be found. "Avery?"

Suddenly, a cake fell from the top of the table down to the floor.

Another.

Then another.

Marcus raced toward the table. But it was too late. Avery had already taken a treat from the pile and shoved it into her mouth. "Thismmmphft tastmmmphft soooo goodmmmphft!"

"Uh, Avery, didn't the contraptionist just tell us not to eat those?" Marcus asked.

Ben and Marcus exchanged a look, then stared at the treats.

Marcus's stomach rumbled. "I guess one wouldn't hurt."

He snatched a treat from the pile.

Ben took one, as well.

Avery reached deep down into the center of the pile. "I bet there's a peanut butter one in here."

She felt the pastries moving underneath. "They're moving!"

Soon treats were cascading off the table on all sides.

Beneath the layer of fresh cakes and cookies was a mountain of moldy candy, moldy pastries, moldy cake, and thousands of maggots.

Avery retched over the pile.

Soon, Ben and Marcus were also retching.

A large gasp came from the far side of the dining room.

Everyone turned to find the tour guide staring at them in complete horror.

Avery turned her head slowly toward the guide.

The guide's eyes narrowed. "Passersby!"

Tam nocked an arrow, aiming it at the contraptionist. But Marcus pushed the tip of his arrow down toward the floor. "Don't kill him!"

The guide charged toward Avery with all his might.

Avery dodged, knocking a pile of vomit-covered treats from the table onto the guide, burying the contraptionist completely.

"Run," Tam said as he led them through the side door.

As they emerged on the other end, they found themselves on a circular patio surrounded by racing clouds. Wind and dust whistled around them. A small band of four contraptionists stood near a machine that resembled the one outside the Creator's Citadel—metal tubes, gauges, and all.

"Burn it!" Tam shouted, racing to the center of a chalk circle that had been drawn onto the black surface. Avery and Marcus trailed Tam as Ben walked toward the rear of the contraption. Soon there was a plume of black smoke spiraling from the machine. Ben turned the dial on the face of the machine to "Rolling Plains" and ran toward the circle.

The guide emerged from the doorway. "Passersby!"

The other contraptionists scrambled in a panic, bumping into their brethren and knocking each other to the ground.

Meanwhile, the fire grew larger and larger around the machine, consuming it entirely. Like before, the dial on the machine spun wildly. Tam aimed his bow and arrow at the spinning dial and fired.

Before the contraptionists could organize themselves, Ben, Avery, Marcus, and Tamerlane were gone.

CHAPTER 11

A Farm in the Valley and Its Unlikely Livestock

Drab dandelions slid majestically across the sky. At two to three feet in diameter, the dried-up flowers swam through the air like lingering jellyfish, squeezing and swelling in tandem, releasing hundreds of parachute-like seeds into the air around them.

Ben's stomach growled. "How much farther is it?"

Tam pointed across the vast green plains toward the mountain range on the horizon. "The Mountain of the Disappearing and Reappearing Sun. That is our destination. The Serene Island is on the opposite side, off the coast. There we will find the sphinx and take its head and finally stop the Fading."

"The sun looks like it's near the peak of that mountain," Ben said.

Tam shrugged. "That's because it *is* near the peak. Right above it, to be exact."

Marcus neared Ben and Tam. "We must climb the peak at night. It's the only way to avoid being burnt to a crisp."

"Burnt to a crisp?" Ben asked. "You mean like a sunburn?"

"No," Marcus said, "I mean burnt to a crisp."

The sun disappeared and was replaced by the black night. In less than a blink, the stars appeared in the sky overhead, sparkling in random intervals. Soon the night winds were cold and the hills around them were filled with the sounds of howling creatures.

"The days and the nights are shorter than ever now," Tam said.

"The Fading" Avery said.

"I'm afraid so," Tam said. "We'd better make camp. Fire will keep the beasts at bay."

"Agreed." Avery nodded, her gaze darting in every direction. "But what will we use to make the fire?"

"I saw a tree when we crossed over the last ridge," Ben said. "I think it's right over this hill. I can go look and see if I can find sticks or something."

"I'll help," Avery said.

Ben and Avery scaled the grassy hill nearby. Sure enough, there was a small tree nestled between two hills on the opposite side. Once they had dropped out of sight from the others, Avery grabbed Ben by his shoulder, spinning him around to face her. "Want to watch the stars with me?"

Avery lay down on the grass, and Ben followed suit.

Avery turned to face Ben. "Sometimes I wish the stars could grant wishes."

Ben stared at the twinkling stars overhead. "What would you wish for?"

Avery shut her eyes. "A family." She opened her eyes. "How about you?"

Ben pondered a moment, then shook his head. "No, it's stupid."

Avery laughed. "No it's not! Tell me!"

"You and Marcus seem so, I dunno, confident. You always seem to know what to do. I wish I could be more like that."

Avery sat up and peered at Ben. "What? You're already confident. You're brave. Bravery by its definition is confidence!"

Ben laughed. "Brave? How?"

Avery's face brightened. "You saved me back at the glass palace. You saved my life. In fact, I've been meaning to thank you."

She was even prettier under the moonlight than usual. Her large brown eyes peered into his, spawning butterflies in his stomach. Ben looked away.

"It was nothing," Ben said. "Anyone would have done the same."

But when he glanced back, he found that Avery's gaze had not shifted. She stared into his eyes. Her blonde spirals moved in the wind, her eyes glistening in the starlight. She leaned in, kissing him on the cheek.

"Not just anyone," she said.

* * *

Avery and Ben appeared at the top of the hill, bundles of sticks and twigs cradled in their arms.

They dropped the bundles at Marcus and Tam's feet. Tam grabbed the driest of the sticks and placed the lower tip against the shaft of another, spinning the branch vigorously between open palms. But there was no flame, not even a hint of smoke. Tam struggled with the branch, then snapped it in two. "Could you have found wetter sticks?"

The wind had grown even colder and Avery shivered. Ben, noticing Avery's discomfort, walked toward the bundle of sticks. "Maybe I can help." Ben pressed his fingers on the sticks. Almost immediately, the wood ignited, and the pile burst into flames.

Both Tam and Marcus's eyes widened in disbelief.

Avery's eyes narrowed. "You're a magic user?"

Ben flinched. "Uhhh. I wouldn't say I'm a magic user. I just learned I could do this, back on the boat."

The flames reflected softly in Avery's eyes "Magic is illegal in Meridia, and rightfully so. Those who use magic become controlled by it."

Ben stared at his hands. "But I don't feel controlled by it at all."

"Okay, genius," Avery said. "What does it feel like when you use it?"

"What do you mean?"

"How did it feel when you lit those sticks just now? I mean, how did your body feel?"

"It . . . it felt good," Ben said. "Like drinking a glass of warm milk on a cold day. I wouldn't say it was anything to write home about though."

Avery walked toward him. "That's what it does. It makes you feel better the more you use it. The greater the spell, the greater the feeling, until you get to the point where you can't stop. If you do stop, you feel weak. You feel sick to your stomach, until you do it again. All the while, it consumes you from the inside little by little until there is nothing left."

Ben fidgeted with his watch. "I didn't know."

"You have to stop using it now!" Avery pleaded, grabbing Ben by his shoulders and shaking him. "Before it's too late. Promise me you'll stop!"

"But . . . I thought it could help us."

"Promise me!"

Silence. Only the crackling of the fire was heard.

"Okay," Ben said. "I promise."

* * *

The sun had already appeared over the mountain for a few moments before Ben and the others headed in its direction. The cool grass felt good under Ben's bare feet, each soft blade slipping between his toes, the beautiful green plains surrounding him on all sides.

Ben caught up to Tam. "How did you learn to fight . . . so well?"

"All translucent elves are born to fight," Tam said.

"But there must be some trick to not getting hit."

Tam shrugged. "The trick to not getting hit is to not be there when the sword lands."

A group of massive gray dandelions fell from the heavens in the distance, almost as if they were falling from one of the slow-moving clouds that was headed east. Still wearing his pajamas, Ben wondered if it was time he found some new clothes.

Not surprisingly, Marcus and Tamerlane fared better when it came to their clothing. Marcus's tunic did a good job of hiding the dirt and the grime. Small, sharp daggers hung loosely from his thick leather belt. He had split his remaining arrows between him and Tam, and they had fashioned some brand-new ones from the sticks that Avery and Ben had gathered; each of them now carried a full load of arrows in their quivers.

"I need new clothes," Ben grumbled to himself, thinking that no one would hear him.

"You and me both." Avery appeared like a ghost by his side. She still wore the tattered, white dress that had been cut at the sleeves and the legs. Like Ben's pajamas, her dress was covered in stains. Her feet were also bare, and her ankles and calves were caked in dried dirt and mud. She smiled warmly at Ben and touched his hand lightly with her fingertips. Ben, both confused and slightly smitten by the attention, wondered why she was being so nice to him after she had been angry the night before.

Marcus slowed his pace until he was walking side-by side with Ben. He pulled him aside as Avery and Tam continued forward. "Ben, I need ask you something. It's serious."

Ben, taken aback by Marcus's tone, nodded. "Sure."

"*Hola. Mi llamo Marcus. Y tú?*"

Ben laughed. "What's that supposed to mean?"

But Marcus didn't laugh. "I just told you my name and asked you for yours."

"Uhhh, my name is Ben."

Marcus sighed. "No, that's not the point. Don't you get it? Someone taught me that language in my dreams. How is that even possible?

Ben stared at him blankly.

"I want you to do something for me," Marcus said.

"Sure, anything."

"Next time I wake up, I want you to interrogate me, ask me everything that I remember, okay? For some reason, I remember my dreams better when I first wake up. Can you do that?"

"Yes," Ben said. "Of course."

* * *

Avery noticed a wire fence about three feet high tracing the ridgeline. Smoke rose from behind a hill. Tam and Marcus nocked their arrows while she drew her blade. Dropping flat to the ground, they crawled up the side of the hill.

The scent of grilled steaks filled Avery's nostrils. Her mouth watered.

Far below, on the other side of the hill, a short creature grilled steaks on a makeshift iron grill. Smoke clouded the air around it and spiraled up toward the sky.

"He's a Boarmin from the Frozen Tundra," Tam whispered. "I can tell from the tusks, even though he clearly tried to file them down to hide his identity. At any rate, his hideous snout gives him away."

Avery marveled at the elf's superior vision. "Is he dangerous?"

"Only dangerous to your coin," Tam said. "Boarmin thrive on bartering. If you make a deal with one, chances are, you got shorted in some way."

Avery sheathed her sword. "Still, we should see what we can barter for. We have a long journey ahead, and whatever that food is is making me hungry."

Marcus's stomach growled. "I agree."

"But what about the fact that we have no money?" Ben asked.

Tam dug into his pouch, producing three coins. He stared at them longingly. "I won these from Char back in the forest. We had a wager over how many arrows it would take to send those two faeries to their graves."

"You shot two faeries?" Avery asked.

"You bet your crown," Tam said. "Despicable monsters. I'd kill every single one if I could."

Avery frowned. "I thought faeries were supposed to be nice and grant wishes."

"They do grant wishes." Tam said, jerking his head at Ben. "If your wish is to be boiled to death and eaten."

Avery glanced at Ben and giggled.

Ben looked at the ground. "I would have found a way out of that net."

"Three coins are not a lot, but at least it's something," Marcus said. "Who's going to do the talking?"

"Not I," Tam said. "Elves are good at many things, but bartering is not one of them. We tend to terminate the other party before the bartering has completed. Besides, I should stay out of sight in case he does not fancy survivors of the Elven Genocide."

"I can talk to him," Marcus said. "But I'm not so sure he'd hear me over the sounds of my stomach. It's really noisy."

"The Queen Regent is our best bet," Tam said. "She has negotiated on behalf of her kingdom, no doubt. Surely, she can barter for some steaks."

"I can certainly try." Avery said, her stomach also growling.

"Here." Tam handed the coins to Avery. "I will be hidden, but nearby."

"I can taste the steaks already!" Avery said unconvincingly.

She scurried down the hill, Ben and Marcus trailing her.

The Boarmin whistled softly to himself, his gaze focused on the dancing flame. He cooked his steaks atop the makeshift barbeque comprised of a pile of rocks with a small metal gate. The aroma of the freshly grilled steaks, with a hint of lime, thyme, and garlic made Avery's stomach growl even louder than before.

"Ex—Excuse me," she said.

This startled the Boarmin. He stumbled backward, a steak dancing precariously on top of his steel spatula. After a little floundering and a bit of improvised acrobatics, the steak wobbled to a stop without falling.

The Boarmin was a short, balding, portly creature with long gray hair on the sides of his head and gray whiskers sprouting from his mouth, ears, and neck. His snout resembled that of a pig's, but was abnormally small for his face. Likewise, the tusks on both sides of his chin had been filed down to unimposing nubs. He wore blue overalls and a filthy white shirt. Three large toes protruded from hairy bare feet.

"Don't you know it's impolite to sneak up behind others?" the Boarmin asked with bulging eyes.

"But, I didn't sneak up behind you," Avery said. "I approached you from the front."

"Do you not see that we are the only ones here? Anyone who approaches anyone out here might as well be approaching from their behind!"

"I see," Avery said. "My apologies then."

"At least you acknowledge your mistakes." The Boarmin placed the steak back on the grill as it sizzled and sputtered, the juices seeping toward its surface.

"Excuse me, sir," Avery said.

"Sir? I am not a Sir! My name is just Clemmons, not Sir Clemmons! I am not a knight no matter what you may think!"

"That's not what I meant at all!"

"Very well, then. What's a sir and why did you address me as such?"

Avery shrugged. "It's just a polite way to greet someone."

"Yes, but what does it mean? If it does not mean knight, perhaps it means dung-scooper or crap-bucket!"

Avery winced. "Heavens, no! It means none of those things!"

"Well," Clemmons said, "It must mean something! I've never heard of a word that means nothing!"

"But the word nothing means nothing," Marcus said.

"It's not a bad word," Avery said. "It means . . ." Avery turned back to Ben and Marcus. "Help me out here!"

"Uh, it means 'sir,' as in 'ssssirrrtainly it's great to meet you!'" Marcus said.

"Oh, I see," Clemmons said. "I like that. So, no way I would be confused with a knight?"

"No!" said Avery and Marcus at the same time.

"Great," Clemmons said. "Well, it was nice meeting you lot. But I must go back to grilling my steaks now! Too-da-loo!"

Avery turned back toward Marcus and Ben. "This negotiation is going terribly."

"Negotiation?" Clemmons ears perked up. "I love a good negotiation!"

Avery turned back toward the Boarmin, but not before regaining her composure and clearing her throat. "We are very hungry and we would like to purchase some steaks from you."

"And who are *we*, might I ask?"

"I am Queen Regent Avery and these are my companions, Ben and Marcus."

"And what of the translucent elf hiding behind the bush on the far hill?"

"Umm . . ." Avery looked back at the bush that the Boarmin indicated. She saw no sign of Tam and wondered how the Boarmin could even see him from this far away. "Who do you mean?"

"Don't play dumb with me, Queen Regent."

"That's Tam. He's with us also."

"You should do a better job of hiding him. Most in Meridia don't have the same sense of humor I do when it comes to the return of the translucent elves. Where do you come from, Queen Regent?"

"The Blue Glass Palace," Avery said.

"The Blue Glass Palace? I've never heard of it. Do you mean the Blue Glass Pile of Rubble? That I have heard of."

"News travels fast," Marcus said.

Avery sighed. "Either way, we would like to buy some steaks from you."

"The steaks aren't for sale." Clemmons turned back to the grill.

Avery scoffed. "What do you mean they're not for sale? What are you going to do with all these steaks? Surely, you cannot eat them all by yourself. There are at least ten steaks here!"

"As I said before, the steaks aren't for sale. I am a broker of dragonwoofs, not a broker of steaks. If I was a broker of steaks, I'd be selling the steaks instead of feeding them to the dragonwoofs that I intend to sell, now wouldn't I?"

Marcus stepped in front of Avery. "If you're selling dragonwoofs, and the steaks are for the dragonwoofs, then it stands to reason that if one buys a dragonwoof, one would get all the steaks as well?"

Clemmons rolled his eyes. "Obviously. One would be an idiot if they could not make that connection."

"Wait, what's a dragonwoof?" Marcus asked.

Avery had read about the dragonwoofs in the library in the palace. Once the scourge of the skies, dragonwoofs, ten to twelve feet in length, would fly over entire armies during battle, breathing fire on unsuspecting infantry and winning wars for kings and queens alike. But after some time had passed, the offspring of the dragonwoofs became smaller and smaller until they were only thirteen inches long. Thereafter, the dragonwoofs could neither breathe fire nor fly at all and soon they were almost extinct.

Avery stepped forward. "We'll buy one."

CHAPTER 12

Where Dragonwoofs Sleep

Avery stared into the Boarmin's dark eyes, awaiting a response, any response.

"One cannot buy a dragonwoof," Clemmons finally said.

Avery sighed. "But you just said you were a broker of dragonwoofs!"

"Yes, I am a broker of dragonwoofs," Clemmons said. "You cannot buy a dragonwoof, but you can buy *three* dragonwoofs."

"What would we do with three dragonwoofs?" Marcus asked.

Clemmons smirked. "That's your problem! They are worthless creatures, as you most likely know. They can't fly, they can't breathe fire. They are nothing like their ancestors. All they do is poop, sleep, eat steaks all day, and poop some more. But as wretched as they are, I can't imagine how much more wretched they'd be if they were separated from each other. A bunch of whining babies they'd be. Not that I care about their feelings or anything. I just don't want people walking up to you on the street and asking where you bought the whiny crabapples and you saying

'Oh, I got them from old Clemmons in the Rolling Hills' and them saying 'Oh, that Clemmons, what a rubbish dragonwoof broker!'"

"Okay then," Avery said. "You've made your point. You will only sell all three. There are three of us here that can take care of them. How many coins do you want for all three?"

"Hmmm. I'll make you a deal. Only five hundred coins for all three, the steaks included. A fine price for the finest bred dragonwoofs in Meridia!"

"But you just said they were worthless!" Marcus.

Clemmons placed his hands on his hips. "I would never say such a thing about my merchandise!"

"Well," Avery said, "We don't have five hundred coins."

"Hmmm. Perhaps I could drop the price if you happen to have something I need."

Avery's eyes widened. "What do you need?"

"Let's see. I would be willing to barter for the shoes of a queen regent!"

"But I don't have any shoes on me," Avery said.

"Oh, that's a shame," Clemmons said. He looked at Ben. "How about shoes belonging to one who can use magic?"

"I can use magic," Ben said.

Avery glared at him.

"Bu-but I promised I wouldn't anymore!" Ben added.

"Besides," Avery said, "He doesn't have any shoes either, as you can plainly see."

"That's too bad," Clemmons said. "I might have given you all three in exchange for the shoes. I do love me a nice pair of magician shoes. How about a pair of boots from two separate translucent elves? Now that is a bargain you cannot refuse!"

Avery sighed, "The other elf who was with us was lost at sea."

"Oh, I see. Did you happen to take his boots before you lost him?"

Avery shook her head.

Clemmons sighed. "Hmmm. You drive a hard bargain. But I am willing to negotiate with the best of them! How about a left boot from one translucent elf and a right boot from another? That's only half the amount of boots I asked you for before! Certainly, that's a great deal for all parties involved!"

"Again, we don't have his boots!" Avery said. "We don't know where he is, so we cannot give you his left boot, both boots, or either of his boots for that matter! How about boots from Marcus here? He was trained by the elves!"

"No," Clemmons said. "I am up to my neck in boots from weeds that have been trained by the elves!"

Avery sighed. "There must be something we have on us that you want!"

"I see," Clemmons said. "You are very good at bartering, Queen Regent. I have to be careful around you. I was unaware that I was dealing with a master." He scratched the top of his head. "Okay. Final offer. I will sell them to you for four coins now and four hundred and ninety-six coins later. That brings you to my original price of five hundred coins! No less!"

"But we only have three coins on us now!" Avery said.

"Sorry. I cannot do it for three. Three is too little. Four, however, is just enough."

"We don't have four coins between us," Avery said. "Couldn't we just pay you three coins now and four hundred ninety-seven later?"

"Sorry. That exceeds my lending threshold, I'm afraid"

"Then we can't buy the dragonwoofs from you," Avery said, defeated.

"Good day then." Clemmons went back to grilling the steaks.

Avery's eyes narrowed. "How about a hundred coins now and four hundred and ninety-seven later?"

This piqued Clemmon's interest. "A hundred coins now? I thought you said you only had three coins."

Avery smirked.

Clemmons grinned. "The negotiation is back on!"

Marcus whispered in Avery's ear. "But we don't have one hundred coins!"

Avery elbowed him and turned her attention back to Clemmons. "Do we have a deal?"

"We have a deal!" Clemmons stuck out his hand.

"Good." Avery shook Clemmons's hand. "Now, I have a question."

"Go right ahead, Queen Regent! Ask away!"

"Do you have a permit to sell livestock within the realm of Meridia?"

Clemmons gaze sank towards the ground. "Well . . . uhhh . . ."

"You are aware that the fine for selling livestock without a permit is ninety-five coins, are you not?"

Clemmons scratched his head. "Uhhh . . . no, I wasn't aware. But no one else needs to know about this little transaction of ours, right?"

"Well . . . as queen regent, I don't think I can look the other way on this. I'm afraid I will need to collect the fine in full."

Clemmons paced back and force across the grass. "How about we deduct ninety-five coins from the upfront payment and call it even?"

"Fine."

"Okay!" Clemmons said. "Five coins it is!"

"But we haven't even broached the topic of tariffs yet. You are aware that there is a tariff imposed on all sales that occur within the confines of the Rolling Plains, are you not?"

"No," Clemmons said, a bead of sweat rolling off his forehead. "How much is this tariff?"

"It's thirty percent along with a ten-percent collection fee. If these were my lands, the tariff would be much cheaper."

"If I deduct these tariffs from the price, what does that leave me with?"

"Well," Avery said. "It leaves you with three coins up front."

"You truly are the master of negotiations," Clemmons said, bowing. "Three coins up front it is. Four hundred and ninety-seven coins later. That is much less than I was willing to let them go for."

Avery handed over the three coins. "Ya know, it's still five hundred coins in the end."

"Yes, but I lost the negotiation!" Clemmons said.

Ben approached Avery. "How'd you do that?" he asked. "How did you know it would end up at three coins?"

"I dunno," Avery said. "I guess I'm just really good at math!"

"Well played, Queen Regent," Clemmons said. "The dragonwoofs and the steaks are yours." He paused. "But! There are conditions that must be met. You must agree to feed them, bathe them, and take care of them. Although I despise the little menaces as much as one can hate a living animal, I don't want other potential customers seeing my dragonwoofs living in poor conditions! I have a reputation to uphold! Do you all agree?"

"We agree," Avery said.

"Okay, you'd better," Clemmons said. "Not that I care what you do with these lazy leeches after you take them with you. But, if one were to check up on you later and find out that you hadn't upheld your end of the bargain, one might want to punish liars such as yourselves! It wouldn't be me, of course. I cannot wait to be rid of the filthy animals, personally." Clemmons walked toward the fence with a plate full of steaks. "Come here you mangy rats. Lunch is ready, not that you lot ever appreciate it!"

Clemmons beckoned Ben, Avery, and Marcus toward the fence. "You need to feed them. It will let them know you are their new masters."

A single dragonwoof meandered toward the fence. At only eleven inches high, the creature was covered in tufts of white fur with black patches. It had a very fine coat with plenty of frill around the chest, legs, and ears. Two disproportionately large ears sprouted out from both sides of its head. A mask of black fur covered both its ears and eyes from rear to front. Its small head was rounded, with a short thin muzzle and tiny teeth. Where the fur ended, a thin layer of scales began, both at the base of its wings and the start of its tail. The olive-colored wings folded at the creature's sides. The olive-colored tail trailed the ground and ended in a scaly tip shaped like an arrowhead.

"I call this one Wolf because she howls at the moon all night and keeps me awake," Clemmons said.

The two other dragonwoofs appeared over the ridge. They looked identical to Wolf in shape and size, except one had red patches of fur and the other brown.

"The red one I named Rooster because he wakes me up every morning with a cockle-doodle-woof," Clemmons said.

"What about the brown one?" Avery asked.

"Oh yeah," Clemmons said. "I almost forgot about the brown one. The brown one is named Sebastian."

"Sebastian?" Avery asked, her eyes widening in disbelief. "Why did you name him Sebastian?"

"I named him Sebastian because he never lets me sleep at night!"

"That makes no sense!" Avery said.

"Makes perfect sense to me! Wait until you try sleeping around this trio of idiots. You'll have bags under your eyes in no time like poor old Clemmons."

"How do we feed them?" Ben asked.

"You feed them steaks, naturally," Clemmons said. "Of course, you'll need to cook them first since these ingrates refuse to eat raw meat."

Clemmons passed a juicy steak from the grill to Avery. She grasped the edge with her fingertips.

"Here," Clemmons said. "Go ahead and feed Sebastian."

Rising, Avery lifted the steak over the fence. Sebastian raced toward the fence on all four legs and jumped up into the air to retrieve the steak. Unfortunately, his pounce was not high enough to reach it. So, Avery lowered the steak to where he could. Sebastian pounced again, yanking it from her hand. He gobbled half of it up, leaving the other half on the grass. Using his nose, he pushed the steak in Avery's direction.

"This one likes you already," Clemmons said. "This is how the dragonwoofs show respect to their master. They share their food."

Avery giggled. "Thank you!"

Sebastian barked in return.

Ben neared the fence and offered a steak to Wolf. Wolf jumped into the air effortlessly and swallowed it in its entirety.

"Sometimes it takes more time before they recognize their master," Clemmons said. "Sometimes it takes a lifetime!"

Marcus also approached the fence with a steak. He held it high over Rooster's head, but the dragonwoof made no attempt to jump in the air. "This one is defective," Marcus said.

"That one refuses to jump for anyone. You have to place the steak on the ground if you want him to eat it. Little mister-prissy-pants he is!"

Marcus dropped the steak on the ground. Rooster sniffed it. After a moment, he took a small bite. Then another. He ate the steak, albeit slowly.

"What if we don't have any steaks to feed them?" Ben asked.

"I'll start you out with a few." Clemmons tossed cooked steaks into a burlap sack. "The rest you'll have to find on your own. I can't do everything for you, you know."

"How will we pay you back what is owed?" Ben asked.

"What was your name again? Eggdens was it?"

"It's Ben."

"Oh yes, my mistake. You were asking about the four hundred and ninety-seven coins you owe me?"

"Yes."

"Do not worry, Ben," Clemmons said. "I will collect them from you when the time comes." Clemmons furrowed his brow as if a thought had popped into his head. "Now, before you go, I need a moment alone with these wretched pests!" He proceeded to shoo Ben, Avery, and Marcus away with a flick of his wrist. They stepped away until he stopped frantically waving his arms.

Once they were far enough away, Clemmons whispered into each dragonwoof's ear, petting them one by one. Wolf licked Clemmons gently on his face. Clemmons stood up and turned toward the group. A single tear rolled down his cheek. "They are ready to go with you." More tears streamed from his eyes. Then he paused for a moment and yelled, "I hate this wind! Always getting dust in my eyes!"

As soon as he said this, he opened the gate, releasing the dragonwoofs into the open.

Wolf, Rooster, and Sebastian bolted out of the gate past Avery, Ben, and Marcus towards the hillside beyond. As the three weeds chased after the dragonwoofs, Clemmons grinned from ear to ear and muttered, "The time has come for dragons and weeds to burn old trees and plant new seeds."

CHAPTER 13

The Principal

World History class was almost over. It was finally Ben's chance to make his move. Summer Poppy was absent today, so there was no way she could interfere. In a few short minutes, the bell would ring, and he could finally ask Taylor to the dance. He sat at his desk, his stomach climbing into his throat with each tick of the clock. As was typical, Mr. Perkins lectured all the way to the top of the hour while the other students stared at the clock in anticipation of the bell. Ben watched as the second hand dawdled past the three, four, five, and six.

"Mr. Young," Mr. Perkins said.

Ben jumped in his seat. "Yes?"

"How hot do you think it has to be for rock to turn into a liquid?"

"Huh? Is that even possible?"

"Is it possible?" Mr. Perkins pushed his spectacles forward toward the tip of his nose. "Why not ask that question to the people of Sicily in 1669?"

The entire class laughed.

"Maaagma!" Mr. Perkins said. "Twelve hundred degrees is the correct answer. At twelve hundred degrees, rocks become magma. You would know that, Mr. Young, if you paid more attention to me and less attention to the clock."

The bell rang, almost to underscore his point. But Mr. Perkins did not walk toward his desk like he normally did. Instead, he placed both palms on Ben's desk.

"Magma," Ben said. "I got it."

That appeased Mr. Perkins about as much as the Sicilian villagers appeased the volcano gods. "I'd like to see you pay better attention to class, Mr. Young. You are throwing away your potential."

Even now, Ben had difficulty listening to Mr. Perkins. He watched Taylor in the corner of his eye as she gathered her books and binder and placed them neatly into her bag.

"Are you even listening to me?" Mr. Perkins asked.

Ben nodded. He attempted to stand up from his desk, but Mr. Perkins smacked the surface with open palms.

"You have the rest of your life ahead of you!" Mr. Perkins announced. "You're wasting it!"

"Won't I always have the rest of my life ahead of me?"

"Excuse me?"

But Ben said nothing.

"Good," Mr. Perkins said as he lifted his hands off of Ben's desk and meandered toward the front of the classroom.

Ben hastily gathered his books and shoved them into his backpack. The zipper caught on the fabric near the teeth. Normally, Ben would wonder why anyone would engineer a quarter-inch seam right next to the zipper, but right now he had bigger things on his mind. He pulled the zipper hard, forcing it over the flap, then jumped out of his chair and ran into the hallway. Ben looked left, then right. He saw Taylor walking down the hall.

He raced after her, but as he got closer, he slowed to a walk and composed himself, then mustered enough courage to tap her on the shoulder.

Taylor spun, her eyes meeting his.

Ben's heart stopped.

Just then, the zipper opened up on his backpack and the entire contents spilled to the floor. Ben scrambled to pick up his stuff as Taylor watched silently. He stood with his belongings mashed between his arms.

"Hey," Ben said, making an effort to stare at her eyes and not at her feet.

"Hey," she said calmly. Almost *too* calmly.

Ben gulped. He shot his open hand out in her direction, dropping his books and binder to the floor. "I'm Ben," he said.

Taylor did not shake his hand. Instead, she snickered. "You're the one who's always getting in trouble in class."

Ben awkwardly retracted his hand.

"You're also the one who didn't know that the Black Death came from rats," she added.

Ben leaned in and whispered. "What if I told you the Black Death actually came from the fleas on the rats?"

Taylor laughed. "I guess you read the textbook after all."

"I did," Ben said, crossing his arms. "It was after I failed the quiz, but I read it."

Taylor laughed. She extended her hand in his direction. "I'm Taylor by the way."

Ben shook her hand. "Yeah, I know."

A moment of silence.

"So, what'd you want to ask me?" she asked.

"Oh yeah," Ben said. "I was wondering . . ."

"Yes?"

But the words seemed trapped in his mouth.

Taylor turned her head to one side. "What is it?"

Ben took a deep breath. "I was wondering if you were going to the dance with anyone tonight."

It almost seemed like an eternity before she answered. Finally, she shook her head. "Not really."

"Would . . . would you like to go with me?" Ben held his breath.

She stared at the ceiling. "Sure, I'll go. But on one condition."

Ben raised his eyebrows.

She squinted. "How good of a dancer are you?"

Ben gulped.

"You do know how to dance, right?"

Ben shook his head before nodding. "Of course I do."

Taylor smiled. "Okay, I'll see you later then." She turned away and resumed her slow stroll down the hallway.

Ben did a fist pump. Taylor looked back, almost catching him.

* * *

Ben arrived at his third period English class, grinning ear to ear.

Like clockwork, students filed into the classroom and took their seats. As usual, Mrs. Pear was late to class. Before long, all of the students were seated at their desks, waiting. Five more minutes passed before she barged into the classroom, stumbling toward the podium, flustered and out of breath.

"Why isn't anyone writing in their journals?" she said. "I thought we discussed that the first ten minutes of class is journal time. That's why I purposefully come late! To give you time to write!"

"What's the topic?" asked Paul from the front row. Paul was the class suck-up. "You didn't assign a topic for us yesterday."

"Oh," Mrs. Pear said as she moved toward the chalkboard. "The topic today is . . ."

She scrawled the words with chalk: *The Mind Is a Prison That the Heart Yearns to Escape.*

Ben dug out his journal from his backpack. It was stained and the binding was worn. He despised these writing exercises and usually resorted to drawing stick figures. Most of the time, the slogans came from trashy romance novellas Mrs. Pear bragged about picking up in line at the grocery store. Ben flipped through the pages in his journal, realizing that there were no blank pages left! Maybe he had gone too far with the stick figure wars last time.

Mrs. Pear fumbled with the power button for the projector. "This thing won't turn on! Stupid machine!"

Paul raised his hand.

But Ben needed a reason to not write in his journal today. "I got this!" he said as he jumped out of his seat.

"Thanks Ben!" Mrs. Pear said. "I didn't know you were so helpful."

Dropping to his hands and knees, Ben crawled underneath the desk and plugged the cord into the power outlet.

Mrs. Pear clapped as the projector came to life. "You're like a regular Thomas Edison!"

Ben returned to his desk to find Marissa Smith smiling at him from the next seat over. She rarely said a word to anybody. Her eyes, nose, and mouth were veiled by the long straight black hair that perpetually hovered over her face. She wore dark colors, usually emblazoned with the name of a band that Ben didn't recognize. She rarely looked anyone in the eyes, so it was surprising to see her smiling at him. Ben smiled back.

Mrs. Pear approached him. "Ben, how do I make the projector have sound?"

But, before he could answer, the classroom door swung open.

A group of overtly cheerful students wearing matching red-and-gold uniforms poured in. One of them, a girl with red hair and freckles, thrust a basket full of flowers into the air. Two other group members, both guys, jumped into the air in unison and cheered, "Carnation sale!"

"We're fundraising for Jason, the South Point Student at Memorial Hospital who has been in a coma for a year," the girl with the freckles announced. "Help the cause by buying a carnation for your girlfriend, boyfriend, or favorite teacher!"

Sure enough, Paul rushed toward the basket and burrowed into his pockets, producing a wad of cash. He purchased a white carnation and immediately handed it over to Mrs. Pear.

"Oh my," Mrs. Pear exclaimed as she placed the carnation over her heart.

The flower brigade prowled the desks, selling carnations to anyone who was willing and pitching carnations to those who were not. In the end, they always made the sale.

Ben, in an attempt to remain inconspicuous, pretended to write in his journal in the hope that they would lose interest and pass him by. He had no need for a carnation. Perhaps, if they had caught him in World History, he would have bought one for Taylor. But the chances of him seeing her at school again today were slim. He tilted his head to find Marissa, also pretending to write in her journal.

But the freckled girl did not buy his charade. "Would you like to buy a carnation? It's for a good cause!"

"I don't have enough money."

"Well, how much do you have?"

Ben reluctantly reached into his pocket and produced two quarters and a nickel.

"Sold!" She handed Ben the white carnation with one hand while snatching the money with the other.

Ben, not knowing what to do with it, immediately turned toward Marissa and handed her the flower.

"You can have this," he said.

Marissa placed the carnation against her nose.

"Thank you," she said as she pushed back her hair, revealing light blue eyes.

* * *

It was lunch. Ben raced into the library, almost knocking down a librarian in the process. He raced up and down the aisles before locating a book entitled *How to Dance – With Step-by-Step Pictures.*

He clutched the book to his chest, pondering the dance and its greater meaning. Certainly, if he played his cards right, Taylor could be his girlfriend by the end of the night. If he had a girlfriend as pretty as Taylor, maybe the other guys would stop picking on him.

Ben read the book, eating the bologna sandwich that his mom had packed for him. He practiced some of the dance moves with an imaginary partner. Some of the other students laughed at him as they walked by, but Ben didn't care.

Eventually, the bell went off, signaling that lunch was now a fleeting memory. Ben went to his locker and began spinning the dial on his dented metal door. Of course, his first attempt at dialing his combination failed, so he had to spin the dial multiple times to the right to reset it before he could try again. Once he finally managed to get the locker open, he noticed a piece of folded red paper jammed through the vent on the door. He freed the note and unfolded it, revealing a heart. He found the following words scrawled on it: *To Ben from Your Secret Admirer.*

Ben's heart skipped a beat. Was it from Taylor? A second bell rang through the courtyard. He was late. Ben stuffed the note into his pocket and raced toward wood shop. On his way, he passed by Marissa, walking alone, smelling the carnation and staring at him. Ben smiled, but she looked away.

* * *

The smell of dust, pine, and acrylic permeated the air. Mr. Anderson stood near the rear of the class demonstrating the band saw to two foreign exchange students. The other students in the class sat at their desks sanding the edges of a small, square piece of wood in an attempt to create an even smaller oval-shaped piece of wood.

Ben pulled the wooden name-for-a-desk he had been working on for the past two weeks from his backpack and applied the finishing touches with ultra-fine sandpaper. The nameplate looked alright, considering it started out as a rather dubious-looking piece of wood.

Ben was getting the hang of cutting, sanding, and even burning color into wood with a handheld propane torch. Even so, Mr. Anderson only allowed him to create a nameplate with the name "Ben" as opposed to "Benjamin," which, according to Mr. Anderson, was "too advanced for this class."

Satisfied with his sanding job, Ben walked over to the vat of lacquer and began varnishing his creation with a paint brush. Although the N in the word "Ben" was disproportionately larger than the B or the lowercase E, he still admired his creation with pride.

Parker and Trey walked over from the old milling machine. Trey hovered near him, sporting a brand-new jersey, presumably purchased by his parents to replace the one that Ben had accidently gotten lacquer on.

Ben sighed. "Can we skip this today?"

"Can we skip this today?" Trey jeered.

Ignoring him, Ben continued to apply a fine coat of lacquer over his wooden name-for-a-desk. He intended to give it to his mom as birthday gift, and he had no intention of letting anyone spoil it for him.

"Hey, he's talking to you!" Parker said.

"Yeah," Trey said. "It's rude to ignore people when they're talking."

Ben kept applying lacquer to his nameplate.

Trey pressed up against Ben with his chest.

"You should take a shower every now and then," Ben muttered.

Trey scoffed. "What'd you just say?"

Ben kept his gaze on the piece of wood as he maneuvered the brush in between the center of the lowercase E.

Trey spun Ben around by his shoulder, forcing Ben to look into his eyes. "I'll kick your ass!" Trey said.

Ben took one step back, the vat of lacquer directly behind him. "The trick to not getting hit is to not be there when the sword lands."

Trey's face immediately turned beet red. "Did you learn that from The Lord of the Rings, queer?" His fist shot toward Ben's stomach.

Ben took one step to the side, dodging the punch.

Trey's fist landed squarely onto the side of the large plastic vat, rupturing it. Lacquer gushed from the fissure, covering the floor with clear coat. Trey slipped and landed flat on his back. The other students clapped—not so much in support of Ben's victory, but at Trey's misfortune.

Mr. Anderson cut the power to the band saw and raised his yellow safety goggles. He glared at Ben first, then turned to Trey as he flapped on the floor like a suffocating fish. "That stuff isn't free," Mr. Anderson said to Ben.

* * *

Ben sat in one of two chairs in front of the principal's desk. Mom sat in the other, still wearing the scrubs she'd worn the night before. Ben avoided the principal's gaze, and instead, looked about the tiny office. The walls were painted matte vanilla, a stark contrast to the thick latex paint that had been slathered onto every surface of the school. The only other things in the room were two nondescript black bookshelves and a placard on the spotless desk that read "Frank DeMarco: Principal."

Principal DeMarco rubbed his balding scalp with anxious fingertips. "Ben is suspended from school for a week for fighting."

"Suspended?" Mom asked.

"But what about the dance tonight?" Ben exclaimed.

DeMarco sneered. His gray suit with the black tie was too small for him, and he grunted between each and every sentence he sputtered. "There will be no dance for you, young man."

Ben shot up from his seat. "Please Principal DeMarco!"

But DeMarco shook his head.

"Since when do you care about school dances?" Mom asked Ben. She turned her attention back to DeMarco. "Don't you think suspension is a little harsh?"

"Not at all, Mrs. Young. We are being very lenient on this matter. Normally, an attack on school property would result in expulsion."

Mom gasped. "Expulsion? My son was defending himself!"

"There is a signed affidavit from another student saying your kid started the fight." Mr. De Marco pushed the folder toward Ben's Mom, but she ignored it.

"A signed affidavit from the other guy's best friend? What are you running here? A kangaroo court?"

"Trey is the only one who had signed witness testimony. The other students in the class claim they didn't see anything until poor Trey was already on the floor with your son towering over him."

"Towering over him?" Mom asked. "Ben is like ninety pounds!"

"Ninety-five pounds." Ben said.

DeMarco sighed. "Either way, this school has a zero-tolerance policy for bullies."

Mom scoffed. "My son is not a bully!"

"Look," DeMarco said. "You're a single mom. I get it. I know you can't be everywhere at once. I know you can't supervise everything your kid does. But these years are very important for Ben's personal development. We call them the formative years. As such, we do our best to instill core values into our students. We lay the foundation. But it is up to you to reinforce these core values when he is not physically on school grounds."

"Core values?" Mom laughed. "You're talking to me about core values? What? Like blaming the victim and protecting the bully? Is that your idea of a core value?"

"I can assure you that's not what is going on here. We take bullying very seriously. In fact, it's in our charter!"

"This is going nowhere!" Mom jumped from her seat, then turned toward Ben. "C'mon, we're leaving."

"But what about the dance tonight?" Ben asked as she dragged him   out   of   the   office.

CHAPTER 14

The Last Inn Before the Mountain

Wolf gawked at Ben, her slit-like pupils dilating within a kaleidoscope of brown and green membranes. Drool strung from the tip of her snout, and her reptilian tail extended toward the sky. Her wings trembled at her sides as she sat on her hind legs, anxiously supervising Ben as he reheated steaks over an open fire.

"You really are just a dog, aren't you?" Ben spun the stick that pierced the steak over the campfire that Tam had kindled a few moments earlier. Wolf let out a small growl and a sharp yelp to signal that she was hungry. Ben and the others had quickly learned that the dragonwoofs were always hungry. In fact, it had only been a couple of days since Clemmons had provided them with the burlap sack full of steaks and those steaks were almost gone.

Luckily for them, they traveled much faster now than before. Yesterday, they had come across an abandoned mule and cart.

"Why would there be a cart here of all places?" Marcus asked.

"It's too convenient," Tam said. "Probably a trap."

The mule was well fed and groomed. Ben, too, wondered where the owner might be. "Whoever owns this cart can't be too far."

"If the owner were here, we would've seen him by now," Marcus said.

Tam nodded. "Anyone dumb enough to leave a cart and mule alone in the middle of the Rolling Plains deserves to have them stolen."

"Either way," Avery said. "If we don't take it with us, this animal could die of thirst, starvation, or worse!"

So, they borrowed the mule and the accompanying cart. It had an unvarnished wooden base with four large wooden wheels. Mounted on the base was a large metal cage with a wooden ceiling. A metal door at the rear of the cage opened outward with a shriek. Judging by the loose feathers and seeds within, the cage had most likely been used for livestock and produce.

Prior to finding the cart, the three dragonwoofs had trailed them on foot. Out of nowhere, they would dart out away from the trail and into the fields toward a rabbit, a bird, or some other wild animal. Although the dragonwoofs had limitless energy when it came to playing and hunting, they could not walk in a straight line for more than a quarter mile before their forked tongues hung limply from their mouths and they slowed to a stop. On more than one occasion, the three dragonwoofs had fallen behind and retreated to the shade of a bush. It was not until two or three hundred feet later that Ben, Avery, or Marcus would realize the dragonwoofs were not with them, forcing them to backtrack.

Although the dragonwoofs were small, they were heavy. It was a chore to carry them, and Ben, Avery, and Marcus were forced to wait for the dragonwoofs on the side of the road while they took repeated walking breaks.

With the cart, however, Wolf, Rooster, and Sebastian were able to sleep in the cage as the mule pulled it along. This allowed them to limit their stops and travel faster across the plains.

Regardless of whether they were sleeping or walking, the dragonwoofs always had a voracious appetite. At one of the stops, Ben threw a small piece of steak above him and Wolf caught it midair.

"Good girl," he said.

Wolf chewed the steak, leaving half of it on the ground. She pushed it toward Ben with her snout.

"That's okay," Ben said. "I'm not hungry, yet."

Wolf whimpered, her large ears drooping.

"Okay. I'll eat some of it. But between you and me, this is pretty gross."

Wolf's tail wagged furiously as Ben leaned over to pick up the steak.

"Yum!" Ben forced a smile. He took a bite of the steak. It still tasted pretty good, so Ben finished off the rest. Wolf rolled on her back, extending her legs into the air as she flopped side to side. Ben rubbed her furry belly just between her scales.

"Cockle-doodle-woof!" Rooster barked as he charged past Marcus toward the hills.

Rooster was the most vocal of the three and seemed to cockle-doodle-woof at anything he deemed bark-worthy, from a bee on the side of the road to a mound of dirt that happened to look at him funny.

At some point during the journey, they had decided to name the mule Bob for no particular reason other than he looked like a Bob. Bob's coat was brown with a coarse black mane. His snout was bright white and his short, thick ears drooped slightly, making him look perpetually drowsy. The mule sauntered down the road, the cart in tow, with little care about his surroundings.

During a roadside break, Ben retreated under the shadow of a large boulder to hide from the unforgiving sun. The grass was cool here, so he lay down and shut his eyes. Not a moment had passed before he felt the blazing sun on his face. He opened his eyes to find that the boulder had completely disappeared. Had the Fading already reached the Rolling Plains?

* * *

The Great Mountain loomed directly ahead of them, splitting the horizon, its white peak a stark contrast to its dark base.

Then, the night sky appeared.

Ben climbed to the top of a large hill and noticed smoke billowing from a cottage at the base of the mountain.

As they neared, they noticed the cottage had been built with cobblestones mashed between square wooden frames. An orange glow danced behind warped glass windows, flickering within. A sign hung from an old wooden post that read: Welcome to The Last Inn Before the Mountain.

"An inn!" Marcus said.

Ben checked the burlap sack for more steaks, but it was empty. "Maybe they have steaks!"

"I'm starving," Avery said.

"You and me both!" Marcus rubbed his grumbling tummy.

Avery pulled back on Bob's reins, leading the mule toward a nearby trough already occupied by a gray horse with long, stilt-like legs and a fat, cream-colored mule with bushy sprouts of coarse black hair near its hooves.

Avery pressed her face against the cage where Wolf, Rooster, and Sebastian lay on their sides, their mouths agape. "You be good while we're inside. We're going to get something to eat and find you some steaks. No barking while we're in there. Can you handle that?"

Sebastian stared at Avery with half-shut eyes, rolled onto his back, and stuck all four of his paws into the air. Rooster barked to signify that he understood that he was not supposed to bark. Wolf slept with her legs stretched straight through the bars of the cage.

Tam pulled his dark cloak from his satchel. "Just in case we run into Elven Genocide sympathizers."

They approached the inn, and Ben marveled at the intricacies of the wall and how each chunk of jagged gray stone was perfectly placed, fitting together like pieces of a puzzle. Small green vines climbed the sturdy wooden supports along all four edges. As they walked by the distorted glass windows, they could hear muffled chatter and music, but they couldn't see anything but the orange glow through the thick panes. They approached a red wooden door.

Marcus raised his fist, but hesitated. "Should we knock?"

Tam grabbed the door handle. "I've never heard of anyone knocking to get into a pub."

The door opened with a loud creak. The music and chatter inside the inn stopped.

A tiny person, about three feet tall, poked his round head outside. His skin was white as snow. He sported oversized round spectacles with golden rims and had short, shaggy gray hair. He wore a white knit shirt with an emerald leather vest. His white leggings were tightly wrapped around his thighs and calves.

"Guests?" he asked as he bowed, exposing the top of his head. Most peculiarly, his bald spot was covered in cracks that looked like a vase that had been shattered and glued back together. As he bowed, white dust sifted from the cracks onto his face.

"I think so," Ben said.

Everyone was silent, both in and out of the inn

"Guests!" the tiny person said. The music and the chatter immediately resumed behind him. He pushed the door open wide then scrambled outside to hold it for the travelers. He scooted by them, revealing a key protruding through his clothes and out his back. The metal bow of the key was made of intricate symmetrical swirls forming a heart. The key rotated slowly in a clockwise motion, ticking as he moved. "I am the innkeeper, Melvin! Welcome to The Last Inn Before the Mountain!"

He stuck his hand out. When Ben shook it, he noticed that Melvin's palm and fingertips were hard like porcelain and ice cold. Even so, Melvin beamed widely, making the handshake seem warmer than it would have been otherwise.

The sights, sounds, and smells of The Last Inn Before the Mountain were overwhelming. In the far corner, opposite a large blazing fireplace, sat a band of five round porcelain men playing instruments ranging from flutes to fiddles to banjos. They looked similar to the innkeeper, but with more colorful hair and less powder on their faces. They stomped their feet in unison as they played. The orange light from the fireplace danced along the walls and ceiling on all sides as if keeping pace with the beat. When one band member stopped, another would run behind him and wind up his key until he started playing again. This occurred multiple times throughout the song.

Other round porcelain men with wind-up keys on their backs sat in wooden chairs at wooden tables, chatting and laughing as they drank ale from wooden chalices and ate a thick, hearty stew from wooden bowls. A few patrons in black robes were scattered throughout the inn, looking slightly peculiar and out of place. But they also enjoyed ale, stew, the music, and the laughter.

The aroma of the stew filled Ben's nostrils, and he could smell hints of garlic, pepper, cheddar, and thyme. This made his stomach rumble like never before. Melvin ushered them toward a circular table at the center of the tavern and pulled out a chair for each of them.

The eastern wall of the room housed a magnificent bar. It was made out of a mahogany tree that had somehow grown a foot high before turning and growing sideways for seven feet, then upwards again toward the roof. Its brown and red bark was covered in a thick coat of lacquer, and it glimmered in the light of the fire. The side of the tree had been expertly filed flat into a smooth countertop, and the part that stretched to the ceiling had been hollowed out and made a shelf that held various wooden jugs and glass bottles containing spirits in vibrant colors. The tree was so perfect it almost seemed as if the inn had been built around it for the sole purpose of using it as a bar.

Behind the bar, stirring a large iron pot of stew, was another porcelain person. The only identifiable female in the room besides Avery, she wore a white cloth apron over a blue knit dress with white hems. Like the others, she also sported a wind-up key that rotated slowly as she moved about the kitchen.

"That's my wife, Hilda!" Melvin said as he snuck up behind Ben, startling him. "Isn't she beautiful?"

She was beautiful.

Hilda had huge, sparkling green eyes and long red hair that plunged toward the ground. As she stirred the pot, she smiled to herself, revealing bright teeth between painted red lips.

"Might I interest you in my wife's world-famous stew?" Melvin asked.

Ben, Avery, and Marcus nodded in unison. Meanwhile, Tam scanned the inn with skeptical eyes from the depths of his hood.

"And you, kind sir or madam," Melvin said to Tamerlane. "Would you like a stew?"

"No," Tam said.

"Okay," Melvin said, defeated. "Three stews it is!" He zipped away from the table.

Avery turned to Ben and Marcus. "We should eat as quickly as possible so that we can feed our dragonwoofs."

Ben and Marcus nodded.

Melvin walked up to Hilda and gave the order for three stews. She snatched a wooden ladle larger than her arm and filled three empty bowls from the kettle with practiced precision. She loaded them on a tray and made a beeline toward their table, then placed the bowls under Ben, Avery, and Marcus's noses. The scent of the spices delighted them. Ben, in particular, thought the stew smelled better than anything he had ever smelled before. His stomach growled in anticipation.

"What's wrong?" Marcus asked Tam. "Aren't you hungry? We've been traveling for days."

"I don't like it," Tam said. "Something isn't right about this place."

"Oh, you're just being cynical, as always," Avery said. "These people are nice!"

"If it smells like a trap and looks like a trap, it's a trap!"

"It *is* a trap," a voice boomed from behind him. "But not one concocted by the celadons, I assure you."

Two large thick-gloved hands fell on Tam's shoulders. They belonged to a hulking beast of a man with green skin. He was covered in dark leather garments from head to toe that smelled of pungent dyes and strong oils. His face was large and sweaty and dappled with dark brown blotches and deep crevices. As he opened his mouth, he revealed jagged canine teeth coated in thick yellow plaque.

"Crap balls!" Marcus said.

Tam, not once breaking his composure, stared straight ahead as the man loomed over him.

"If you do not remove your hands," Tam said, his fingers creeping toward the dagger on his belt, "It will be you who has found themselves in a trap."

But the man did not budge. Instead, he stood there, his hulking shadow looming over them. "I have been awaiting your arrival." His hands slid off of the elf's shoulders. "I've been waiting here for quite some time."

The man walked around the table and dragged a large wooden chair toward them.

Ben and Marcus scooted their chairs closer to Tam and Avery. The man took a seat, his massive body landing with a thud. His bulging black eyes shifted left and right as he scanned them slowly, his breathing labored and heavy.

He spoke, "Allow me to introduce myself. I am—"

"You are a goblin," Avery said, her voice both confident and filled with wonderment.

"Indeed I am."

"One of three remaining in Meridia," Avery said.

"One of two. The Dread Pirate Arnaud recently perished from the gout. He was one hundred and fifty-two years old."

Avery placed her finger on her lip. "You don't strike me as a cleric. That leaves only one goblin left. You are The General of One Thousand Wars sent by the Sovereign to kill us."

CHAPTER 15

The General of One Thousand Wars

The General of One Thousand Wars grinned, the reflection from the fire dancing across his dark, penetrating eyes.

"How did you find us?" Avery asked.

"The question is not how I found you. The question is: why."

"I already know why," Avery said. "You are one of the Sovereign's three generals."

"Yes," the general said. "Still, the question is not so much why I found you; the question is: why haven't I killed you yet?"

Tam removed his blade from his belt underneath the table as Avery's fingers slid to the hilt of her sword. Meanwhile, Marcus leaned forward and grasped the bow leaning against his chair.

"Others have tried," Avery said, clutching the hilt of her sword as she slowly eased it out of her sheath. "In fact, another one of the Sovereign's generals tried to kill us. You should ask him how that went."

The general laughed. "I appreciate your gumption, Queen Regent. You remind me of a goblin with that mouth of yours. But do not make the mistake of comparing me to that buffoon."

Avery sat up straight in her chair. "You serve the same master in the same capacity. At some point, comparisons must be made."

"You are mistaken, Queen Regent. I do not serve the Sovereign. I merely complete contracts on his behalf. Either way, I think you will find me a much more formidable opponent than the weed commander who leads the Iron Pike Army."

"Okay, I'll bite," Ben said. "Why haven't you killed us yet?"

"That is a compelling question with a compelling answer," the general said. "I admire that you were the only one in the group to not reach for a weapon underneath the table."

Avery and Marcus's eyes widened. Tam remained cool and focused.

The general smirked. "There will be no need for weapons. Not yet, anyway. On my honor, you will not be harmed before the next sun appears. Not by me."

"On your honor?" Avery asked. "What's stopping the four of us from killing you where you sit, *on your honor?*"

"What is stopping you indeed? Do you see the man behind me in the corner wearing the dark robes just beyond the reaches of the firelight?"

Avery tilted her head, peering behind the general. Sure enough, there was a man in the corner, just as the goblin had said.

"I see him," she said. "And?"

"I paid him fifty coins to sit there and enjoy a bowl of stew and drink a mug of ale. This tavern is famous for their beef stew and their ale, as you may already know. I paid several people in this very inn to do just that: enjoy a bowl of stew and drink a mug of ale. And that is what they will continue to do as long as you have a drink, eat some stew, and engage in conversation with me."

"Do you think a handful of drunks in an inn can take us out?" Tam asked.

"Oh, they're not here to 'take you out' as you so aptly put it. No. They are here to kill the aging tavern owner, his pretty wife, and any other porcelain person in this tavern who is unfortunate enough to be in the same room as three weeds"—the general paused and stared intently at the cloaked figure in front of him—"and a translucent elf who cannot follow simple instructions. Now, put your weapons away!"

Hilda walked toward the table. "Is there anything else I can get you all?"

"Yes." the general said. "Ale for me and ale for each of my new friends!"

"No ale for me!" Avery said. "I'm not old enough to drink!"

Hilda looked at the general, confused.

"Like I said, ale for everyone at the table. And bring the hooded fellow some of your famous stew. He has had a change of heart and cannot wait to try it!"

"Wonderful!" Hilda said. "Five ales and one famous stew!"

But before she could zip away, the general placed his hand softly on her shoulder.

"I am not done. I need you to cook up three steaks and place them in a clean burlap sack.

"But, I don't have any steaks to cook," Hilda said.

"Use the same fine meat you use to make your famous stews. I am certain the three pets will not know the difference."

"You want to feed the main ingredient of my world-famous stew to . . . pets?"

"I will pay double."

Hilda paused. "Whatever floats your cat!"

The general handed Hilda a bag of coins. "I will pay for everything, including any food or drinks consumed by my friends or their pets. Run along, now."

The general returned his attention to the companions. "Such a nice girl. Hopefully nothing bad happens to her."

"You know about our dragonwoofs?" Avery asked.

"I assure you, they are unharmed. The same privileges apply to them as to you. No one in your party will be harmed before the next cock crows. You have my word. You also have my word that you will be dead before tomorrow's night appears, but let's take it one step at a time, shall we?"

They stared back at the goblin, uneasiness in their eyes.

"On that note," the goblin said. "You can eat your bowls of stew. I assure you they are not poisoned."

Hilda arrived at the table with a tray full of thick wooden mugs, each filled to the brim with ale. She placed a mug on the table in front of each person, then departed as fast as she had arrived.

"A toast!" the goblin said. "If you're old enough to die, you're old enough to drink with me."

They reluctantly clashed their mugs together against the general's and moved them toward their lips.

Avery lifted the mug, bracing herself. Although she had never tried ale before, she knew deep down that it would be utterly disgusting. Her lips touched the outer edge of the mug as the thick fluid drained into her mouth. She shut her eyes, expecting the most sour and bitter taste on her tongue.

Surprisingly, the ale tasted like water.

Avery peered back into the mug to see if she had been duped. Sure enough, the ale in the cup was light amber with a foamy top.

She took another sip. It tasted exactly like water. She took another sip.

Water.

Then another.

More water.

"Does this taste like water to anyone else?" she asked.

Ben and Marcus looked back at her with uncertainty in their eyes. They were hesitant to speak. Did they think it tasted like water too?

But before Ben or Marcus could say anything, the general snatched Avery's mug from across the table, peering inside. He inhaled deeply. "This is most definitely ale!"

"No," Avery said. "It's most definitely w—" Marcus kicked her beneath the table before she could finish her sentence.

"It's ale!" Marcus said. "I've never had ale before, but I am certain this is what ale is supposed to taste like, right Avery?"

"Most definitely," Ben said. "This is most definitely the best ale I have ever had. Avery, you should give it another sip, I think."

"Okay, if you guys say so." Avery took another sip from her mug. "I don't think—"

Again, Marcus kicked her under the table.

"Oh yeah," she squealed. "This is most definitely ale!"

"Yes," the general said. "The finest ale in all of Meridia. Perhaps the queen regent has built up a tolerance for ale to the point where it tastes like simple water! Perhaps you have goblin blood in you after all!"

"Oh, joy," Avery said.

Relieved, Marcus turned back to the general. "Why must we drink and converse with you? What's in it for you?"

"I've been a general for many decades. I've been in countless wars."

"Oh, you can't count to a thousand all of a sudden?" Avery asked.

"I can. But to win one thousand wars, that is something else entirely."

"I've read everything there is to know about Meridia," Avery said before draining the mug of ale.

The goblin followed suit as if it were a competition, slamming the empty mug onto the heavy oak table.

Avery continued. "I imagine, like most things in history books, that a thousand wars is a gross exaggeration."

"Another round," the general said to Hilda before turning back to Avery.

"Exaggeration or not, I earned my name because I have been in more wars than any other general in the history of Meridia. I've seen every tactic and I've seen every maneuver. After you have experienced as many wars as I have, you start to realize that there are only a finite amount of moves. After a while, wars become a lot like chess. The movements become more and more fixed, the tactics are repeats of tactics you have witnessed before."

Hilda dropped off a fresh round of ale.

"On a long enough timeline, wars will be fought the same way they were fought before," the general said. "The enemy flanks from the east when you send a contingent to the south. The enemy moves their cavalry from the west when you plant your scouts in the mountains to the north. Victories are repeated, along with losses. When you learn all the moves, you start to unveil the patterns. When you unveil the patterns, you know the outcome of the battle even before it begins. Once you know the outcome, you can never lose. For this reason, I do not dabble in wars any longer. They are beneath my intellect."

The goblin took a massive gulp from his mug, emptying it completely. Avery did, as well. Like clockwork, Hilda arrived with two fresh mugs.

"That is why I quit being a general and became a bounty hunter. Bounty hunting is a much more intimate activity. Individuals are more unpredictable than the masses. Each hunt is different from the last. I feel an exhilaration, now, that I stopped feeling when I was winning war after boring war. That is why I have chosen to hunt you, and that is why I am talking to you now. I love learning more about my prey before I hunt and kill them."

"But won't bounty hunting repeat itself the same way if you keep doing it long enough?" Avery asked. "Why not quit while you're ahead?"

The general held his mug high above the table. "To quitting while you're ahead!"

Avery stood from her seat, wooden mug in hand, before clashing it against the general's.

"You are wise beyond your age, Queen Regent, but I am not one to breech a contract that I have already committed to."

"Why accept contracts from the Sovereign?" Avery asked. "Someone with your talent should be able to find a more reputable employer, no?"

The general laughed. "The Sovereign's reputation is only strengthened by having me in his employ. Besides, the Sovereign has a unique taste for carnage that perfectly aligns with my talents. He also pays handsomely. When he announced that he needed three weeds hunted and killed, I would have jumped at that opportunity alone. When he added a translucent elf from the Red Forest to the contract, I almost did it for free. You see, the killing is what drives me. Trinkets and all that other nonsense are secondary distractions as far as I am concerned."

Ben moved his hand over his wrist. The goblin picked up on this.

"Oh, I see," the general said. "The trinket is a timepiece. It all makes sense now. No wonder he offered so much gold for it."

"I thought you said you were doing this contract for free," Avery said.

"I said I almost did it for free. Like most inhabitants of Meridia, I have my vices. Ale being one of them." The general took a long drink from his mug.

Avery shrugged. "After we take care of you and that pathetic Christopher, maybe we'll pay the Sovereign a visit." Avery chugged the rest of her ale. The general gulped his down as well.

"He employs three generals, you know," the goblin said. "They are spread far and wide. You've already met that idiot, Christopher. Now, you've met me. Pray you never meet the third. She is ruthless beyond words. But, for what it's worth, I play fairly. Not like the other two. You can rest easy now that I have found you. I promise you that your deaths will be clean and honorable."

Tam sipped his ale slowly. "Goblins are smart, but they are no match in single combat to an elf."

"That is true of many goblins. But I am unlike other goblins. My expertise in combat is derived from my ingenuity."

"You are right about one thing and only one thing." Tam slurped from his bowl of stew. "This stew is delicious."

"I look forward to doing battle with you. The translucent elves' reputations precede you."

"You should have found us earlier," Avery said. "There were two elves in our party then."

"Now, that would have been something. Two elves in a fight to the death with a goblin."

"My bets are not on the goblin in that scenario," Avery said as Hilda delivered new mugs of ale. Avery drank heavily from her mug, and, seeing her, so did the general.

Again, the goblin grinned. "We will see tomorrow how well one elf and three weeds fare against the General of One Thousand Wars."

"Maybe we should go now?" Ben whispered into Avery's ear. "You know, to get a head start?"

"I think I'd rather stay here and have a few more drinks with our new friend," Avery said loudly.

The general held up his mug for another toast. "Cut from the same cloth!"

"You said you wouldn't kill us until tomorrow," Avery said. "Is that a promise?"

"Yes," the general said. "I promise to kill you tomorrow after the cock crows but before the night appears."

Marcus shot a glance toward Avery. What are you doing?

Avery returned the favor by kicking Marcus underneath the table.

"I propose a drinking contest," Avery announced.

The general smirked. "You are aware that a goblin has never lost a drinking contest?"

Avery's eyes narrowed. "Then you have nothing to fear."

"What are the terms?" the general asked, his head swaying back and forth from the ale. "Certainly, you do not think I will call off the contract if I lose?"

"Of course not," Avery said. "If I win you must simply tell me how many wars you have really won. The real number. Not the one in books."

"I've never told anyone that number."

"I am not finished. Once you have told me that number, you must pay that number to me in coins. Let us hope, for my sake, that the history books are not a complete exaggeration."

The general pondered for a moment. "I accept those terms if I am defeated. And if I win?"

"Name your price," Avery said.

The goblin's face brightened. "There is a sword. A sword created by the ancient citizens of the Incriminye intended to keep peace. A sword that changed from white to red if it touched the blood of another. This enabled the Incriminye to know if a capital crime had been committed within their walls."

Avery revealed her short sword and slammed it on the table. "Take a good look. Before long, I will paint this sword bright red with Christopher's blood."

The general stared at the blade's satin-like white surface, drool forming in the corner of his mouth. "You are a goblin, indeed. If circumstances were different, I might have taken you on as an apprentice. You could have been the daughter I never had."

Avery smirked, her small hands clutching the large mug. "Bottoms up, pops."

* * *

The sun beamed brightly from every window in the inn.

When The General of One Thousand Wars awoke with slobber running down his chin, he found himself seated at the same table and in the same chair he had been the night before. Except now, the three weeds and the translucent elf were nowhere to be found. In their place were four stacks of wooden mugs, each piled five to ten high.

Melvin, the innkeeper, waddled over to the general as cheery and friendly as ever, the wind-up key on his back spinning slowly. "You're awake!" he said. "I am deeply sorry you had to sleep in these conditions, but you were out cold and you were far too heavy for me and Hilda to move!"

"How long have I been out?" the general asked.

"Quite some time. That weed girl drunk you under the table. It's not surprising though. Ale does not have the same effect on weeds that it has on us!"

The general grasped Melvin's collar and pulled him toward his growling face. "What do you mean?"

"Well . . . well, you know," Melvin said, sweat and white dust dripping from his porcelain forehead. "If a weed drinks ale, they might as well be drinking from a well. I've seen it before."

"How long has the sun been in the sky?" the general asked.

"Long enough for the night to appear any moment now.

"No!" The general released Melvin's collar, rising from his chair and breathing heavily.

At that moment, the night appeared outside the thick glass windows. Melvin scurried toward the fireplace to light it.

"Clever girl," The General of One Thousand Wars said.

"Who now?"

"My daughter," the general said.

"Your daughter? I don't think I've seen anyone around here who would fit that bill."

The goblin cleared his throat. "Which way did they go?"

"I think they were headed toward the mountain. They did leave a cart behind with a mule. Apparently, the mule's name is Bob.

They said I could keep him as long as I took care of him and fed him. I sure do like animals."

"Good for you." The general grasped his forehead in pain.

"Those are some swell friends you've got. Hilda and I can definitely use the cart to make our deliveries. It's dandelion pie season!" Melvin paused. "Oh, one other thing . . . your friends, they took another bag of meat with them for their pets. They went ahead and put it on your tab. The girl said you wouldn't mind."

CHAPTER 16

The Queen Bee

"**X** equals three because of the inverse relationship with Y," Avery said with confidence. It seemed that everyone's eyes had been fixed on her the moment she walked into class.

Of course, the van taking her from the group home had been late by at least fifteen minutes. Samuel, the van driver who doubled as the maintenance guy, had forgotten it was the first day of public school for the eighth graders.

"That's correct," Mrs. White said. "Perhaps you can use those computational skills to get to class on time tomorrow."

Everyone laughed.

But Avery ignored them. The only thing on her mind were the fosters who were coming to see her on Saturday.

Mrs. White shushed the class and pointed at the student next to Avery. "Veronica, it's your turn to wow us with your math skills. Problem number eight, please."

Veronica Miller rose from her seat. She was definitely pretty, probably the prettiest girl Avery had seen at school so far. She had long black hair and her clothes looked brand new. She wore several silver bracelets on her right wrist that jangled as she wrote on the whiteboard. When she finished copying the problem from her text book, she turned and faced Mrs. White.

"You're not done yet," Mrs. White said, "You need to solve it before you can sit down."

"I don't know how," Veronica finally said.

Mrs. White sighed. "Who can help Miss Maybelline?"

Avery shot out of her seat. "I will!"

Avery adjusted her oversized glasses and examined the board. She turned toward Veronica. "This is a tough one." Avery grabbed a marker and wrote several equations on the board. "X equals one or X equals negative one. But since one is a removable discontinuity, the answer is negative one."

Mrs. White clapped. "Very good, Avery."

Avery and Veronica returned to their seats. Veronica scribbled a note and handed it to Avery. Avery read the note: "Hallway. After class."

The bell rang, and Avery gathered her belongings and headed for the door.

Veronica stood at the other end of the hallway, facing away from Avery. Her hair was smooth and vibrant—everything that Avery's tangled mess was not.

Avery reached into her backpack and found her asthma inhaler. She took one quick puff and walked in Veronica's direction. Veronica turned as Avery approached her.

"You really understand this stuff, don't you?" Veronica asked

Avery blushed. "Understand what?"

Veronica laughed. "Math, silly."

Avery watched as Veronica was greeted, hugged, and/or kissed on the cheek by almost everyone who walked by. Eventually, Veronica resumed walking down the hallway with Avery in tow.

"You're from that exchange program, aren't you?" Veronica asked. "The one for orphans?"

Avery looked down at her clothes. She wore the same white polo and blue pants that Mrs. Dewey had given her, Stephanie, and Tracy to wear. "Yeah, is it that obvious?"

Veronica laughed. "You all wear the same clothes and you started the semester a week after everyone else. So I'd say, yeah, it's pretty obvious." Veronica stopped in the middle of the hallway, turning to face Avery. "Anyway, onto the real reason I asked you to walk with me. I was wondering if you'd be up for tutoring me in math. Obviously, I need some help. Please say yes! Please!"

Avery laughed. "You want me to tutor you in math? I mean, you're already in the advanced class, aren't you good at it already?"

"Yeah, I'm good at it. But I'm not great at it. You solved an equation that I, in a million years, couldn't have ever solved."

"I don't know," Avery said. "Our van picks us up from the school right after the last bell. When would we have time?"

Veronica shrugged. "We'll make do. Lunch, nutrition break, study hall, whatever works."

Avery pondered for a bit. Veronica gave her sad eyes in response.

"Okay, I'll tutor you," Avery said

Veronica sighed in relief. "How much?"

Avery laughed. "Nothing of course."

"Thank you," Veronica said. "You don't know what this means to me. I owe you."

Avery laughed again. "Nah, you don't owe me anything."

"I'll be the judge of that, orphan girl." Veronica walked toward an open classroom door. "Can you start tutoring me during nutrition break today?"

* * *

Avery arrived to her first period math class to find a boutique shopping bag waiting for her on her desk. She had tutored Veronica yesterday during nutrition break, lunch, and study hall. On top of that, anytime she had finished a class, Veronica was outside waiting, textbook in hand, anxious to ask a new question. Avery started to question what she had gotten herself into.

"Surprise!" Veronica said. "I put together a week's worth of clothes for you. Some of them are new, most of them are from my closet. I think you'll like them."

Avery riffled through the bag. There was an assortment of blouses, skirts, T-shirts, and jeans. "Why? You didn't have to do this!"

Veronica smiled. "I just thought you might want to wear something other than your standard issued uniform.

Avery laughed. "I'll have you know that standard issued orphan uniforms are a hot commodity around these parts." She pulled a long white dress from the bag and held it up in front of her. "This is beautiful!"

"You should wear that to the dance on Friday," Veronica said. "You're going, right?"

Avery stared at her blankly. "I—I don't . . ."

"Wait, you're going, *right*?"

Avery took off her glasses and rubbed her face. She put them back on, blinking her eyes rapidly. "Even if I were allowed to go, I'm not really the *go to a dance* kind of girl, if you know what I mean. Look at me."

Veronica stared at Avery intently. "What are you talking about? You're so pretty, Avery."

Veronica flipped her own hair from side to side and smiled.

Avery attempted to flip her hair. Sadly, her frizzy ends got caught in the hinges of her glasses. She removed them to untangle the loose strands.

Veronica ran her fingers through Avery's hair. "Meet me at my locker after class."

Veronica's locker was one of the few peppered with an absurd number of notes and stickers. Veronica dialed the combo and opened the door. More notes fell to the floor, which Veronica ignored. She pulled out a small plastic bottle and handed it to Avery. "I usually use this after P.E., but you can have it. Put it in your hair after you shower tonight. Leave it in overnight. Don't wash it out until morning. It'll make your hair look just like mine. Well, it won't be the same color, but you get the idea."

Avery stared at the bottle. "Do you think it'll work?"

"I'm positive."

"How positive?"

"About fifty dollars positive. That's how much the full bottle costs."

"No way," Avery said.

Veronica reached deep into her locker and pulled out a large barrel of a brush. "Here," she said, handing it to Avery. "Do you have access to a blow dryer?"

"Yes, but I never use it."

"Start using it. Do you know how?"

Avery shook her head.

"No worries. I can teach you. Do you have contacts for your eyes?"

Avery flinched. "What?"

"You know, contacts." Veronica pulled the skin below her eye.

But Avery couldn't see anything. "No, it's not covered by my medical plan. It's considered cosmetic."

"What's your prescription?"

"What's my what?"

"Your prescription, you know, for your glasses."

Avery shrugged. "I have no—"

Veronica pulled a pair of glasses from her locker and handed them to Avery.

Avery stared at Veronica's glasses. They were way cooler looking than her glasses.

"Try them on," Veronica said.

Avery took off her glasses and put Veronica's on.

Veronica pushed her nose into Avery's face. "Can you see?"

Avery looked around and gasped. "Yeah! I think so"

Veronica grinned. "Cool, that means we're the same prescription!"

"How is that possible?"

Veronica smirked. "Must be fate, orphan girl. You can borrow my glasses."

"Really?"

Veronica shrugged. "Yeah, my dad's an optometrist. I can always get new ones."

"Why are you doing all this for me?"

Veronica smiled. "I owe you, remember?"

"No you d—"

Veronica laughed. "You know those movies where the popular girl helps the new girl, only to turn on her halfway through?"

"No, our TV doesn't work."

Veronica laughed. "It doesn't matter. Either way, I'm not the girl in those movies. I refuse to be a cliché. Besides, it's not me helping you. It's you helping me, right? See you at nutrition break."

* * *

Thursday night, Avery sat on the couch reading books with her new glasses.

Tracy approached Avery in tears. "We have to tell Mrs. Dewey that we can't go to South Point anymore," she said, her voice cracking.

"Why?" Avery asked, "What's wrong?"

"All the girls there hate me. They hated me from day one! I tried to fit in with them, but I hear things. They call me poor. They call me all sorts of things behind my back!"

"What about the boys? Certainly, the boys must like you."

Tracy threw her arms into the air. "The boys are the worst! I made out with this boy, Glover, beneath the bleachers during lunch today. Now, I'm on some slut-shaming wall in the boys' bathroom and no one will leave me alone! By fifth period, everyone was making kissy faces at me in class. It's absolutely the worst! I can't take it anymore! We have to tell Mrs. Dewey! Public school is no place for nice girls like us!"

"Calm down," Avery said. "It's going to be okay. You just have to give it more time."

"More time? I won't last another second there! Going to that school is the worst thing that has ever happened to me in my life!"

"There's a dance tomorrow night," Avery said. "I already asked Mrs. Dewey if me, you, and Stephanie could go. It'll be fun. You'll see"

Tracy crossed her arms. "It's going to be dreadful. All those idiots running around like they own the place!"

"I think you should give it a chance. Maybe you'll meet a nice boy. A football player or something. You never know."

Tracy peered at Avery suspiciously. "What happened to your face?"

"What?"

"Something's different about you."

Avery touched her temples. "New glasses! Can you believe it?"

Tracy bared her teeth. "No, it's not just that. It's your hair. Your clothes. You've been hanging around that Veronica Miller chick, haven't you?"

Avery grinned. "Yeah, we're friends."

"Well, I wonder if she'll stay friends with you once she finds out your M.O."

"My what?"

"Your modus operandi. You stole my idea. You're trying to become popular at school so you can land a rich foster!"

Avery winced. "I didn't *steal* your idea. I don't know what you're talking about."

"You know exactly what I'm talking about. Still, I wonder if they're going to want to adopt you once they find out."

Avery grasped Tracy's shoulders. "You can't tell anyone, you promised!"

Tracy pushed Avery's hands away. "I guess you shouldn't go to that dance tomorrow, huh?"

* * *

Avery spent the morning looking over her shoulder, wondering when Tracy was going to pop up and cause trouble. She approached Veronica during their lunch tutoring session. "Veronica, I have something to tell you."

Veronica put down her pencil. "What's up?"

"I can't go to the dance tonight."

"What?"

Avery stared at the floor. "I'm sorry."

Veronica stood up. "Hold on, you can't bail on me now. I put a lot of work into this, you have to go!"

"A lot of work? What're you talking about?"

"Meet me in the faculty restroom after school. The one near the trailers. I'll show you then."

That night, Avery met Veronica in the bathroom like she'd been instructed. She opened the door and found that the countertops had been covered with an assortment of blushes, eye liners, and lipsticks. There was even a blow dryer plugged into a socket underneath the sink. Veronica stood in front of the mirror in a black slip dress and flats. She immediately turned her attention toward Avery. "Love the dress."

Avery wore the white dress. She grinned. "Thanks. It's one of yours."

Veronica laughed "I know. Are you ready for some makeup?"

"Mrs. Dewey always says I'm too young for makeup."

"Mrs. Dewey isn't here."

Veronica began applying eyeliner to Avery's lids. "Don't squint." As soon as she finished with Avery's eyes, she applied lip liner and lipstick.

Avery sighed. "Listen—"

Veronica laughed. "Don't talk. You'll mess me up!"

Veronica grinned. "Ta-da!" She beamed. "You look beautiful."

"Really?" Avery asked.

Veronica pulled Avery toward the mirror. "Really."

Veronica snatched a circular pad and began powdering Avery's face. "You were saying?"

"One of the girls from the home is saying I'm using you because you're popular. It's not true."

Veronica kept powdering Avery's face. "I know. We made a deal. That's why I'm helping you and you're helping me, right?"

"I know," Avery said. "It's stupid, but she knows something about me and has threatened to tell certain people if I go to this dance."

Veronica stopped powdering. "Oooh, a secret? Like what?"

"I don't want to get into it. The point is, I have fosters coming to see me tomorrow. If they found out about it, they might not want anything to do with me."

Veronica grabbed Avery's shoulders. "Fosters? They might adopt you, right?"

Avery shrugged. "Yeah."

"Let's say everything works out. You'd live with them forever, right?"

"Yeah, well, until I turn eighteen."

Veronica laughed. "So, forever."

"I guess so."

"Maybe you should just tell them the truth before this other person has a chance. Don't you want to live with people that appreciate you for who you are?"

"I think so," Avery said.

"Oh," Veronica said. "I almost forgot."

She handed Avery a contact lens case.

"What is this?" Avery asked.

"You didn't think I was going to let you wear glasses to the dance, right?"

"What? But how?"

"If our glasses are the same prescription, that means our contacts are the same prescription too. At least for one night. The trick is, you have to let me touch your eyeballs."

"Ew" Avery said.

* * *

The ballroom was nothing like Avery had ever seen before. Sure, it was just the school gym with a facade of cheesy decorations, but it was overwhelming nonetheless. The ceiling glittered with an assortment of sparkling lights. Banners and black curtains lined every wall. Music pumped in sync with the lights as lasers moved across the dance floor.

No one was dancing. In fact, most of the students stood around drinking punch.

Beth Chang, president of the Associated Student Body, approached the microphone on the stage. "Testing. One. Two. Testing. Okay, it's that moment everyone's been waiting for! Earlier tonight, we crowned Glover Andrews as the king. Now, it's time to crown the Queen of South Point for all of eternity . . . or at least until we have another dance! Votes have been cast. And your new queen is . . ."

Veronica whispered into Avery's ear, "I hope you don't mind. I know the president of the ASB. She owed me a huuuggge favor."

Beth cleared her throat. "Avery Hopewell!"

Avery's eyes opened as wide as saucers.

"Go get your crown, Queen Avery," Veronica said.

Avery stepped on the stage and the crown was placed on her head. She was overcome by the attention from the cheering students. Regardless, she couldn't help but feel a sense of déjà vu. She scanned the crowd to find one set of eyes glaring back at her. They belonged to Tracy.

The curfew imposed by the group home cut her victory short, however, and soon she was whisked away by the same tiny van that she had arrived to school in.

The entire way home, Stephanie gushed. "I can't believe you were named queen! I love your dress. I love your makeup. I love your hair!" Stephanie went on and on as Tracy sat in the back of van, sulking.

As the van drove through the neighborhood, Avery could not help but notice a mailbox in someone's yard that had been painted a bright, ugly yellow.

They reached the group home, and the three girls opened the gate. Avery headed toward the front door, a spring in her step. She grasped the plastic crown, staring at it in admiration. Suddenly, someone tugged on her hair from behind, pulling her to the ground and knocking the wind from her lungs.

Tracy straddled her chest, screaming and slapping her face with all her might. "You humiliated me in front of everyone!" She smacked Avery in the face again.

But Avery did not fight back. In fact, Avery could not breathe at all. Her lungs had collapsed into a little ball in her chest. She gasped for air, but the more she tried, the more her lungs burned.

Stephanie tried to pull Tracy off, but Tracy elbowed her, knocking Stephanie to the ground.

Samuel, the driver, just now realizing there was a fight, stepped out of the van and headed toward Tracy and Avery. But he was a slow man and couldn't move fast enough.

Avery's inhaler was on the grass beside her. She reached for it, but her fingers fell short. Beyond the inhaler was Barney the goat, appearing from the side of the house.

Barney charged Tracy, knocking her off of Avery with a well-placed head butt. Tracy screamed as she flew across the yard. Barney raced after her, ramming her again and again until Tracy hopped the fence, tearing her clothes in the process. Barney, content with himself, trotted toward Avery, then kneeled beside her and licked her face.

* * *

Even though the meeting room was just the living room decorated with an assortment of plastic flowers, it still looked nicer than usual. Waiting for her on the couch was a well-dressed couple. They smiled and stood up as soon as she entered the room.

The man extended his hand. Avery shook it, noting his soft skin. The woman gave her a big hug.

"What happened to your eye?" the woman asked.

"Oh," Mrs. Dewey said. "Our little Avery had an accident last night. She had to make a quick trip to the hospital, but she's okay. She's going back in a couple of days for a follow-up."

The woman beamed. Her smile seemed so warm and genuine, Avery didn't know what to think.

"Do you want to tell us about it?" the woman asked.

Avery turned toward Mrs. Dewey. Mrs. Dewey nodded ever so slightly.

"Okay," Avery said. "It involves a school dance, asthma, and a goat. But I need to tell you something else first. I might be a bed-wetter."

CHAPTER 17

The Stone Keeper

The night had already appeared over the mountain trail. Soot rose from the ground with each step. The higher up the mountain that they climbed, the fewer plants, bushes, and trees they found around them. Guided through the haze only by moonlight, they trekked across jagged rocks and faded trails. At times, the path was so steep that Ben, Avery, Marcus, and Tam dropped to all fours so they could climb it. This seemed to amuse the dragonwoofs, who were already relegated to traveling on four paws. Vertical or horizontal, the three dragonwoofs maneuvered the trail with ease, their short legs moving rapidly over the rocks and crevices, paws coated in gray soot. The dragonwoofs managed to stay three paces behind the travelers at all times, their split tongues hanging low from their gaping jaws.

Marcus struggled with each step, his knees moving side to side as if his legs were rubber bands.

Ben approached him, soot covering both his face and pajamas. "You okay?"

Sweat tumbled down Marcus's forehead, forming small beads of ash that became bigger and bigger before rolling off his chin. "I'm not used to this. The climbing, I mean."

As expected, Tam traversed the trail with little difficulty. The translucent elf glided over the rocks, never losing his footing. His burlap poncho had been completely transformed to gray by the hovering ash. "We must move faster. That goblin will catch up to us at this rate."

"He's nursing the biggest hangover of his life right now," Avery said. "I'd be surprised if he even woke up to see the sun today." She coughed heavily, hacking ash from her lungs. Tam handed her a piece of torn fabric from his burlap poncho. She immediately placed it over her mouth and nose.

"You should have let me cut his throat while he was snoring," Tam said.

"We'd be no better than The Ghastly Four if we did something like that," Avery said.

"Yes. But The Ghastly Four don't have to look over their shoulders the rest of their days."

Avery's bare feet were filthy and covered in cuts. "We have nothing to worry about as long as we cross the peak before the sun appears."

Wolf followed Ben intently, nipping at his heels and whimpering. Ben stopped to lift her from the ground. Her leathery wings and front paws draped over Ben's forearms while her rear paws and scaly tail dangled below his arms. At twenty or so pounds, Wolf was quite heavy for her size. Even so, Ben made an effort to pick her up every now and then, even if it was to only carry her a short distance.

"We must make haste," Tam said. "The sun will appear in the sky directly above the peak, making it impassable."

"How much longer until the sun appears?" Marcus asked, panting.

"Not long. With the Fading getting stronger, it could happen any minute. We must hurry." Then Tam stopped dead in his tracks. "Everyone, to me!"

Marcus raced toward Tam, pulling his bow from his back. "What is it?"

But Tam remained mum, staring at the path ahead. Ben and Avery raced toward him. All three dragonwoofs growled.

"It's happening," Tam muttered. "It's happening now."

Ben studied the path, but he could not see or hear anything out of the ordinary. The trail made its way down into a valley and in and around rocks, small hills, and ridges, before heading up the side of the tall white mountain in the distance. But as he peered at the valley, he noticed the air became blurry.

Then it happened.

In a blink, the valley and everything in between vanished. The tall white mountain lunged toward them and was now towering over them. The path that had led down into the valley a moment ago now led straight up the side of the mountain.

"What just happened?" Ben exclaimed. "Where did everything go?

"What once was never was," Tam said.

"That was the Fading?" Avery asked.

"Yes," Marcus said.

"It's worse than I thought," Ben said

"Come," Tam said. "We must cross the peak and get to the other side before everything we know is gone."

They climbed higher and higher toward the top of the mountain, their surroundings now a stark contrast to the lower trail below. At this higher elevation, the dark-gray ash and jagged rock had been replaced by a white ash resembling snow. It was soft under their feet.

Soon, they found themselves in a flat area illuminated by the moon and shrouded by a low-hanging mist, the perimeter lined with ancient stone structures. The columns and statues were now reduced to half-broken pieces and rubble, six to ten feet tall in size. An eerie cold filled the air around them.

Avery shivered. Sebastian wrapped his paws and wings around her ankle. He was also shaking. Sebastian stared back at Avery, too scared to bark or whimper.

"It's a graveyard," Tam said. "Look."

The mist shifted back and forth along the ground as if it were being inhaled and exhaled by an unseen force. They caught glimpses of small black rocks that had been meticulously stacked one upon another like markers. The mist shifted again, revealing more and more grave markers in the distance.

"There's at least a hundred of them." Ben pulled his hands into his pajama arms and held them across his chest to escape the cold.

The mist parted, revealing a large, dark gray stone statue perched upon a massive stone block. It stood at least six feet high, had four legs and huge folded stone wings draped along both its sides. Its face was a cross between a snake and a bear, with two huge incisors that protruded upward from its bottom jaw, as if frozen in perpetual anger. It had the body of a mountain lion, its muscular legs supported by jagged stone claws ending in enormous talons, and a thin, long tail with a serrated tip.

"It looks like a gargoyle," Ben said

"There are stories of a keeper." Avery's voice faltered, "one who watches over those who attempted to escape the wrath of the Clumsy King. Long ago, three hundred of the Clumsy King's peasants fled to the mountain to avoid his persecution. In response, the Clumsy King placed armies on both sides of the mountain for weeks, preventing escape from either side. After weeks of agony and despair, the peasants died with nothing but ash in their bellies. It is said that the keeper protects the graves of the dead, waiting for the day when the Clumsy King or any of his descendants attempt to scale the mountain. Legends say that the keeper will spring to life and kill anyone foolish enough to topple any of the grave markers, even if it's by accident."

"When the sun decides to retire, wolfbats and other creatures of the night spread like an unkempt fire," Tam said under his breath, drawing his bow and arrow.

Marcus walked toward Avery, his eyes bulging. "You knew about this all along? It never dawned on you to tell us about this before we climbed the entire mountain?"

Avery shrugged. "I didn't think the legend was real. I'm still not sure it is. I only read about it in one of the books back at the palace. For all I know, it is just another fairy tale."

"Really?" Marcus exclaimed. "Don't you get it? Even the fairy tales are real!" Marcus kicked into the ground, creating ashy clouds.

"What has gotten into you, Marcus?" Avery asked. "As long as you don't knock over any markers, we don't have anything to worry about."

Marcus grasped his head. "Oh, I see. You think I'll knock over the markers because I'm fat."

"I didn't say that."

"You're worried that I'll knock over everything like the clumsy fat ass that I am and wake the keeper!"

Tam peered at Marcus. "Brother."

But Marcus ignored him. "I guess little-miss-skinny-dress would never knock over the markers. She's too perfect."

Ben grasped Marcus's shoulders from behind. "What's gotten into you?"

Marcus shifted his weight backward, knocking Ben onto the ground, white ash exploding around him on all sides. "Oh, I guess you're her big tough boyfriend now."

"I'm not her boyfriend," Ben said, wiping traces of blood and ash from his nose.

"What're you talking about, Marcus?" Avery said. "Why are you saying these things?"

Marcus kicked ash in Avery's direction. "Shut up, Anna"

Avery looked at Marcus, perplexed. "Anna?"

Marcus laughed. "You know what? I changed everything for you. I started running because of you. And I hate running!"

"Calm down," Avery said.

"I'm tired of it," Marcus said. "I'm tired of everyone thinking I'm fat. This is the way I am. I can't help it!"

"No one is saying you're fat," Avery said.

"They all do," Marcus said.

"Who?" Avery asked.

"Them." Marcus stepped backward, the heels of his boots a foot and a half from the nearest grave marker

"Marcus, watch out!" Ben said.

Avery inched her way toward Marcus with her hands held high in the air. "Look Marcus, we're friends. We would never say or even think those awful things about you!"

Tam approached Marcus as well. "My brother. What the queen regent says is true. I only know you as the greatest warrior I have ever encountered aside from my own brother."

"That's not true," Marcus said.

"Listen to me closely," Tam said. "If you knock over that marker behind you, we all die on this mountain."

Marcus stopped in his tracks. He looked over his shoulder and stared at the rock pile just inches away from his boot. A single bead of ashy sweat rolled off his chin, landing one inch away from the marker.

He blinked rapidly, then turned back toward Avery, Ben, and Tam. "I'm sorry. I don't know what just came over me."

Avery smiled warmly. "It's okay, just step away from the marker."

Marcus nodded. But instead of moving away, he fainted and collapsed in place, his limp body crashing onto the marker, scattering the pile of rocks in every direction.

"What just happened?" Avery raced to Marcus.

"He fell asleep," Tam said.

The ground shook below their feet.

"The keeper," Avery said.

Rising, Tam readied his bow.

All three dragonwoofs ran off, escaping down the same trail they had come from.

"Wolf!" Ben shouted. "Sebastian! Rooster!"

The statue of the keeper awoke with a thunderous crack. Ash scattered on all sides. The stone columns surrounding them rattled as chunks of chipped stone and rock careened toward the earth, slamming into the ash. The black markers shook as well, but strangely, not one of them fell.

The statue slinked off its perch slowly, landing on the ground on all fours, bursting thick white clouds in every direction. Dust poured from the joints of all four of its lumbering legs. The stone around its gaping mouth, nose, and eyes cracked and snapped as the beast opened its jaws, emitting a deafening wail. The keeper took one long look at Marcus's limp body, then lurched toward it, heavy stone claws scraping the earth each time it lifted its massive legs. The ground shook with each step it took toward Marcus.

"It's going to kill him!" Ben yelled.

"No." Tam aimed at the creature with his bow. "We will kill it first."

Avery unsheathed her white blade.

"Careful." Tam released an arrow into the beast. The tip of the arrow smacked into the back of the keeper's head, then ricocheted back toward the ground. "No matter what happens, you must not knock over any of the markers, or else it will turn its attention to you."

Undeterred, Avery charged the stone beast, her bare feet moving swiftly through the soft ash, and slammed the sword into the creature's backside. But the blade deflected off the hard stone and sparks erupted into the air. Avery lost hold of the hilt and the sword sailed from her grasp, landing directly on top of a marker, toppling it.

The keeper spun around, roaring.

It sank low to the ground and charged Avery on all fours, stone teeth bared between snapping jaws. Avery jumped back, but tripped and fell, raising a cloud of ash. The creature stood over her, its stone teeth looming inches from her face.

The keeper cocked its head back, ready for the kill. Then it shrieked loudly and jerked its head sideways.

In the distance, Ben stood near the marker he had just toppled.

The keeper, forgetting that Avery was even there, charged at Ben. It closed the gap in no time at all. But then an arrow slammed into the side of its face. It didn't penetrate the creature's stone hide, but the monster jerked its head to one side, eroded stone nostrils gaping and incisor teeth gnashing. From only a foot or two away, Ben could clearly see the creature's beady eyes. Unlike the rest of its stone exterior, the keeper's eyes were jet black and seemed alive as they moved in their thick sockets.

"Its eyes!" Ben said. "Aim for its eyes!"

The beast lunged for him. Ben, dodging clumsily, slipped on the ash and landed flat on his back. The keeper leapt forward, clearing Ben entirely. It spun, enraged, sending white ash into the open air.

But Ben was nowhere to be seen. Only Tam, two feet in front of the keeper's face with an arrow aimed straight at its eye.

Tam released the arrow. A spurt of black, tar-like substance erupted from the socket. The keeper roared. Tam nocked the last arrow from his quiver, but the stone creature spun, toppling him to the ground with its jagged stone tail. Tam stood to find that he had landed on top of a marker. The black rocks had scattered in every direction.

The keeper leapt toward Tam, spreading its stone wings. Tam rolled backward, missing the beast's crash by a fraction of a moment. It slammed into the ground, shaking the earth around it. Tam spun, his bow at the ready. He released the arrow point-blank into the creature's good eye. A black tar-like substance poured out of both its sockets.

But this did not deter it. It roared loudly and charged Tam again. This time, Tam leapt into the air and landed on the small of the creature's back. He gripped its wings as it slammed head first into the stone pedestal at the center of the graveyard. He released his dagger from his belt and rammed it into the creature's scalp, stabbing it over and over. The sharp blade deflected off the unyielding stone surface, shooting sparks into the air.

The stone keeper howled, then rolled on its back, attempting to crush Tam. But Tam dove off the creature's side before it could do so. As the creature rolled, all four legs in the air, Tam slammed his blade into the joint between its front leg and chest, snapping the blade off at the handle, lodging it at the joint. The beast screamed and rolled upright, its leg immobile.

The keeper charged toward Tam with its three remaining legs, knocking the elf off his feet and catapulting him into the air. Tam crashed onto the ground as dark blood flowed out of a freshly opened wound on his forehead.

"It can still see!" Tam said, rising.

Again, the keeper charged him. Tam dropped flat to the ground on his back as the creature raced over him. He grasped a second blade from his belt and slammed it into the crevice between the creature's hind leg and groin. It was a direct hit. Black ooze spilled from the joint onto Tam's face.

The keeper roared, staggering sideways across the ground, clouding the air with bursts of ash.

Tam stood up, intent on sending the creature to its grave. But the stone keeper had other plans. It spun quickly, smacking its stone tail on the back of Tam's head, knocking him straight into another stone marker, scattering it.

The creature grimaced, then charged Tam's unconscious body.

Avery flanked the keeper and stabbed it in its hind leg, the blade jostling in its joint. Avery grasped the hilt and pulled with all her might. But before she could release the blade, the creature spun around, knocking her flat to the ground with its thick stone head. It lunged toward her, all four of its legs slamming into the earth on both sides of her body. It hovered over Avery, snarling. Avery squirmed underneath, barely dodging the keeper's attempts to snap her head off. Just when she thought she was done for, a small dragonwoof with brown spots dashed toward the stone keeper and began gnawing on its front leg.

Sebastian barked at the keeper as he scurried between its legs taking tiny nips at each opportunity, before latching onto the creature's stone tail with his tiny jaws. Annoyed, the keeper jerked its tail up and down, but Sebastian held on for dear life.

The keeper howled in frustration and whipped its tail with enough force to finally dislodge the dragonwoof. Sebastian was catapulted into the air toward the white stone columns on the outer perimeter. Missing the pillar by inches, Sebastian sailed right past it and disappeared off the edge of the mountain.

"Sebastian!" Avery yelled.

The keeper returned its attention to her, spreading its wings wide, using its huge stone arms to pin her down to the ground. Avery looked out the corner of her eye and found Ben with his arms stretched toward the creature, trembling.

"Don't do it," Avery said. "The magic will consume you."

CHAPTER 18

The Mountain of the Disappearing and Reappearing Sun

The keeper wrapped its jaws around Avery's head, ready to crush her with its teeth.

Ben clenched his eyes shut and stretched his arms toward the stone creature. He could feel the warmth moving through his body toward his hands.

A stream of flames shot from his fingertips, hitting the creature on its side. The beast screeched, releasing Avery. The keeper turned to Ben. He blasted it again with fire magic. Enraged, the monster shifted its weight to its back legs, ready to charge. Ben stretched his arms out again. But, before he could do anything, a massive goblin ran past him.

The goblin slammed a huge double-bladed sword onto the creature's outstretched stone wing, shattering it into pieces. It recoiled and shrieked.

"The General of One Thousand Wars," Avery muttered.

The goblin leapt onto the keeper's back and rammed the double-bladed sword into the creature's shoulder, dislodging chunks of gravel and stone. He hopped off, landing heavily on both boots, and swiped at the keeper's legs with all his might, knocking it onto its back.

The general turned toward Avery. "Collect your companions and run, Queen Regent. I will take care of the keeper."

"Why are you helping us?" Avery asked.

"How else will you stay alive long enough for me to make good on our wager? I owe the queen regent a gold coin for every war that I fought in and won."

"But you were trying to kill us before!"

"Back at the inn, I promised to kill you after the cock crowed and before the night appeared," the general said. "That day has since come and gone. I am no longer a threat to you."

Avery's eyes narrowed. "I don't believe you."

"Perhaps the queen regent has made quite the impression on an old goblin. Especially one who was never afforded the opportunity to have a daughter of his own. Besides, when else would I have the chance to face a stone keeper in single combat?"

The keeper writhed, trying to right itself.

"Go now!" the general said.

Avery snatched her blade off the ground and ran toward Ben and Tam. "Let's go!"

Tam looked at her, then stared back at the general in disbelief. "Why is he here?"

"I'll explain later! Grab Marcus!"

Tam heaved Marcus's unconscious body onto his back. The stone creature roared, then righted itself. The general slashed at the creature's head, but it moved out of the way and the blade hit the ground, instead. The monster ignored the general and galloped after Avery and her companions.

Seeing this, the General of One Thousand Wars raced toward the nearest marker. The keeper stopped dead in its tracks as the black rocks toppled to the ground. It turned to face him.

"That's right," the general said. "Your fight is with me, now!"

The keeper charged the goblin, catching his arm between gnashing stone teeth. Green blood sprayed into the air. The general stabbed the creature's throat, chunks of gravel bursting free.

* * *

Tam carried Marcus on his back, Avery and Ben leading the way. The moon beamed overhead, casting a cold glow over the ashy trail.

Beyond them, the silent peak loomed in the distance against a backdrop of star-cluttered sky.

The silence was shattered by a screaming howl from down below.

"The general." Avery looked down the trail. "He's losing the fight!"

"Good!" Tam said. "That'll be one less problem we have to worry about!"

But Avery was frozen. She stared at the trail behind them. "I'm going back for him."

"What?" Ben asked.

"I'm going back for the general," Avery said. "He saved our lives. We owe him the same."

Tam scoffed. "The only thing we accomplish by going back down there is dying right next to him!"

Avery raised her sword to the night sky, the ghostly moonlight gleaming off the white blade. "Since when are elves afraid to die?" She raced away.

Tam turned to Ben. "It's up to us now, weed. It's up to us to cross this mountain and stop the Fading."

But Ben stared behind them. "I'm going with her."

"Have you both gone insane?" Tam asked.

Ben shrugged. "The mind is a prison that the heart yearns to escape."

* * *

Green blood flowed from The General of One Thousand Wars' arms and legs, his sword broken halfway down to the hilt. Beyond him, the keeper readied for another attack.

Avery arrived, huffing and puffing, with Ben right behind her. She ran at the monster, sword drawn, and leapt into the air, slamming her blade onto the beast's tail and severing it. Ben flanked the creature, flailing his arms and shouting, distracting the beast. The general launched his broken sword overhead onto the creature's remaining wing, shattering it into three massive slabs. The move snapped the last shards of metal from the sword's hilt.

The creature howled, then staggered sideways.

The general dropped the hilt of his sword into the ash as Ben and Avery flanked the beast, but every time they moved, it followed them.

"How come it can still see us?" Ben asked.

"Maybe those aren't its eyes," Avery said.

Ben noticed that the ground trembled with each step the creature took. But, no matter how hard the earth shook beneath his feet, the grave markers did not topple.

Ben raced toward the nearest grave marker, plucking a rock from the top of a stack. He rubbed it between his fingers, cleaning off the black soot. They were not rocks at all.

They were eyeballs.

Ben watched as each black eyeball in a nearby stack of markers turned toward him. The keeper charged in his direction. Ben quickly knocked over the marker nearest to him, scattering the eyes onto the ashy ground. As he did, the stone creature stopped dead in its tracks. Another stack of eyeballs turned toward Ben before the creature resumed its charge. Instead of fighting the beast, Ben raced toward the markers, scattering them.

The General of One Thousand Wars watched. "Of course!" He approached a marker of his own.

With his open palm, he scattered the black eyeballs. Avery knocked over a marker, as well.

Indecisive about which person to attack next, the stone keeper stood, paralyzed, as the markers toppled around it one by one.

Soon, all the markers were scattered. The beast let out a giant roar. The arrows lodged in both its eye sockets trembled, the black tar-like goop seeping down both sides of its face. The keeper whimpered, then collapsed, the arrows falling from its sockets.

Avery neared the creature, her blade at the ready. "It's almost sad. The creature's only desire was to protect these graves. Now it has no purpose."

"Now would be a good time to get back to the peak!" Ben said.

The earth rumbled beneath their feet.

The multiple black objects from the grave markers moved across the white ash, rolling toward the stone keeper.

"We must go," the general said. "Now!"

Hundreds of eyeballs rolled across the ash and converged at the base of the keeper, each one clamoring to get as close as possible. The stone creature tilted its head toward the ground, allowing two of the eyeballs to roll up the sides of its face into its empty sockets. The beast bellowed, then stood on its feet. With its new eyes, it turned to face them.

"This creature has more eyes than we have blades to poke them out," the general said.

"How do we stop it?" Avery asked.

"We can melt it," Ben said.

"Melt it?" Avery asked. "What're you talking about?"

Ben stared at the creature. "Stone becomes magma at twelve hundred degrees."

Ben aimed his fingertips in the creature's direction, ready to shoot at it with flame. But the general pushed his hands downward. "Weed, your powers are not strong enough to melt it. Besides, the magic will destroy you if you use it."

Avery smirked.

"But there is another solution," the general said. "There is only one thing hotter than any magic in this world!"

"You don't mean—?" Avery asked.

"Lure the beast toward the peak!" The general ran across the graveyard and up the trail.

The creature charged Avery. Just as it was about to slam into her, an arrow struck the joint above its front leg, toppling it to the ground.

Avery turned to find Tam nocking an arrow from a nearby ridge. She clambered up the trail as Tam closed the gap behind her.

The stone creature, blades and arrows lodged in each leg, hobbled after them.

Avery looked back down the trail to find Tam hot on her heels.

Tam beamed. "Elves are never afraid to die, Queen Regent."

Ahead, the General of One Thousand Wars scaled the steep trail, green blood streaming down his arms and face. "Almost there," he said, his pace faltering.

Ben passed him.

Then Tam.

Avery stayed at his side.

Finally, they reached the top.

The peak was a charred plateau surrounded by sheer cliffs on both sides. There was the Rolling Plains and Red Forest to the east, the Calm Sea to the west, the Mountains of Pariah to the north, and the Drowned Swamps to the southeast.

The general pointed to a trailhead at the northern edge of the plateau. "That path leads down the other side of the mountain. If you are already on the trail when the sun appears, you should be safe. Go now!"

"You first," Avery said.

"No. I will stay here to ensure the beast does not follow."

Avery crossed her arms. "No way."

"Have you ever heard of the green flash?" the general asked. "It happens right before the sun appears. You head down the trail. When the green flash appears, the stone creature will no longer be of this world."

Avery gasped. "But you'll die!"

"No," the general said. "I will finally live."

Avery stomped her bare feet. "Sounds like a load of crap to me!"

"There is no time to argue! You must head down the trail now! Take this with you." He handed a pouch to Avery.

Avery stared at the bag, confused. "What is it?"

"Four hundred and ninety-seven gold coins."

"One for every war you fought and won?"

The general smiled broadly. "I would not be standing here if I didn't win."

Tam promptly disappeared down the mountain trail, followed by Ben. But Avery did not follow. Instead, she stood there, staring at the General of One Thousand Wars. Just beyond the general, on the other side of the charred plateau, stood the stone keeper.

Before she could warn him, the beast charged.

Without a moment of hesitation, the general pushed Avery toward the trailhead, then turned to face the stone creature. But it was too late. The keeper rushed at the general midair with snapping jaws, toppling him to the ground.

Ben ran toward Avery to pull her away from the edge of the plateau.

Suddenly, the sky around them turned green.

Frozen by panic, both Avery and Ben were paralyzed. It would have been futile for Ben to wrap his arms around Avery in an attempt to shield her from the sun that would soon vaporize them both, but he did anyway.

The general, meanwhile, used every ounce of strength he had left to push the stone keeper off his body. Once on his feet, he dove toward Avery and Ben, knocking them down the trail.

Then, just as quickly, he leapt off the northern cliff of the mountain.

A blinding light filled the sky as fire consumed the peak of the mountain. The keeper melted into orange liquid.

Avery raced down the winding trail, trying to get a better view of the cliff that the general had leapt off of. But when she finally found a vantage point, she saw that the cliff dropped straight down the side of the mountain, thousands of feet below.

She fell to her knees and let the tears flow.

CHAPTER 19

The Run

Anna's brown eyes were narrow and alluring; each time Marcus gazed into them, his heart trembled.

Today, those eyes also brought frustration. It had gotten to the point where he could not look into them anymore, so instead, he opted to stare at his massive driveway.

"We've been friends for as long as I can remember," Anna said.

"Best friends," Marcus said.

"Yes, best friends, exactly. You're like my brother."

Marcus shoved his hands in his pockets. "I don't get it. We like watching the same movies. We like talking about the same stuff."

"I told you I already have a boyfriend."

"And he treats you like garbage. How many times have you complained to me about him?"

Anna stared at the ground. "It's complicated."

"Nah, you make it complicated." Marcus looked into her eyes. "I'm trying to make it simple."

Anna buried her face in her hands. "I'm sorry. I just don't feel that way about you."

Marcus paced back and forth across the driveway. "What does he have that I don't have? Is it because he's good at soccer?"

Anna crossed her arms. "Of course not."

Marcus raised his gaze from the concrete. "Is it because I'm fat?"

Anna gasped. "No! Definitely not. Look, I already told you why."

"It's not my fault. I get it from my parents; it's genetic."

"Your parents are both fit. They work in TV."

"My mom and dad work in an office," Marcus said. "I'd hardly call that TV."

"They work for a studio. They have corner offices. Look. I'm not going to argue with you about this. I already told you my reasons."

Marcus shrugged. "It's because I'm fat."

Anna sighed. "I didn't say—"

"Is it because I'm homeschooled?"

Now Anna was pacing. A plane flew high above, tearing the silence.

"My parents make me do it," Marcus said. "It's not my fault they hire private teachers!"

Anna sighed. "You don't get it, do you? I think we need a break. I'm going to stop coming over to your house for a bit. Maybe that'll help clear your head."

"Fine!" Marcus said. "But don't come crawling back when our shows start up again!"

Marcus watched her walk away.

As Marcus entered his house, he was greeted by the familiar scents of the foyer. An unsettling concoction of glass cleaner, bleach, and furniture polish assaulted his nostrils, indicating that the maid just finished cleaning this portion of the house.

The house itself had a modern look. As he walked down the hall, he caught his reflection in the rather large mirror. His short black hair was especially curly today. His gut stuck out, but he didn't care. The phone rang from the kitchen. Marcus answered it.

"Mom?"

Mom sounded exasperated. "Did the maid come yet?"

Marcus glanced around the foyer. "I think so."

"Look, honey. Me and your dad are going to be home late tonight."

Marcus sighed. "Again? But it's Sunday."

"I know. Order yourself a pizza if you get hungry. There's money on the counter."

"But I had pizza yesterday."

"Order different toppings. I have to go. I love you, Marcus."

"I love you too, Mom."

* * *

Marcus's game room was loaded with every video game system imaginable. Shelves lined every wall in the room and were crammed with movies, board games, toys, and comic books. The far wall housed two compact fridges: one for sodas and one for snacks.

At the center of the room, in front of a huge TV, was a leather couch with cup holders built in.

Joe, a friend he had met one day at the comic book store, sat on the couch. He was older than Marcus and sported a neck beard over his pale, acne-prone skin. He wore a t-shirt with the words "High Score" printed on the front.

Marcus maneuvered through the final level of the game with ease.

"Does this game have codes?" Joe asked.

"What's that?" Marcus asked, smashing a slice of pizza into his mouth.

"You know. Codes for extra men or invincibility or whatever."

"I dunno." Marcus shot an enemy on the far side of the screen while yelling, "Boom, headshot!"

"You're the headshot king!" Joe said. "What other games do you play?"

"I like strategy games. You know, the kind where you can move your military units around the board and flank the enemy."

"Like chess?"

Marcus laughed. "Sort of."

"Give me that." Joseph yanked the controller from Marcus.

Marcus stood up and approached the mini fridge. "Want anything?"

"What do you have?"

Marcus shrugged. "Everything."

Marcus snatched a can from the fridge and chucked it toward Joseph, throwing it beyond his reach. He grabbed a new can from the fridge, walked over, and handed it to him.

"So, where's your mom and dad?" Joseph asked.

"Working," Marcus said.

"It's like nine o'clock on a Sunday."

Marcus shrugged. "Mrs. Matheson is here on weekdays during the day," Marcus said. "She's my teacher. I have a Spanish tutor on Saturdays, Clara."

"Is she hot?"

"Who, Clara?" Marcus laughed. "Nah, she's like a hundred years old."

"Yeah, is she hot?"

Joe chugged the soda and crushed the can against his forehead. "Listen, I gotta bounce." He handed the controller back to Marcus.

"You don't want to watch a movie or something?"

"Nah, I got to get ready for school tomorrow."

Marcus shrugged. "Yeah, I don't have that problem. School comes to me."

"Must be nice." Joseph left, but not before taking another soda from the fridge.

Now, the house was empty.

Marcus shut off the TV.

Silence.

The empty TV screen reflected his image like a mirror. Marcus stared at himself for a bit. He began to recall all of the names that the other kids had called him at school. Lunchbox. Cheeseburger. Those were just a couple. He remembered begging his mom and dad for homeschooling every day before they finally broke down and gave him what he wanted.

* * *

It was dark outside. Marcus exited his home in running shoes, basketball shorts, and an old T-shirt. He charged down his winding driveway, out the gate, and into the road.

The streets were quiet. Only a handful of street lamps flickered in the distance. He stared down the empty street ahead of him—the pavement seemed to go on for miles and miles.

Then he ran.

Marcus raced down the street, his stomach bouncing over his hips like a water balloon. The more it hurt, the harder he ran. He did not stop. He ran faster than he had ever run before. The pain in his legs compared little to the burning in his chest and the stabbing pain in his stomach. He ran faster. Seconds became minutes. Minutes became an eternity. He passed by a blue house.

A green house.

He even passed by a house with a yellow mailbox in the yard.

He kept his head down, intent on running across the entire city if that's what it took for Anna to love him back.

CHAPTER 20

The Serene Island

Ocean salt and rot lingered in the night air.

The water was still and opaque. Its reflective surface gave off the impression that a person could walk upon it if they were so inclined.

But Avery knew better. *When the sun decides to retire, wolfbats and other creatures of the night spread like unkempt fire.* She knew that all manner of beasts lurked just beneath the inky depths.

Large, white rocks split the horizon, but as the raft drifted closer, Avery realized that they were not rocks at all. They were statues of ancient warriors in thick armor and massive triangular helmets with spears and swords in their deathly grips. The chalky figures pierced the black water like knives, their torsos escaping the obsidian depths below as their blank, expressionless faces stared listlessly across the Calm Sea.

Ben sat with his legs crossed near the rear of the raft, clenching and unclenching his hands, sweating. Avery knew it was the magic building up inside him, seeking release from his fingertips. She promised herself she would keep an eye on him to ensure the magic did not take control like it had done to so many before him.

She patted her right side, feeling for the bag of gold coins she had secured to her sword belt underneath her dress. The coins jingled within—all four hundred and ninety-seven.

Soon, the raft was surrounded by countless white statues, each staring at the boat with hollow gazes. Small, black cats with glowing eyes perched on the statues; their thick, onyx fur matted with dried ocean salt.

"Salty cats," Tam said. "One for every ship and captain that has gone down at sea. They never leave the ocean."

The salty cats watched the raft glide by, only their eyes moving. The dragonwoofs growled at them, but the cats ignored them, their ghostly stares unbroken.

Avery scratched Sebastian behind his ears. After scaling the peak, they had found all three dragonwoofs eagerly awaiting them at the base of the mountain. Last she saw them; all three dragonwoofs had ran down the wrong side of the mountain. Not to mention that Sebastian came back, only to be thrown off the side of a cliff! Either way, Avery was pleased that the dragonwoofs were safe.

Wolf, Rooster, and Sebastian paced from one end of the raft to the other. Rooster didn't even perform his routine cockle-doodle-woof that everyone had grown accustomed to. It was clear that the dragonwoofs did not like the idea of being stranded on a wooden raft in the middle of the sea.

Marcus slept on the side of the raft. As they had descended the mountain, Tam had revealed Marcus's sleeping body behind a bush. They'd manufactured a makeshift stretcher comprised of sticks, leaves, and roots to drag him down unscathed. At the bottom of the mountain, they'd found themselves only twenty paces from the Calm Sea, with a wooden raft tied right there on the rocky beach. Avery had called out to see if the owner was nearby, but her cries were only returned by the soft sounds of the waves washing lazily onto the shore. Even so, she couldn't help but wonder whose life they had complicated by borrowing the raft.

Once aboard, they sailed west toward the ocean horizon for an entire day. Now it was night. Avery watched the stars overhead. They began to disappear one-by-one, leaving holes in the sky. Then they disappeared in bunches, five or ten at a time, creating dark gaps.

Tam also looked at the vanishing stars. "The Fading," he said.

The raft trembled and Avery could feel the air being sucked out from around her.

"Stay together!" Tam dragged Marcus's snoring body closer to Ben. "Ben's trinket will protect us from the Fading!"

Avery blinked. The stars appeared to shift closer, as if the sky had shrunk. The wind howled around the raft and the water churned. The distant horizon was bounding toward them.

Then, the wind stopped and a tiny dot appeared on the horizon.

"The Serene Island," Tam said.

But as they sailed closer, dark clouds filled the sky, blocking the stars completely.

"A storm," Tam said. "We have entered the Great Desert."

"Desert?" Ben asked.

Soon, the sky rumbled and blinding flashes of light lit up the clouds above. Small particles, neither rainfall nor drizzle, fell from the night sky and landed on Ben's face with a sharp sting. He swiped his cheek with his fingertips, rubbing the residue between his finger and thumb. "Sand?"

Indeed, it was raining sand.

Avery tried to shield her eyes, but the sand fell so heavily that it cascaded down her body like a waterfall. In seconds, yellow sand had covered the raft.

It began to sink.

"We have to keep the sand off!" Avery said, eating some in the process.

They kicked mounds of sand off the raft as fast as they could. The downpour was relentless, and soon they were on all fours in an attempt to bulldoze the sand off the raft with their arms. They even had to push it off of Marcus's slumbering body so he wasn't buried alive. Even the dragonwoofs helped, digging into the sand with their front paws and pushing piles off the edge of the raft with their noses. But the faster they worked, the faster the sand fell. The raft sank inch by inch.

Just when the raft was about to sink completely, it stopped. There was no longer an ocean around them, only wet sand. But the sand kept falling, and soon the wet sand was replaced by golden dunes all around. Then, the sand stopped falling entirely, revealing miles of dry desert in every direction.

The sun appeared. Hot light beat down on their heads. They were surrounded by scorching desert with no signs of trees or cloud cover in sight.

Marcus finally woke.

He turned to Avery. "I'm sorry. I'm so sorry about what I said earlier!"

Avery smiled. "Don't worry about it. You weren't being yourself."

Ben ran up to Marcus. "What do you remember?"

Marcus grasped his forehead. "I remember Anna. I like her, but she doesn't like me in the same way. I think it has to do with my weight, so, I run. I hurt myself running, but I keep going. I run so far, I pass a yellow mailbox that I've never seen before."

Avery grasped Marcus by his shoulders "A yellow mailbox?" What do you remember about the yellow mailbox?"

Marcus shook his head. "I don't know."

Tam walked over to them. "Time is moving faster than ever in Meridia. We must hurry before it is too late."

Ben wrapped his pajama top around his head like a towel, a futile attempt to block the sun. Wolf walked over to the portion of the ground covered by Ben's shadow and lay down on the sand behind him.

Avery marched forward, her tattered dress still covered in dark stains and soot. Sebastian trailed her, whimpering. Avery picked Sebastian off the ground, relieving his paws.

"I wish someone would pick me up." She hugged Sebastian to her chest. "You're not the only one with bare feet on the hot sand."

On the horizon, she noticed a shimmer of metal glinting in the sunlight.

"Do you see it, too?" Marcus asked as he came up beside her.

"Beware of mirages," Tam said as he peered at the object suspiciously.

"Can you see what it is?" Avery asked. "With your amazing eyesight, I mean."

"Survivors of the Elven Genocide do not fare well in desert climates. Our senses are stifled by sand. Our skin is tortured by the sun." Tam pulled his cloak tighter around his face, obscuring his eyes beneath the depths of the hood.

"We should go check it out," Avery said.

They trudged forward over the tall golden dunes toward the shimmering light. But the farther they walked, the farther away the light shined.

It became so hot that Avery dropped to her knees, exhausted. Her mouth was as dry as the sand around her.

Tam appeared over the top of the sand dune in front of them. "You need to see this."

They followed Tam with the dragonwoofs in tow. As they reached the peak of the dune, they spotted a massive mound of sand below.

At least fifty yards wide, the mound was a perfect circle, the sand upon it raked into a perfect spiral toward a black dot at the center. Circling the outer perimeter of the mound was a continuous stream of water. At two feet wide, the stream had no beginning and no end, but flowed briskly clockwise.

Avery raced down the sandy slope toward the stream. She dropped to her knees and scooped handfuls of water into her mouth. Wolf walked up to the stream as well, lapping up the cool water with his split tongue. Sebastian and Rooster followed suit.

"Where did this come from?" Marcus asked.

"What do you call any land mass that is surrounded entirely by water?" Tam asked.

"An island," Ben said. "The Serene Island!"

Kneeling, Tam scooped water into his cupped hands as well, the liquid barely discernible against his translucent skin.

Ben glanced at Marcus, and vice versa, then they dunked both their heads into the shallow stream.

After drinking their fill, they hopped over the stream and made their way toward the center of the mound. The wind blew softly as they neared the center, their footprints and boot prints scattering the perfectly drawn spiral beneath their feet.

Near the center of the mound was a deep, dark pit filled with howling winds.

"It must be the entrance," Tam said. "This is where we'll find the sphinx and take his head."

Ben peered over the edge of the hole. It looked like an old well, lined with stone on all sides. It was pitch-black, too dark to see anything. A cold draft flowed upwards from its depths.

"How do we get down?" Ben asked. "There's no ladder or anything."

"I guess we jump," Tam said.

"Jump?" Avery asked. "But we have no idea how deep it is!"

Ben snatched a small pebble from the sand and dropped it down into the pit. He held his ear close to the opening, but any sounds were drowned out by the wind below.

"One of us needs to test the height of the fall," Tam said.

"Test the height of the fall?" Ben asked.

"The one who suggests it should be the one who tests it," Avery said.

"I was not speaking of me," Tam said. "I speak of those who know how to fly already." He glared at the three dragonwoofs where they stared at him blankly from the sand.

"No way," Ben said. "You heard the Boarmin. They can't fly!"

"I know at least one of them can." Tam walked toward Sebastian and snatched him off the ground. Sebastian yelped, his panicked eyes looking straight at Avery.

"Don't you dare do it!" Avery said.

"We both know he can," Tam said. "We saw it on the mountain."

"What we saw was Sebastian getting thrown off the edge of a cliff," Avery said. "What we didn't see was him flying!"

"How else is he alive then?" Tam asked. "Think about it. How are any of these dragonwoofs here now? We saw them retreat down the wrong side of the mountain. How did they beat us to the other side? I'll tell you how. They can fly. All three of them!"

"Put him down," Avery said.

"Our elders used to have a saying," Tam said. "You can store a dagger in a scabbard forever to keep it free from nicks, but in the end it is useless. How will these creatures learn to use their abilities if you keep sheltering them?"

"You are not dropping Sebastian down that hole," Avery said. "End of story."

Tam placed Sebastian back down on the sand. The dragonwoof trotted toward Avery, but not before growling at Tam and kicking sand back in his direction.

"Fine," Tam said. "How do you propose we get down there, Queen Regent?"

"What about rope?" Marcus said. "Couldn't we just lower one of us down?"

"What rope?" Tam said, "None of us are in possession of rope."

"We can use our clothes," Avery said. "Daisy chain them together."

"Yeah," Marcus said. "Like Cinderella with her hair!"

"Rapunzel," Avery said.

Marcus started prying off his boots. But before he could even get one boot off, Wolf pranced straight toward the pit and peered into its depths, barking.

"What is it, girl?" Ben asked.

Wolf looked back at Ben. She paused, then leapt into the pit.

"Crap balls!" Marcus said.

Ben, Avery, and Marcus raced toward the edge. They peered into the pit's dark depths, hoping to see some sign of Wolf below. But Rooster cockle-doodle-woofed and leapt over them, followed shortly by Sebastian!

There was a period of silence followed by a single bark. Another. Then another. Soon, all three dragonwoofs barked below.

"I can hear them!" Avery said. "It doesn't sound that deep!"

But the barking turned into howls.

"Something's down there with them!" Ben said.

Avery looked at Ben knowingly. "The sphinx."

Ben stood up, took a step back, and leapt in.

Avery screamed, but regained her composure long enough to hold her ear toward the pit. But again, all she could hear was the wind and the dragonwoofs.

"I'm okay!" Ben finally said.

"How deep is it?" Avery asked.

There was no answer.

Rising, Avery turned to Marcus and Tam. "Race you there." She spun and jumped into the pit.

Avery fell with her eyes squeezed shut, the cold wind barreling into the space between her dress and skin. She fell faster and faster, bracing for an impact that did not come. Avery opened her eyes only to find more darkness around her. She plunged deeper, falling even faster, her stomach crawling into her chest. Soon, the screaming howl of the wind became unbearable. She tried to yell, but the wind whipped her voice away.

Soon the cold wind was replaced by a warm breeze. Her descent slowed until she was floating softly over a warm cushion of air, the darkness around her broken by a sharp white light. Avery rubbed her eyes. She could now see that she was entering a humongous chamber comprised of white marble walls covered with countless black cracks and crevices. On all sides of the chamber stood pillars, also made of cracked white marble. Down below, Ben chased the three dragonwoofs. Beyond them was a gigantic glass box at the center of the cavern. Avery blinked, straining to see what manner of creature was pacing left and right inside. The creature looked at her and smiled.

The sphinx.

Wolf, Rooster, and Sebastian were headed straight for it.

She yelled a warning at the top of her lungs, but Ben could not hear her. Her feet finally hit the cool stone floor and she raced after them.

"Avery!" Marcus said as he and Tam descended from the top of the cavern behind her.

She turned back long enough to shout, "We gotta stop them!"

Her lungs began to burn deep inside her chest. She collapsed on the cavern floor, huffing and puffing. Eventually, Marcus and Tam arrived beside her, lifting her from the ground.

"Are you okay?" Marcus asked.

"I'm fine," Avery said, coughing. "We have to stop them! They are headed straight for the sphinx!"

* * *

"Wolf! Sebastian! Rooster!" Ben yelled as he raced after the fleet-footed dragonwoofs. But they did not stop, fixated on the peculiar creature inside the box.

As the dragonwoofs neared the box, they stopped barking and sat down. Ben finally caught up them.

Standing inside the glass box was a large creature that resembled a lion. Seven feet tall and ten feet long, it slinked across the floor on four muscular legs ending with massive knife-like claws. Surrounding its intelligent eyes and massive jaws was a thick, coarse, buff-colored mane that drooped over its neck and shoulders.

"Visitors?" The sphinx asked, his voice deep and powerful. "When was the last time I received visitors?"

CHAPTER 21

The Sphinx of Fact

Avery, Tam, and Marcus stood in front of the large glass box. Tam nocked an arrow and aimed it at the sphinx inside.

"Are you the Sphinx of Fact?" Ben asked.

"Are you Ben the Weed?" the sphinx asked.

Ben stepped forward. "How do you know me?"

"How would I know anything if I were not the Sphinx of Fact?"

"We've come for your head," Marcus said.

The sphinx laughed. "My head? What could possibly compel you to come for my head?"

"The Creator is sick because of you!" Tam said. "You are the cause behind the Fading. You are the reason why Meridia disappears into nothingness as we speak!"

"Am I now?" the sphinx asked. "And what makes you think such?"

"The Creator told us so," Ben said.

"Did he? Are you certain those were his words?"

Ben shrugged. "Well, we didn't talk to him directly."

The sphinx paced back and forth within the box. "Can I ask you a question? Why would I want Meridia to disappear when it is my sole purpose to maintain its memories? Can you not see the records of Meridia all around you?"

Ben looked around. There wasn't a single book in the cavern as far as he could see.

"If you're not responsible for the Fading," Avery said, "why would the Creator want your head?"

"Would not it be because he needs it to help stop the Fading?"

"Okay," Avery said, "How does taking your head stop it?"

The sphinx stopped pacing and stared directly at Avery. "How does it not?"

"You speak in riddles," Avery said.

The sphinx resumed pacing. "Have I yet to ask you a single riddle?"

Avery approached the glass. "I meant you make no sense."

"Do not I make anything but sense?"

Avery scoffed. "Why do you only speak in questions?"

The sphinx grinned. "What is the worth of a sphinx who does not ask questions?"

Avery faced the others. "This is pointless."

"Let's just take its head and be done with it," Tam said.

"What if you did not need to take my head?" the sphinx asked. "What if I gave it to you willingly?"

"You'd give us your head willingly?" Avery asked.

The sphinx stopped pacing. "Why not? It's just one of many books in this chamber, is it not?"

Avery peered at the white marble pillars and walls. Something wasn't right. The dark cracks and crevices were too uniform, too symmetrical. She walked toward the nearest column to investigate. Upon approaching the column, she realized that it was not made of cracked marble at all. It was made up of thousands upon thousands of books that had been meticulously stacked. In fact, stacks of books comprised every single wall and column in the cavern.

"The sphinx's head is a book?" Avery asked.

"When was it not?" the sphinx asked.

Avery scanned the thousands upon thousands of books. "Which one is it?"

The sphinx resumed pacing. "Which one indeed?"

Avery approached the glass. "Aren't you going to tell us which book it is?"

The sphinx sat on the floor. "And why should I answer your question when I have a question of my own?"

"What's your question?" Avery asked.

The sphinx smiled. "What if I were to ask you a question that could not be answered with a yes? What question would I ask?"

"Are you serious?" Avery asked. "Are we doing riddles now?"

But the sphinx did not answer.

Tam approached the box. "Are you dead? That's the one question that can never be answered with a yes."

The beast stood up on all fours and cleared his throat. "What belongs to you but others use it more than you do?"

Avery furrowed her brow.

Ben stepped toward the box. "Your name."

The sphinx's face brightened. "What is it that has four legs, one head and a foot?"

"Four legs, one head, and one foot?" Marcus said. "That's easy. It's a bed."

The sphinx paced back and forth. "Are you ready for the actual questions?"

"What do you mean?" Avery asked. "Those weren't the actual questions?"

The sphinx grinned. "Why is it that when I give it food, it will live, but if I give it water, it will perish?"

"How many of these riddles do we have to answer?" Ben asked.

But the sphinx did not answer the question, only repeated his own.

Tam stepped toward the glass box. "I know this, I know from living in the Red Forest during the dry season. It lives when you give it food and perishes when you give it water because it's fire."

The sphinx paced back and forth. "Is that your answer, translucent elf and survivor of the Elven Genocide?"

"It is."

"Is he right?" Avery asked.

The sphinx sat down and faced Avery. "Would not you know if he was wrong? What runs, but cannot creep? What has a mouth, but cannot speak? What has a head, but cannot see? What has a bed, but never sleeps?"

"I think I got it," Ben said. "A rose has a bed but doesn't sleep. It also has a head that does not see and it does not speak. A rose is the answer!"

"Is that your answer, weed who appeared in the Red Forest?"

"Yes."

The sphinx frowned. "Can a rose run but not creep?"

Ben fell to his knees as wrinkles covered his skin from head to toe. His skin dried up and his hair fell from his scalp. He screamed.

Avery raced toward Ben. "What's happening to him?"

"What happens to those who are ignorant?" the sphinx asked. "Do they not grow old and die ignorant unless they change their ways?"

Ben writhed on the ground as dark spots appeared over his withered skin.

"Change him back!" Avery said.

But the sphinx repeated his question, "What runs, but cannot creep? What has a mouth, but cannot speak? What has a head, but cannot see? What has a bed, but never sleeps?"

"A river has a mouth, a head, and a bed," Marcus said. "It also runs but doesn't creep. It's a river!"

"Is that your answer, weed trained by the translucent elves?"

"Yes," Marcus said, bracing for the worst.

The sphinx smirked. "What is weightless, but you can unmistakably see it? Why, when you put it in a bucket of ale, does the bucket become lighter?"

Marcus pondered a moment, then blurted out, "Air!"

The sphinx resumed pacing. "Is that your answer?"

"Yes?"

"Can you unmistakably see air?"

Marcus crumpled to the floor as wrinkles covered his body. His boots slid off as his feet shriveled like raisins. "Crap balls," he said.

The sphinx repeated the question, "What is weightless, but you can unmistakably see it? Why, when you put it in a bucket of ale, does the bucket become lighter?"

"It's a hole," Tam said. "A hole is the only thing other than a goblin that would make a bucket of ale immediately lighter."

The sphinx's eyes narrowed. "Is that your answer?"

"Yes."

The sphinx smiled. "What is lighter than a petal, yet the strongest knight cannot hold it for much more than a minute?"

"We are done answering your riddles, creature." Tam aimed an arrow at the glass box.

"Is that your answer, translucent elf and survivor of the Elven Genocide?"

"No," Tam said. "But this is." Tam released the arrow. It took flight and pierced the side of the glass box. But the box did not shatter.

The sphinx frowned.

Tam tumbled to the ground, his organs shriveling and darkening underneath his translucent skin.

"This is madness!" Avery yelled.

"Is that your answer, Queen Regent?"

Avery shook her head. "No!"

"What is your answer then?" the sphinx asked.

"Light as a petal yet the strongest knight cannot hold it for more than a minute," Avery said, her words cracking in her cough-racked lungs. "It's breath! A knight cannot hold its breath!"

The sphinx smirked. "The holes in my eyes are square, not round. I have horns, but they make no sound. I eat everything around, on mountains and in town, but I'll return to you with cheese by the pound. What am I?"

Avery pondered the riddle. Her face brightened. "You're a goat."

The sphinx walked from one end of the huge glass box to the other, revealing a massive blue book.

"*The Sphinx's Head*," Avery whispered in awe. "It was inside your box this entire time."

"Out of all these books, if only one was written in its entirety by you, would not you keep it close to you at all times?"

"I guess so," Avery said.

Avery looked at the old, shriveled versions of Ben, Marcus, and Tam. "What about my friends? Will you turn them back to normal?"

"Once they leave this place, will they not be in the same state they were in before they arrived?"

"You better hope so, for your sake," Avery said. "So, how do I get the book out of the glass box?"

"How can one shatter glass? Is that the question you ask?"

Avery took her white blade from underneath her dress. She walked toward the large glass box, intent on smashing it to pieces. She paused. "Who put you in there? Who didn't want you to get out?"

The sphinx grinned. "Did someone put me here to keep me in, or did someone put me here to keep others out?"

"It matters little." Avery raised her short sword high in the air. "Either way, we need that book and there's only one way to get to it."

The familiar clickety-clack of iron boots made Avery hesitate. She spun around to find a boy with long, black hair dressed in all-black garb approaching her. He wore a heavily soiled bandage wrapped tightly around his shoulder. He glanced at Ben, Marcus, and Tam curled up on the floor. "Didn't anyone ever tell you that winning battles is a young man's game?"

Ben, Marcus, and Tam tried to grab Christopher with their shriveled hands.

Christopher turned to the three dragonwoofs sitting near the glass box. "I always wanted new pets. Maybe I can train them to fetch my slippers."

The dragonwoofs growled at Christopher.

Christopher looked at the sphinx and grinned. "The Sphinx of Fact. At last, we finally meet."

Like the dragonwoofs, the sphinx growled and bared his teeth.

Christopher sneered at Avery. "It took us quite some time to fix the mess you made of the contraption back at the citadel. I had contraptionists working around the clock to make it usable. One even perished from exhaustion"

"You monster," Avery said. "How did you find us?"

"I didn't. I came here to collect the sphinx's head. But unlike you, I'm not talking about a book. You being here simply allows me to kill two little birds with one stone."

"Let's start with this little bird then." Avery positioned her blade at the ready.

Christopher was unfazed. "Fortune smiles upon me today, Queen Regent. Can you imagine my delight when I learned I could travel directly to the Serene Island using the newly repaired contraption? No stops at the Rolling Plains. No treks over The Mountain of the Disappearing and Reappearing Sun. Just a non-stop flight to the island."

"Your story lacks truth," Avery said. "You can't beam to the Serene Island. It's out of order."

"Yes, it was out of order," Christopher said. "But thanks to you, that is no longer the case. Whatever you did to make the sand fall from the sky to form this island enabled me to beam here directly." Christopher paused. "I'm being selfish. Perhaps I should rephrase. Whatever you did allowed *us* to beam here directly. I don't like to travel alone, as you know."

Dozens of Iron Pike Army troops descended from the pit entrance, filling the cavern with the clamor of charred iron boots and massive seven-foot pikes. The soldiers assembled behind Christopher. At two hundred strong, the Iron Pike Army stood in perfect military formation.

Christopher laughed. "Put your silly weapon down, Queen Regent. You cannot fight the entire Iron Pike Army with one sword and three little dogs."

"No," Avery said. "But I can die trying."

Christopher grinned. "Yes, you can die."

Avery circled Christopher, her sword at the ready. "I have one question for you before I slice you open in front of your men."

"Go on." Christopher said.

"Why is the Sovereign melting watches and clocks at the Tower of Continuance?"

Christopher shrugged. "What are you talking about?"

Avery's eyes narrowed. "We saw it with our own eyes."

"Did you now? I had heard rumors that you were running amok under our noses at the Tower of Continuance, but I thought the tales too outrageous to believe."

Avery nodded. "We destroyed the contraption there, as well."

"Quite impressive for a motley crew of weeds and an elf. I will answer your question about the trinkets. But first, I have one of my own. Haven't you noticed that the sun appears and disappears faster than ever before?"

"Yes," Avery said.

"You see, trinkets, with their methodical ticks and methodical tocks are sooo painfully slow."

"I saw the master clock at the Tower of Continuance," Avery said. "I saw how the hands spun around the face faster than any clock I've ever seen."

"Once we have destroyed every trinket in Meridia, there will only be one remaining: The master clock at the Tower of Continuance," Christopher said. "He who controls the last clock in the world controls the flow of time."

"To what purpose?"

"The Fading, of course," Christopher said. "Speeding up the flow of time has enabled the Fading to spread faster than ever before, allowing it to consume the land and everything in it. We have found and destroyed every trinket in the realm except one. This trinket's mere existence prevents the Fading from sprinting across the realm in a single blink."

Ben covered his antique watch with his shriveled hand.

"Nevertheless," Christopher said, "the Fading grows stronger, and soon it will consume the land regardless if we find this last trinket or not. It's only a matter of time."

"Why would the Sovereign want this?" Avery asked. "Why would he want the Fading to destroy everything in the world, including himself? It makes no sense!"

Christopher sneered "Oh, you still don't know, do you? It was not the Sovereign's plan to destroy this world with the Fading. No, that plan came from another. We are simply pawns in a greater game, he and I. We both serve a greater power. It is *his* will that brings the Fading upon Meridia."

Avery pondered a moment before the realization hit her.

"It can't be," Avery said. "That's impossible."

Christopher smirked.

"You lie!" Avery said. "The Creator would never destroy his own world!"

"Do I lie?" Christopher turned to the sphinx. "Tell her. Tell her this one last fact before you die."

The sphinx glared at Christopher, then lowered his gaze toward the floor.

Christopher grinned. He marched toward the glass box containing the sphinx. "You know what happens next. There is no sense in destroying the world if you don't destroy its records. Or its record keeper."

Christopher spun to face his army. "Burn this cavern to the ground and bring me the beast's head!"

The soldiers shifted their pikes forward.

But Avery did not wait for them to attack. Instead, she raced toward Christopher with her sword raised high. She leapt into the air, pointing the tip right toward his head.

Christopher waved his hand in the air, forming an electrical sphere around his body. Avery crashed into the shield with a sharp crackle and fell unconscious to the floor below.

At that moment, a platoon of fifty soldiers broke ranks and rushed toward the glass box. Meanwhile, the remaining soldiers scurried toward the perimeter of the cavern, lighting torches and setting the walls and columns aflame. The smell of burning pages, ink, and glue filled the air as everything blazed a brilliant orange.

Christopher stared at Avery as she lay on the floor, his blackened veins distending throughout his body. He turned to where her companions lay, helpless. Christopher lowered his shield and stepped between their trembling old bodies. "All of you will perish today. But not before the Sphinx of Fact."

The soldiers surrounding the sphinx's glass box bashed into it with the blunt ends of their pikes. The dragonwoofs, in an attempt to stop the soldiers, nipped at their heels as they scurried between the soldier's thick iron boots. The iron-clad soldiers paid the dragonwoofs little mind, however, and continued hammering at the glass as the sphinx anxiously paced from one end to the other. Soon, cracks formed.

Soldiers on one end of the glass box managed to create a hole big enough for two of them to squeeze into. As they climbed into the box, the sphinx attacked them, decapitating one with his teeth and ripping the other into two separate halves with his claws, spraying black blood onto the inner glass walls.

Other soldiers were not as eager to enter. Instead, they continued bashing on the glass in unison, creating a web of cracks from one end of the glass to the other.

The cracks grew deeper and longer. Then the walls shattered to the floor, taking the glass ceiling with them. The soldiers readied their iron pikes as they surrounded the sphinx on all sides, approaching him with trepidation.

The sphinx leapt over the ring of soldiers, landing just outside of it. He mauled the soldiers on the outer edge of the circle, ripping iron plated arms from iron plated torsos. Black blood spilled onto the floor. Chaos ensued, and soon many soldiers ran away from the beast with their arms held high above their heads.

Christopher hunched over Avery and snatched her sword from the ground. He pointed the tip of the blade toward her throat. She awoke, her eyes groggy and unfocused. Christopher sat Avery upright on the ground with his free hand and positioned the white blade, ready to separate her head from her body.

Ben struggled to his feet, his knees shaking. His knees gave out, landing hard on the stone floor. His eyes met Marcus' and Tam's, who also struggled.

But before Christopher could swing the blade, he was hit from above by a burst of flame.

Sebastian flapped his olive-colored wings in the air like a bird, expelling a thin stream of flame from his mouth toward Christopher. Then all three dragonwoofs were in the air, raining fire down on the Iron Pike Army. Some soldiers retreated toward the far corners of the cavern while others flung their spears into the air in an attempt to strike the dragonwoofs. But the dragonwoofs dodged the projectiles with ease and launched more fire into their ranks. Christopher raised his hands, shooting flames of his own as the three dragonwoofs whizzed over his head.

The sphinx continued to fight off the Iron Pike Army soldiers, tearing limbs and heads off one by one. But soon the creature was overpowered by sheer numbers. More and more soldiers circled around him. One stabbed him in his hind leg, and he roared in pain. Another managed to drive his pike into the creature's neck. Soon, the sphinx toppled to the ground as more and more soldiers landed blows.

Christopher laughed giddily as the sphinx collapsed. He turned toward Avery with his arms outstretched, flames forming between his fingertips.

Ben attempted to stand again, his eyes fixed on Christopher. His knees and legs shook uncontrollably, but he used what strength and willpower he had left to stand.

The sphinx turned his head toward Ben. With his dying breath, he spoke. "You have been burdened with age. But with great age, comes great knowledge. With great knowledge, comes great wisdom. With great wisdom, comes great power!"

Ben felt an unbelievable surge of energy course throughout his body. He shut his eyes as warmth traveled under his skin. While the years brought upon him by the sphinx had been unkind to his body, his mind benefited tenfold. It felt as if he had been training in the art of magic for decades. His veins distended and blackened and time seemed to slow to a crawl, his aches and pains replaced by an overwhelming euphoria. Ben could feel a massive force moving from the core of his being, out his arms, and toward his fingertips. Ben knew that if he released a force this great from his body, he would likely die. But he didn't care. He would do anything to save Avery's life, even if it meant sacrificing his own.

Ben pointed his trembling hands at Christopher.

"What do you think you're going to do?" Christopher said, laughing. "I have been honing my magic for over two years! You have been in Meridia for two weeks!"

Ben peered over his shoulder to ensure that Marcus and Tam were safely behind him. He glanced at Avery and motioned her toward Christopher with a single nod of his head. She looked back at him, tears streaming from her face. She shook her head. "Don't do it," she pleaded.

But it was too late.

An incredible stream of flame launched from Ben's fingertips.

Christopher attempted to summon an electrical shield around his body for protection—but not before Avery ran toward him and embraced him tightly with her arms, ensuring that she was also surrounded by it.

The flames struck the electrical shield with a deafening crack, encompassing it on all sides, burning everything and everyone behind it in flame. The fire stretched across the expanse of the entire chamber, consuming the whole of the Iron Pike Army. Soldiers screamed as the dragonwoofs circled the air overhead, howling in victory.

Christopher screamed, his arms extended outward, using every bit of strength he had left to keep his shield intact. But soon his powers began to wane. Meanwhile, Avery hung onto Christopher tightly as his electrical sphere became smaller and smaller around them.

Finally, the flame ceased shooting from Ben's fingertips and he collapsed to the ground, wisps of smoke curling up from his wrinkled hands.

Christopher retracted his electrical shield, stumbling as he turned to see his entire army had become nothing but charred corpses. He fell to his hands and knees.

Avery snatched her blade from his feet and held it high over his head. "This is for Sebastian and the other automatons."

Christopher laughed. "You finally get your revenge, Queen Regent."

Avery flinched. "Revenge?" At that moment, she thought of a yellow mailbox. She remembered a girl straddling her chest as she lay on the ground. "This is revenge," the girl said. "Revenge for going to the dance and humiliating me in front of everyone."

Avery rested her sword by her side. "I won't take your pathetic life."

Christopher grinned and reached into one of his pouches.

Avery turned around to see Ben collapsed on the floor. "Ben!"

She started to race toward him, but heard something behind her.

She spun around, sword in hand.

Christopher ran into the tip of the white sword with his chest, painting the blade a brilliant, bright red.

In his grip was an iron dagger, hovering mere inches from Avery's face. It dropped to the floor with a clatter.

She released her fingertips from the hilt, then stumbled backward, her eyes wide. She cupped her face in her hands, unable to comprehend what she had done.

She had just killed another weed.

Avery dropped to her knees, sobbing.

But the flames grew hotter.

She raced toward Ben, her bare feet moving over the stone floor as the book walls and columns burned. The three dragonwoofs trailed behind her, inches from her heels.

When she neared Ben, she noticed he had turned back into his young self.

Wolf raced toward Ben and pounced on his chest, but Ben was unconscious.

Avery turned to find that Marcus and Tam were also their young selves. "Help me get him out of here!" she said.

Tam flung Ben over his shoulder.

Marcus approached the body of the sphinx as it lay near the shattered glass box, blood seeping from his multiple stab wounds.

He crouched near the beast's large head, petting it lightly with his fingertips, then noticed a blue object lodged underneath his body and pulled it out. On the cover were the words "*The Sphinx's Head: A History of Meridia.*"

The fire grew, turning the room into an inferno. "This place will burn to the ground any moment," Tam said. "We have to get out of here!"

Tam carried Ben across the burning cavern as Avery and Marcus followed.

They stood underneath the entrance high above. Soon, they began to rise into the air toward the portal.

Once on the surface, Tam lay Ben face up on the sand. Avery knelt beside him, but Ben did not move. His eyes remained shut and his chest did not rise.

"You saved me." Tears streamed down her face.

Marcus touched Avery's shoulder. "He sacrificed himself for all of us."

Avery wiped the tears from her eyes. She leaned over and kissed Ben on his forehead.

Ben's eyes sprang open. "Am I dead?"

"No!" Avery said, tears running down her face. "You're not dead! You're not dead at all!"

Marcus ran toward Ben. "Thought we lost you there, buddy!"

Even Tam smiled.

Marcus handed the book over to Avery and Ben. They opened it. On the white parchment was a single riddle: "What lies behind the door with a two, a three, and a seven, where guests wish for hello, not goodbye, where the only key required is the face of a ticking clock."

CHAPTER 22

The Coma Ward

The short, metal bench with olive-colored vinyl cushions had likely been purchased by the hospital for the sole purpose of clashing with the pastel-green walls. Ben had already been sitting there for an hour and seven minutes when Ellen, one of the nurses who worked closely with Mom, approached him. She was a short, portly woman with a jolly smile.

"Hey, Benjamin" she said, adjusting her pink scrubs. "Your mom is going to be another thirty minutes. She got pulled into another exam. Everything cool here?"

"Everything's, um, cool here," Ben said.

Ellen smiled and bustled down the corridor.

Ben riffled through the gift bag at his feet, even though he knew that the contents had not changed since he'd last checked five minutes ago. He found the same wooden name-for-a-desk and the same birthday card as before.

Mom had already worked a double today. If she worked any longer, she would be clocking a triple. Ben promised himself that if he ever became successful, he would make sure she never had to work again.

Unfortunately, his prospects of success were already waning. He had been suspended for two weeks at school. Normally, not having to go to school would have been a celebration. But suspension was more boring than he had anticipated. Besides, he at least wanted the opportunity to explain to Taylor why he was forced to stand her up at the dance.

Soon, another thirty minutes had passed, and he found himself fighting to stay awake. His head bobbed up and down as his eyelids became heavier and heavier.

He awoke to find a familiar gray cat at the other end of the hallway, staring at him. "Finny?"

Finny rose and disappeared down the hallway under the dying light of a flickering fluorescent bulb.

Ben stood and ran down the hallway after his cat.

Soon, he found himself enveloped in complete darkness. The only thing visible was a distant, flickering strobe. He moved toward the light.

A door slid open beside him with a shrill ring, revealing close walls and a well-lit square of tile. An elevator.

He entered the tiny space just as the doors slapped shut behind him. He looked up and down the walls, but there was no control panel.

The elevator dropped sharply for several stories, then slid open, revealing another dark hallway. Ben exited the elevator to find Finny, purring softly.

"Finny?"

But Finny spun around and scurried in the opposite direction. Ben chased after him, careful to avoid the toppled wheelchairs and IV bag holders that lined both sides of the hallway. The lights flickered overhead, creating a disorienting strobe. He timed his movement with the flashing light so that he wouldn't run into anything.

He spotted a soft, white light emanating from a room at the far end. This particular light was inviting and didn't flicker like the others.

He entered. Standing at the center was a young boy, around thirteen years of age, wearing a freshly laundered hospital gown. He smiled at Ben, his black hair hovering over his pale forehead.

Where had he seen this boy before?

Then, he remembered the same boy peering at him high above from a window of a white citadel at the center of the sea.

"You're the Creator, aren't you?" Ben asked.

But the boy did not answer.

"We've been trying to find you. Me, Avery, Marcus, and Tam."

Again, the boy did not answer. Instead, he turned away.

"Is it true that you created the Fading? Why would you want to destroy everything and everyone you helped create?"

Finny entered the room and approached the boy. The boy crouched down and picked up the cat. He turned and faced Ben again.

The boy spoke calmly. "I have a question of my own. How does one escape a cell where the captor never leaves his post to eat or sleep?"

"What?" Ben asked.

"What may seem like a world to some has become a prison for others. When the bells toll at the tower, the bells will no longer toll in our ear. Only then will we be free."

The boy placed Finny on the ground.

"The reach of the Fading has grown since you left," the boy said. "The sickness spreads from within. There is little time left. Find me here, but don't look for me there."

"Find you here?" Ben asked. "Do you mean the hospital?"

"Find me behind the door with a two, a three, and a seven, where guests wish for hello, not goodbye, where the only key required is the face of a ticking clock."

Ben flinched. "The sphinx's riddle?"

"Find me here but do not look for me there," the boy repeated.

Suddenly, there was a loud crash.

Ben awoke, finding himself back on the small metal bench.

Strewn across the floor were prescription bottles and inhalers in tiny cardboard boxes. Standing in front of him was a skinny girl, about the same age as him, with blonde hair and large glasses. Both her eyes were blackened and she had cuts and scrapes on both arms.

"It's you," she said, her hands trembling.

Ben stared at her. He recognized her, but from where? The more he tried to remember, the more it made his head hurt. But he persisted. Even then, he could only remember bits and pieces. He remembered a forest with a red sky, a glass palace, a tall white citadel, and a massive black tower with a large clock. He remembered walking across vast grassy plains and scaling a mountain with no shoes on.

His headache grew with each fragmented memory.

He remembered an inn at the base of a mountain and a large cavern filled with books. He remembered a massive beast pacing back and forth inside an enormous glass box.

The pain was sharp and throbbing.

"Are you okay?" the girl asked.

"Yes," Ben lied.

He pressed his fingers deep into his temples. Finally, the pain subsided. He remembered the open sea. He remembered the crashing waves. He remembered the ocean breeze blowing the girl's hair back, revealing large brown eyes. Then, he remembered calm seas with a glass-like surface. He remembered the moon illuminating the girl's skin with a soft blue glow. He remembered the girl smiling back at him. Was he dreaming?

"A-Avery?"

"Yes!" she said. "Ben?"

"Ben stood up from the bench, almost tripping over a rogue prescription bottle.

Avery lunged forward, hugging Ben tightly.

"These are mine," she said, indicating the scattered bottles on the floor. "I can be quite clumsy sometimes."

Ben crouched down to help her pick them up. Avery did the same, their eyes meeting halfway.

"It's really you, isn't it?" Avery asked.

Ben plopped the bottles and boxes into her white paper bag.

"What happened to your eye?" Ben asked.

"It's a long story," Avery said. "It involves a jealous roommate and a goat."

Ben laughed. "Really?"

Avery adjusted her glasses and pulled her matted hair. "Sorry, if I knew I was going to run into you, I would have dressed the part."

"You look amazing," Ben said.

Avery laughed. "I . . . I'm supposed to meet Mrs. Dewey in the waiting room."

Ben looked her in the eyes. "Do you want to come see something with me first?"

* * *

They stood in front of an elevator.

Ben paused a moment before speaking his thoughts aloud, "Find me behind the door with a two, a three, and a seven, where guests wish for hello, not goodbye, where the only key required is the face of a ticking clock."

Avery furrowed her brow. "What are you talking about?"

"It's the sphinx's riddle," Ben said. "Remember from the book?"

"I think so."

Ben stared at the ground. "I saw a boy in a dream. He said the same words to me."

"Who did what now?"

But Ben did not answer.

Avery began murmuring to herself. "The two, the three, and seven is most likely a room number."

"I agree."

"Where guests wish for hello, not goodbye," Avery added.

Ben scratched his head. "Where would you wish for hello, not goodbye?"

Avery paused. "You don't think the riddle is referring to the coma ward, do you?"

"It could be. But what about the rest of the riddle? What about the part about a key being a face of a clock or something?"

Avery shrugged. "Where the only key required is the face of a ticking clock?"

Only a moment had passed before they both yelled, "Visiting hours!"

Ben pushed the button to call the elevator. The doors closed and the elevator hummed to life. Soon, they were dropping.

When the elevator stopped and the doors squealed open, Ben almost expected the hallway to be filled with darkness.

Instead, the hallway was well-lit and had the same pastel-green walls and the same white-and-green checkered floors that he had seen on the fifth floor.

They exited the elevator, stopping in front of a sheet of paper that had been taped to an easel. Imprinted on it were the words: "Coma Ward: Visitation Hours Are Strictly Enforced."

Avery raced down the corridor.

Ben chased after her.

"Visiting hours are only open for the next ten minutes," she yelled back at him.

Ben watched the room numbers pass by.

231.

233.

235.

She stopped just short of 237, causing Ben to crash into her.

In front of her was a red door.

As they neared it, Ben could hear light sobbing on the other side.

They opened the red door.

Inside, a boy lay on a mechanical hospital bed. All manner of machines and tubes protruded from his body. He looked to be about Ben and Avery's age.

A shrill, repeating beep came from a machine near the bed.

But it wasn't until Ben neared the bed to get a closer look, that he realized he was staring at the same boy from his dream.

"Who is he?" Avery asked.

But before Ben could answer, a woman cleared her throat from the shadowy corner of the room. "Are you his friends?" The woman wiped fresh tears from her eyes. "I'm glad he has friends who care enough to visit. I'm Annabelle."

Avery stepped forward. "I'm Avery, and this is Ben."

"How do you know my boy?"

"We don't—" Ben said.

"He's our friend," Avery said. "From school."

"Did you also know the boys who did this to him?" Annabelle asked. "The ones who called him names and painted our mailbox yellow?"

Ben flinched. "What?"

"They painted your mailbox yellow?" Avery asked.

Annabelle rubbed her eyes. "They bullied him, you know. They bullied him into jumping off that overpass. They knew what would happen to him."

"I'm sorry," Avery said, a tear now streaming down her face.

"Affluenza," Annabelle said. "That's what the lawyer calls it. The boys who did this won't face any charges. Their lawyers say it was Jason's choice in the end. No one put a gun to his head, they said. But I know better. They pushed him. They pushed him until he couldn't take it anymore. His so-called friends."

"Will he be okay?" Ben asked.

Annabelle shook her head. "The doctors say that he may never wake up. But as long as I can see the lines moving on that machine, I won't give up. Not as long as I can hear the beeps. I'll wait for him to wake up. As long as it takes, I don't care. But the doctors say his brain activity is slowing down. If it stops completely, it won't be in my hands any longer. It'll be at the mercy of the hospital and insurance. They'll pull the plug. I won't have a choice."

"The Fading," Ben muttered.

Avery heard him. She neared the bed and stared at Jason.

"I'm sorry for what happened," Ben said to Annabelle.

"Bless you," Annabelle said. "Bless you for coming, but I want some more time alone with Jason, if you don't mind."

Avery grabbed Ben by his shoulders as they left the room. "That was him, wasn't it?"

Neither of them said a word as they took the elevator to the fifth floor. They walked toward the waiting area. After turning a corner, they could hear a doctor speaking to a patient in a nearby examination room.

"You have to take baby steps," the doctor said. "You can't run a marathon without running a mile first!"

"Okay," a voice said. "But I ain't gonna stop running!"

"Baby steps first, Mr. Cooper. I don't want to see you here again for another sprained ankle!"

The patient exited the room right in front of Ben and Avery. He was a large boy about thirteen years old with black skin and short curly black hair. He wore basketball shorts and a T-shirt, and had a bandage wrapped taut around his left ankle. He looked up at Ben and Avery a millisecond, then dropped a bundle of elastic bandages onto the floor.

"Crap balls!" he said.

* * *

There was a jingle and a jangle before the door opened, revealing a dark room. The scent of dust filled the air. Ben entered the small space, clutching an array of different colored keys in varying sizes hanging from an oversized metal ring. Avery and Marcus followed him with trepidation.

"I'm supposed to meet Mrs. Dewey in the waiting room!" Avery said.

"Shut the door behind you," Ben said.

"Did you steal those keys?" Avery asked.

"No. My mom works here. I'm just borrowing them."

Marcus shut the door behind them just as Ben yanked a rusted beaded cord above his head, dousing the room in a dirty yellow light. A single bulb swung back and forth from a fissure in the concrete ceiling, sending shadows crawling in each corner. The room was small and filled with a hodgepodge of shelves of varying heights, colors, and materials. Some shelves held old faded blankets and linens that had yellowed over time. Others contained old plastic bins and bedpans. Mop buckets populated the dark corners.

Ben dashed toward a shelf, grabbing an armful of blankets.

"Lock that door," Ben said to Marcus as he dumped the bundle of blankets and sheets on the floor.

Marcus locked the door behind them with a loud *click*. Ben dropped down on all fours and spread the blankets across the floor between the metal shelves.

"So, let's get down to it," Marcus said. "What exactly did he say to you?"

Ben struggled to remember. "He said something about being sick."

"We knew that already," Avery said. "That's why we went halfway across Meridia to find the sphinx's head in the first place."

Ben stared at the ceiling. "He also said something about being a prisoner or something."

"Whose prisoner?" Marcus asked. "The Sovereign's?"

"He didn't say."

What else did he say?" Avery asked.

"He mentioned something about if the bells toll in the tower, the bells will stop tolling in his ear."

"That makes zero sense," Avery said. "How can bells in a tower keep bells from tolling in your ear? Are you sure you heard him right?"

Ben shrugged. "Pretty sure."

"Well, there's one way to get the right answers," Marcus said. "We go back there and ask him the right questions."

"So, we just show up to the citadel unannounced?" Avery asked. "Need I remind you that didn't work out too well for us last time."

"This time, we have something he needs," Ben said. "We have the book."

Avery paused, staring at the blankets under her restless legs. "There's a problem. All this excitement . . . I'm not tired at all. I don't think I could go to sleep right now even if I tried."

Ben produced a bottle of unopened cough syrup from his front pocket"

Avery grabbed the bottle. "Where did you get this?"

"I grabbed it from a crash cart in the hallway," Ben said. "Cold medicine always makes me tired; I figured it could help us sleep."

"It makes me sleepy too," Avery said. She opened the cap and sniffed the contents. "It smells like an old shoe." She reluctantly took a sip. "Ugh! This stuff is weapons-grade. It tastes terrible!"

She handed the bottle to Ben.

Ben stared at the bottle before taking a sip. The syrup slid down the back of his throat like a slug down the side of a stucco wall. "Ackkk! You aren't kidding!"

Avery sat down on the blankets. She began to sway back and forth softly, her eyelids becoming heavier with each passing moment.

Ben attempted to pass the bottle to Marcus, but Marcus was already sound asleep on the blankets with no assistance whatsoever.

When he turned toward Avery to tell her, she, too, had already fallen asleep.

Soon, Ben felt his own legs crumpling under his weight. As his head hit the blanket, he wondered if it would have been a good idea to kill the light in the supply room before they fell asleep.

CHAPTER 23

Return to the Creator's Citadel at the Center of the Sea

B en could feel the sickness brewing from the deepest pit of his stomach. It spread into his arms and legs and soon his body was covered in a cold sweat. His veins pulsed under his skin. If only he could release the magic from his fingertips one more time, maybe the sickness would be released with it.

Ben held his head over the green water as it sped by below him. He had already vomited five times. Even though there was nothing left in his stomach, the urge to vomit did not stop.

Avery patted him softly on the back. "There, there. The sickness will go away. I promise."

But Ben could barely hear Avery's words. Instead, he heard the voices in his head.

Release the magic
Release it now and all will be better.
Release it.

Release the magic before it's too late.

Ben held his fingertips out over the moving water. He could feel the warmth building beneath his skin.

"No!" He yanked his hands back to his side.

Ben's muscles clenched up and he struggled to move. He vomited again and collapsed on the raft, then stared blankly at the sky as it cycled from day to night and back once more.

* * *

Ben was uncertain how much time had passed before he was able to move again. But once he could, he realized the sickness had all but passed. He was grateful for the care given to him by his friends. Even the three dragonwoofs tried to help by licking his face when the pain became too unbearable.

Ben wondered if the severity of his sickness was a result of the sphinx's aging curse. He had definitely used powers much more powerful than he could have otherwise. But, what if the sickness was this bad each and every time he stopped using magic? Either way, he had no intention of finding out. He promised himself that if he made it through this, he would never use magic again.

The fog hung low over the colorless sea and the sky was oppressed by dark clouds, illuminated by a distant, shrouded sun.

Find me here, but do not look for me there. The Creator's words weighed heavily on Ben as they approached the citadel from the west.

Even with his sickness, the journey via a creaky wooden raft from the Serene Island to the Creator's Citadel was shorter than Ben had expected. Tam had attributed the shorter journey to the Fading, stating that it was "now devouring parts of the sea in its quest to consume all of Meridia." The Creator had told Ben that the Fading had been spreading, but he never figured it was this bad.

Ben took a moment to stare at his wristwatch. Suddenly, the minute hand moved! He blinked in shock. But upon further examination, he found the minute and the hour hand both pointing at the twelve, the same position they had always pointed to. Had he imagined it?

"I think it's safe to say you have the last trinket in Meridia," Marcus said. "You better keep it close."

Ben traced his fingers around the solid band. "Not like I have much of a choice."

Then the raft came to a halt.

"We're here," Tam announced.

The gray ocean froth clung to Ben's bare toes with each sopping step across the white marble platform. At the opposite edge, beyond the Creator's Citadel, were the craggy silhouettes of black ships swaying back and forth with the ebb and flow of the gentle tide. No doubt the ships were now abandoned, a remnant of the Iron Pike Army who lay dead deep within the lair of the sphinx.

The citadel loomed directly overhead. What once was a beacon of hope at the center of the Great Sea now stood a cold, barren structure. The tower appeared lifeless, transformed gray by the dark sky and ocean surrounding it. Its front entrance hung open, the splintered red wood of the tiny door flapping against the frame to and fro as the ocean breeze willed it.

"Why's the door open?" Avery asked. She splashed toward Ben with sodden feet.

Marcus ran up behind them, pressing *The Sphinx's Head* against his chest.

Marcus whistled for the dragonwoofs to follow, but Wolf and Sebastian didn't budge. Rooster stretched his paw from the raft to the marble platform below, but upon touching the cold sea water, he quickly retracted it back to the safety of the raft.

Ben worried that he, Avery, and Marcus would awaken at any moment to find themselves in the small, dank storage room, or worse, be discovered in their hiding place by nosy hospital staff.

But, it was clear that the Fading was spreading faster than ever before. This was their last chance to speak to the Creator before the world was swallowed whole.

Ben caught up to Tam. "What happens to weeds when . . . you know . . . we die?"

"Only dead weeds know the answer to that question," Tam said.

Ben stopped to stare at the sky. The clouds racing overhead reminded him of the sky at the Tower of Continuance.

"When the bells toll in the tower . . ." he said to himself.

Suddenly it hit him. He raced after the others. "Hey guys," he said. "I think I'm starting to understand!"

But no one heard him. Ahead, Avery, Marcus, and Tam crawled through the tiny unguarded doorway of the citadel.

He followed them in.

Goosebumps rose on Ben's arms and he shivered in the sudden cold. Everything, including the walls and floors, was sterile white. Even the air tasted sterile.

Ben looked up. The inside of the tower was hollow all the way up to the ceiling, ten stories above. At the center of the circular chamber sat a pearly throne made of the same white marble as the walls and floors. Standing at almost twenty-five feet high, the base of the throne looked like a pillar of light as it shot upwards from the floor towards the ceiling.

Seated at the very top was a frail boy around thirteen years of age, with pale skin and black hair. His long, skinny fingers grasped the outer edges of the pew; both his legs folded toward the far edge. He stared intently at them with waiting eyes.

Ben caught up to Avery, Marcus, and Tam. The red door fluttered behind him. But that noise was quickly drowned out by a shrill beeping sound that filled the chamber. Repeating over and over, the noise reminded Ben of the life support machine he had seen in the hospital.

"When the bells toll at the tower, the bells will no longer toll in our ear," Ben said to himself again. "When the bells toll at the tower, the bells will no longer toll in our ear. When the bells toll at the tower, the bells . . ."

He attempted to speak up, but the boy on the throne spoke instead. His voice was soft but commanding. "Who dares approach the Great Creator?"

Avery cleared her throat. "Queen Regent Avery, my lord. These are my companions, Marcus and Tamerlane from the Red Forest, and Ben from uhhh—"

"We have gone on a quest for you and brought back *The Sphinx's Head*," Marcus added.

"A quest for me?" the boy asked. "And what should I do with this head of a sphinx?"

"You asked us to find it for you," Avery said.

The boy yawned. "Did I, now?"

"Well," Marcus said. "You didn't ask us directly. Your doorman asked us."

"Doorman?" The boy said. "I do not know of any doorman."

"His name is Sir Reginald," Avery added. "He answered the door when we were last here at the citadel."

The boy sighed. "Can't you see my door is broken? Why would I have use for a doorman? Perhaps you confused my door with the many other red doors in Meridia."

"Something's not right here," Marcus whispered.

Avery stepped forward. "At any rate, we have *The Sphinx's Head* with us now. The doorman said you were ill and that it would cure your sickness."

This piqued the boy's interest and he leaned forward in his throne. "Did he say that? This so-called doorman. Is that exactly what he said?"

Avery nodded.

"Bring it forward. I would like to see this head of the sphinx with my own eyes."

Marcus stepped forward with the book.

"Wait!" Ben said.

The boy gripped the edge of his throne. "Who are you to interrupt the Creator?"

"I'm Ben. We met in the hospital."

The boy stared at Ben. "I know of no such meeting taking place."

"When the bells toll at the tower, the bells will no longer toll in our ear," Ben said. "That's what you said. I have solved your little riddle. You're not the Creator." Ben paused. "You are the Sovereign!"

Both Avery and Marcus recoiled. Tam nocked an arrow.

The boy squirmed, receding as far back into his seat as the hard marble surface would allow. His eyes narrowed.

"You created the Fading to destroy Meridia and everything in it, didn't you?" Ben asked. "You built the Tower of Continuance to control the speed of time so that the Fading would spread faster! You aimed to erase the Creator's thoughts so that the doctors would pull the plug on his life support. That's what you meant by stopping the bells in his ear, didn't you? You seek to murder the Creator!"

The boy clapped slowly. With a flick of his wrist, the book jumped from Marcus's arms straight up into the air and onto his lap. He turned the pages. "This does not look like the head of a sphinx to me. I'd expect it to be far bloodier with two eyes and a snout."

"I only have one question for you," Ben said. "What's in it for you?"

The boy continued to flip through the thick pages. He pondered a moment, then lifted his gaze back at them.

The boy spoke. "It's all here in this book. Didn't you bother to read it? No? Well, allow me to summarize. At the start, the Creator made this world and everything in it so that he would have something to do while he slept. You see, the Creator had somehow fallen into a long slumber—one he could not awaken from.

"The coma," Ben said.

"The ageless sleep," the Sovereign said. "And while he slept he dreamt of the trees, he dreamt of the mountains, he dreamt of the deserts, and he dreamt of the sea. He dreamt of the disappearing and reappearing sun, the moon, and the stars. He dreamt of the faeries, the Boarmin, the porcelain people, the wolfbats, and even the translucent elves. Then, after he had created and built everything he could dream of, he invited other weeds to partake in his creation—to frolic in his playground, if you will. He watched them play from afar in his white citadel in the middle of the sea. You see, he only intended to watch you until he woke up. But he never woke up, did he? No, he just kept dreaming and dreaming. Day after day and night after night he toiled with his creation. But like anything, boredom and monotony set in. Soon, his creation became his prison. That is when I came into the picture. That is when I convinced him he would never wake up. You see, the Creator is weak. I, however, am strong. I will do what it takes to be free, even if it means the ultimate sacrifice. I have the strength to do what must be done whereas he only has weakness!"

The Sovereign pointed his fingers at the ground near them. A pillar of searing-hot flame erupted straight into the air.

The Sovereign tossed the book into the center of the fire. The pages crackled and popped as they burned. A pillar of black smoke spiraled into the air and the stench burning pages permeated the hollow tower.

"To destroy a world, you must first destroy its records," the Sovereign said.

"What have you done to the Creator?" Ben yelled. "Where is he?"

"You still don't get it, do you?" the Sovereign asked. "I am the Creator. I always have been. We are one and the same!"

"You lie!" Marcus said.

The boy laughed, "One side of the Creator represents hope and happiness. One side represents anger and boredom. It was only a matter of time before I was able to completely take over. The Creator, as you know him, is dead!"

With a flick of his wrist, he encased both Ben and Avery in a massive block of clear ice. Frantic, Avery pounded on the inner walls with her open palms. Ben did the same, but the ice was too thick to break. With another flick of the Sovereign's wrist, the cube of ice trapping them began to rise into the air, and soon, Avery and Ben hovered high above the ground. The temperature inside the cube dropped, raising the hair on both of Ben and Avery's arms and legs. Their bare feet curled over the icy floor below them.

Tam released his arrow at the Sovereign, the fletching screaming as it took flight.

But the Sovereign held out his palm, causing the projectile to career around the throne completely, striking the chamber wall far behind him.

Tam nocked another arrow and aimed it at the Sovereign. The boy flicked his wrist in Tam's direction, but Tam rolled out of the way just as a cube of ice began to form around him. The cube materialized, empty, then shattered to the ground next to him.

Tam released his arrow into the air. It flew toward the Sovereign with a sharp zip. The boy waved his hand, forcing the arrow to veer away from him. It landed with a thump, piercing the backing of the throne just a few inches from his head. Angered, the boy flicked his wrist again, attempting to trap the elf in yet another block of ice.

But just as he extended his fingers in Tam's direction, an arrow slammed straight through his palm from below. Black blood sprang from his wound and the Sovereign howled in pain. He peered down below to find Marcus nocking a replacement arrow.

The Sovereign turned his gaze toward the top of the tower and thrust his arms high above his head.

Deafening thunder emanated from the ceiling high above, followed by a loud crack. Creeping, drab daylight poured down crumbling tower walls high above. The Sovereign grinned as the skylight illuminated his throne.

A moment later, huge slabs of marble fell from the ceiling and walls. Tam and Marcus dodged left and right as the slabs crashed around them. From inside the cube, Avery held Ben tightly as several pieces slammed into the ice around them, tilting their icy prison as they hovered high in the air.

Tam and Marcus dove behind a large slab of newly landed marble, using it as makeshift cover.

Once the dust had settled, Tam shouted at the Sovereign, "You cannot create, you can only destroy!"

The Sovereign clenched his teeth. "The Fading serves a greater purpose than you will ever understand. It is my crowning creation. Perfect in almost every way. Soon you and your wretched friends will all perish!"

"No!" Marcus said from behind the marble slab. He shot another arrow at the Sovereign. But the Sovereign placed his good hand in front of him, forcing the arrow to divert its course yet again. He plunged his arms into the air, causing the tower to crumble further. More slabs fell to the floor from above, just missing Marcus and Tam.

"Your heroics bore me," the Sovereign said. "Let's raise the stakes."

With a snap of his wrist, he moved Ben and Avery's cube of ice over the blazing column of fire he had used to burn the book. Flames crawled up the cube on all four sides causing the inner and outer walls to sweat.

Meanwhile, Marcus and Tam slipped between the marble slabs and debris in an attempt to flank the throne.

"How dare you say that I do not know how to create," the Sovereign said. "I designed the magic cube with the perfect thickness—the insides will fill up with water, drowning you, before the outer edges are melted completely through. You will die long before your cold, wet bodies spill out!"

Ben pressed his hands against the ice, but nothing happened.

The Sovereign grinned. "Your magic is useless here, weed."

An arrow screamed past the Sovereign's face, just missing him. The Sovereign turned to Marcus. Marcus ducked behind the slab of marble and nocked a new arrow.

The Sovereign lifted his uninjured palm into the air, forcing the massive marble slab to lift off the ground. "You think you can hide from me?" He flipped his fingers upwards as the slab and accompanying debris rose at least thirty feet into the air.

Marcus, completely exposed, stood alone, aiming an arrow at the Sovereign from the ground below.

He took the shot.

But the Sovereign held out his free hand, forcing the arrow to miss its intended mark again. He chuckled, then realized something wasn't right. "Wait," he said. "Where's the elf?"

Another arrow came from high above, slamming into the Sovereign's good hand, pinning it against the rear of the white marble throne. He looked up to find Tam perched atop the levitating slab.

"Take him out!" Tam yelled at Marcus below.

Marcus nodded. He had already nocked his last arrow.

The Sovereign now turned to Marcus. His eyes widened in fear as Marcus assumed a perfect stance and slowly aimed the arrow at him from the ground below.

"You can do it, Marcus!" Avery yelled from the floating ice above. The cube was now half-full of water and quickly filling as the ice melted around her. Ben echoed her words as the water reached his chest.

Marcus took a deep breath and exhaled. "Boom, headshot," he said.

Then Marcus, along with his bow and arrow, dropped unconscious to the floor.

Marcus awoke to the sounds of pounding fists and the sharp rattling of a doorknob. He spun around quickly to assess his surroundings. It took a few moments for him to regain his composure and recall why he had locked himself in this cramped supply room to begin with. He peered down near his feet to find Avery and Ben curled up and asleep on the sheets and blankets below. He heard a gruff voice from outside the door. "Is someone in there?" The question was followed by more pounding and the rattling of the doorknob.

"I can see a light underneath the door!" a female voice said.

Marcus dragged Ben toward the far corner of the room, beyond the reach of the overhead light. Despite all the jerking and the pulling, Ben did not wake up from his slumber. Nor did Avery when Marcus pulled her toward the corner in a similar manner. What was in that cough syrup, anyway?

"I'm going to buy you guys some time," Marcus whispered. "Make it count!"

Suddenly, he heard the jangling of keys just outside.

"Are you sure that's the right key?" a female voice said.

"Yes," a male voice said. "This has every key."

"Good. Someone forgot to stock bedpans in the main storage room and these patients won't stop peeing!"

Marcus scampered to where the sheets had been spread onto the floor and bundled them into a ball. He raced back to the far corner of the room and draped them over Ben and Avery. He turned back to find the key ring Ben had taken earlier sitting on the middle of the floor. Marcus raced toward the keys, but before he could snatch them up, the door flew open revealing a short, portly lady with pink scrubs. Her nametag read "Ellen."

Behind her was a tall, lanky man in dark blue coveralls. He wore an oversized tool belt containing all manner of spray bottles and sported a fairly robust, albeit well-groomed, mustache.

Marcus shuffled forward, standing in front of the keys so they couldn't see them.

"What are you doing in here?" Ellen asked. "This room is off limits to patients!"

A bead of sweat rolled down Marcus's forehead and splashed onto the soiled concrete below. "*Dónde está el baño?*" he said. "*Me pis mis pantalones!*"

Ellen stared at Marcus blankly, then turned toward the Janitor. "What did he just say?"

The janitor shrugged. "How would I know?"

"Aren't you Mexican?"

"My parents are Mexican. I'm from New Jersey!"

Ellen sighed, then turned her attention back to Marcus. "Where are your parents? *El family?*"

Avery moaned from the back corner of the room.

"What was that?" Ellen asked as she peered into the dark corner with suspicion. "I thought I heard something."

Marcus kicked the keys under a nearby shelf and clenched his stomach with both his hands and let out a very loud fart.

The nurse jumped into the air.

"*Necessito Pepto Bismol!*" Marcus said.

"Okay, okay," Ellen said. "Does your stomach hurt?"

"*Mi gato es verde!*"

"Wait a minute," the janitor said. "This kid is African-American. Why is he speaking Spanish?"

"Maybe he's from Rio de Janeiro," Ellen said.

"They speak Portuguese over there, don't they?"

"I think you're thinking of Portugal."

"*Mis pantalones son muy grandes!*" Marcus said.

"Well, either way, we need to find this boy's parents before they start asking a bunch of questions," Ellen said. "I don't think the hospital can survive another lawsuit!"

"Come with us, kid," the janitor said. "We'll help you find your parents."

"*Mi perro es intelligente!*" Marcus said.

Escorted by the two hospital staff members, Marcus left the supply room. The janitor peered into the room suspiciously and locked the door behind them.

* * *

The Sovereign growled with glee as Tam and Marcus, both trapped in a large cube of ice of their own, levitated high above the shattered marble floor. Bits of debris and dust fell from the sky overhead. High above, the upper walls of the tower were completely destroyed, revealing the gray clouds racing overhead.

Tam tried to wake Marcus from his slumber, but his efforts were futile.

The Sovereign sat upon his throne. "Who would create such a despicable species?" he said to Tamerlane. "Elves are only good for one thing: battle. Normally, I would appreciate that quality. But I'm tired of your insolence!"

With a flick of his wrist, a new ring of fire materialized on the floor below. He moved the cube containing Tam and Marcus directly over the flames. The fire licked the sides of the ice, and soon water began filling the hollow cube from inside.

Tam propped Marcus up against the back wall. He checked both his quiver and Marcus's only to find them empty. He pulled a dagger from his belt and began scraping at the ice walls from inside, snapping the blade from the hilt. Defeated, he sat down on the pooling floor next to Marcus. "This is it for us, my brother. I don't see a way out."

Meanwhile, in Ben and Avery's cube, the fluid inside was now at least three-quarters full, allowing enough room for their heads above the waterline. Gasping, Avery grabbed onto Ben's pajamas. "What do we do?"

"I don't know," Ben said.

"You have to think of something! We're going to die!"

Ben took a deep breath and turned toward the Sovereign. "Jason. That's your name, right?"

The boy looked at Ben suspiciously.

Ben continued, "We met your mother, Annabelle."

The Sovereign, slightly alarmed, beckoned Ben and Avery with his fingertips, pulling the floating cube directly in front of him. The water sloshed around in the cube, submerging both Ben and Avery before settling.

The boy stared through the clear ice into Ben's eyes. "You lie!"

"No. We spoke to her."

The Sovereign gazed upon Ben and Avery, his fingers tapping the throne.

"She misses you, Jason," Ben said. "She misses you more than anything!"

For a split moment, Ben could almost see a tear materialize in the corner of the boy's eye. But then the boy scowled. "You are mistaken. The mother I knew did not protect me. The mother I knew would not miss me!"

Suddenly, deafening thunder filled the sky. Ben peered toward the top of the tower to find a bright light descending. Was the sun crawling toward them?

The Sovereign grinned. "The Fading spreads faster than ever before. One trinket remains in Meridia. One trinket keeps it from spreading across the land in a blink of an eye. But even then, the Fading persists. Any moment now, it will consume everything and everyone in Meridia. The bells at the Tower of Continuance will toll, and the Fading will vanquish all of creation."

As the light crawled further down the sides of the tower, Ben could hear the faint sound of bells tolling in the distance.

"It's happening," the Sovereign said. "You have lost everything."

A blinding light surrounded them, moving closer and closer, tighter and tighter. Soon, everything around them—the walls, the sky, the floor, and even the Sovereign—was consumed in blinding white light. Ben peered at the other floating cube to see both Tam and Marcus disappear into the light. The light squeezed tighter around them, and soon only Ben and Avery were left.

Ben and Avery threw their arms around each other.

Ben shut his eyes and braced for impact as the light inched nearer.

The light roared and crackled.

Then everything was silent.

Ben opened his eyes to find himself still trapped in the cube, Avery clutching him tightly. He peered to his left to find Marcus and Tam floating in the cube beside them. He looked straight ahead to find the Sovereign still seated on his giant throne, in complete shock.

"The Fading," the Sovereign said. "What did you do?"

The watch around Ben's wrist glowed faintly.

"It can't be!" the Sovereign said, finally noticing the trinket. "It was here this entire time?"

"It wasn't true what you said earlier," Ben said. "About your mother, I mean. She waits for you in the hospital every day. She waits at your bedside in hopes that you wake up."

The shrill repeating beep filled the citadel chamber, louder than before.

"You need to wake up, Jason!" Ben said.

The Sovereign lowered his hands as tears formed in his eyes. His scowl melted into a frown.

Ben peered into the boy's eyes. Something was different.

"Tell my mom I love her," Jason said. "Tell her the next time you see her."

"Why not wake up and tell her yourself?" Ben asked.

Jason shook his head. "I can't wake up. I've tried again and again. Now *he* has taken over."

"The Sovereign?" Ben asked.

Again, Jason nodded.

"The Sovereign is a manifestation of my grief and anger. Once, I was able to control him, but soon, he controlled me. He'll be back any moment. I will use what power I have left to free you from his icy prisons, but you must do something for me in return."

"What?" Ben asked.

"You must kill him."

"But doesn't that mean you'll die too?" Avery asked.

"There's no time left," Jason said. "He's coming."

With that, Jason dropped both cubes onto the floor, shattering the ice around them. Water gushed around Ben and Avery onto the floor. They fell to their knees, taking in huge gulps of air. Tam and Marcus poured out of their respective cube as well. Tam snatched a sliver of ice from the ground and nocked it into his bow and aimed it at the boy.

But Tam was too late. The Sovereign created a new cube of ice around the elf before the ice could even go airborne.

The Sovereign turned to Ben and Avery. Again, he flicked his wrist in their direction encasing them in a new cube of ice. He created a new ring of fire on the floor, larger than before.

He motioned the cubes over the fire, and once again, the cubes began to fill with water from within.

"Your ruse was clever but short lived," the Sovereign said. "Now you will die and I will extract the trinket from your dead body."

Suddenly, a sliver of ice penetrated the Sovereign's chest, piercing his heart. Black blood poured freely from the wound. The Sovereign peered below toward the ground to find Marcus with his bow aimed in his direction. He gasped.

The fire beneath the cubes of ice disappeared without a trace.

Both cubes fell to the floor, shattering into a million pieces, releasing Ben, Avery, and Tam.

A loud crack filled the sky. It sounded like it came from halfway across the world.

The boy slumped over and smiled. "Thank you."

With that, he disappeared.

The Creator's Citadel began to crumble around them.

Ben, Avery, Marcus, and Tam raced toward the tiny exit of the tower as slabs of marble toppled and slammed into the floor on all sides.

They dove through the entrance into the open air, landing on the large marble platform. With a loud thundering snap, the entire citadel collapsed behind them, imploding. Dust and debris filled the air around them, blinding them with massive puffs of white.

The dragonwoofs, Wolf, Rooster, and Sebastian, watched them with blank expressions from the safety of the raft.

Then, the ground beneath them moaned and snapped.

Was the world ending?

The white marble shook beneath their feet and cracked, creating huge fissures immediately filled by the hungry sea as they hurried toward the wooden raft. With each step, the floor disappeared into the ravenous ocean behind them. Ben lunged forward, barely catching the starboard edge with his fingertips. Marcus did the same, then Tam. Avery was not so lucky; she missed the edge of the boat and, instead, sunk toward the dark depths below.

Ben dove after her.

The water was peaceful. There was almost a silent tranquility beneath the deep blue depths as massive slabs of marble sunk slowly into the sea around him. There was a small, glowing object below. Ben swam faster and deeper than he had ever swam before. He reached out toward the glowing white object just as it reached back toward him. He felt fingertips, then a hand and pulled it toward the surface.

He gasped for air as he emerged from the depths below. A moment later, Avery appeared, gasping as well.

Marcus and Tam pulled them onto the raft.

The world did not end. In fact, the ominous racing clouds from before were now still and pierced by white beams of light from the sun. Ben stared at the horizon as the wind blew softly into his face. The light from the sun lit up the sea around them, making it look like molten silver for miles around.

He checked his watch to find the hands travelling slowly around the face. Even though the hands moved, time seemed to slow down around him.

"Why?" Ben asked.

"Why what?" Marcus asked.

"Why are we still here?"

Avery stepped toward the edge of the boat, the wind wrapping her wet hair around her face.

"We stopped the Fading!" Marcus said. "We stopped the Sovereign! We saved the world!"

"You saved us!" Ben said. "How did you get back here so fast?"

"Oh," Marcus said. "Some nurse and some janitor found me hiding in the room. But don't worry! I hid you in the corner. Then I pretended I only knew Spanish. They took me down the hall and made me sit on a bench while they went looking for my quote-unquote parents. Joke's on them though; both my parents are at work! Anyways, I fell asleep on the bench in like two seconds. Now I'm here. Oh, by the way, you're still asleep in that disgusting supply room!"

Avery patted the sides of her tattered white dress in a tiny panic.

Just then, her coin pouch bobbed up to the surface of the water near the raft.

Avery snatched it and unraveled the twine near the top.

She stared into the opening. "They're gone."

"What's gone? Marcus asked.

"The coins. The four hundred and ninety-seven gold coins the general gave me."

"Did you lose them?" Marcus asked.

"It looks that way," Avery said. "But the bag is still tied shut!"

"How can four hundred and ninety-seven coins vanish?" Ben asked.

"There's something inside!" Avery dug deep into the tiny sack. She produced a miniature scroll of paper from the bag, about one inch wide. The paper was wet, but still intact. She gently unrolled the scroll, careful not to tear the delicate paper. The more she unraveled it, the longer it became. Soon, the edge of the paper hit the floor of the raft. Printed on the scroll was the following:

"Greetings weeds (and elf). Thank you very much for making good on your promise to pay me back my 497 coins. I trust that the three dragonwoofs in question have served you well and will continue to do so in the future. Either way, no refunds. Thank you and good luck. Your humble dragonwoof broker, Clemmons."

"The dragonwoof broker?" Ben said.

"How is that possible?" Avery patted down her dress in continued disbelief.

Tam, completely disinterested in the conversation, stood near the edge of the raft, surveying the silver ocean with eager eyes.

Avery stood next to him. "Do you think Char is still out there?"

"I know he is," Tam said.

"We'll find him," Marcus said.

Avery turned toward Ben, the ocean wind running through her hair. "What happens now?"

Ben paused. "We dream."

EPILOGUE 1

Homecoming

The hallway smelled like wet paint and body odor. It was filled to the brim with students. Taylor was talking to Summer near her locker, but Ben didn't care. He walked over and tapped her on the shoulder. "Taylor?"

She turned to face him. "Yeah?"

Ben looked her in the eyes. "Look, I wanted to apologize for not showing up to the dance."

"Oh," Taylor said. "No biggie." She leaned in. "Oh, wait, you didn't think we were going together, did you?"

Ben furrowed his eyebrows. "Actually, yeah."

Taylor laughed. "I only said I'd meet you there, right?"

Summer giggled.

Ben sighed. "Well, either way I just wanted to say I was sorry."

He turned to walk away, but Summer stopped him. "Ben?" she said.

Ben spun around.

Summer's eyes narrowed as she spoke. "The next time a girl says she'll go to the dance with you, maybe you shouldn't blow her off."

"I know," Ben said. "I got suspen—"

"Maybe you don't understand the hierarchy around here," Summer said. "So, I'm going to spell it out for you nice and clear. Girls like *us* don't go to dances with nerds like *you*."

Taylor, uncomfortable, looked away.

Summer continued, "Next time there's a dance, I suggest you stick with your own tragic gene pool."

But then Taylor and Summer's eyes widened in unison.

Ben felt a tap on his shoulder.

He turned to find Avery standing before him. Her hair tumbled over her shoulders and she wore a white top with a plaid skirt and matching knee-length socks. Ben's heart jumped into his throat. She was beautiful.

"Hey Ben," Avery said. "I wanted to ask you a question."

"Yeah, sure."

"Will you go to the homecoming dance with me?"

Ben beamed. "Of course."

Avery grabbed Ben's hand. They walked down the hallway, leaving Taylor and Summer with their mouths open.

"Thanks," Ben said.

"For what?" Avery asked.

"For asking me to the dance."

"You don't need to thank me, silly. I *wanted* to ask you."

Ben paused. "Wait, have you been putting notes in my locker?"

Avery scrunched her face. "What?"

Suddenly, a large boy appeared from around the corner, almost crashing into them.

"Crapballs!" the boy said. "I've been looking everywhere for you two!"

Avery and Ben stared at him in shock. "Marcus?" they exclaimed.

Marcus unfolded a page from a newspaper. "Have you seen this yet?"

The headline read "Local Teen Wakes-Up from Coma After a Year."

"We did it," Marcus said. "We saved him!"

Ben stared at the article in shock. "No way!"

Principal DeMarco appeared from around the corner. "There you are!" He snatched Marcus by the collar. "You don't go to school here!"

"Wait, I can explain," Marcus said. "I know I'm homeschooled right now, but my parents are in the process of enrolling me!"

"You can come back here when they do," DeMarco said.

* * *

Avery watched the houses pass by as the van drove her through the neighborhood. Samuel, the driver, whistled a tune. She looked at the seat behind her, almost expecting Tracy to be there ready with insults. But Tracy had been kicked out of the home for days. Avery looked to her side to find Stephanie snoring. She returned her attention to the window and watched as she passed a house with a yellow mailbox. She smiled.

Mrs. Dewey was waiting in the front yard with Barney when the van dropped Avery off at the group home. She raced toward Avery and hugged her. "They said yes!"

"Who?" Avery asked.

"The Smiths! They're going to adopt you, Avery! You're finally going home!"

EPILOGUE 2

The Painted Canyon

Marissa packed the earth around the stem with a delicate touch, careful to ensure that she did not damage her newest addition: a delicate blue flower with frosted white tips that glowed softly during the night.

She was rather pleased with her collection. She had obtained flowers from all four corners of the continent as a result of her recent expedition. Truth be told, her original reason for traveling had little to do with collecting flowers. Regardless, she had already secured four of the five "things" that she had been tasked with finding. The collecting of flowers simply acted as a nice diversion to the long treks through thick forests, deep swamps, and barren wastelands.

Marissa, content with the state of this particular flower, scanned her greenhouse from end to end. On a sun-filled day, the petals, with their array of colors and patterns, would produce a kaleidoscope of radiant blues, greens, yellows, oranges, whites, blacks, and reds. But today, the sun was dull and its light strained to even penetrate the clouds above. Fortunately, the glass walls and arched glass ceilings had done a superb job of trapping the sun's heat and keeping out the sharp winds that often invaded the Painted Canyon.

A small irrigation ditch ran through the soil from one end of the greenhouse to the other, supplying fresh water to the flowers from an outside stream. The water reflected Marissa's cold blue eyes. She shut them to focus on the tranquility of her greenhouse, surrounding herself with the sounds of blissful silence and trickling water.

Someone cleared his throat behind her. Marissa turned around to find her commanding officer standing at the entrance of the greenhouse. Colonel Gobea wore fitted crimson-red armor from head to toe that had been fashioned from lava glass. At the center of his breastplate was the golden insignia of a coiled snake.

"What is it?" Marissa asked, unable to hide the annoyance in her voice. She stood, revealing the same lava-glass armor beneath her thick red woolen cloak. Lightweight and malleable, the lava-glass armor afforded her agility and speed without sacrificing its ability to absorb a direct strike. She pushed her long black hair away from her face.

"Apologies, General," he said. "But, word arrives from the citadel. He has summoned you and your army."

"Has he now? And here I was, running trivial errands across the continent for relics while the other generals were free to run amok and conquer the realm. Why summon me now, I wonder? What has prompted this sudden change of heart?"

"Both the Iron Pike Army General and the General of One Thousand Wars are dead."

"At whose hand?" Marissa asked, her lips curling.

"They say three weeds and two survivors of the Elven Genocide are responsible."

"Interesting," Marissa said, her eyes widening. "Two out of three of his generals are dead? This never would have happened if he would have sent me to begin with."

A deafening crack came from outside.

Marissa exited the greenhouse with Gobea in tow. She peered beyond the Painted Canyon at the distant horizon and watched as the Tower of Continuance crumbled to the ground.

"It appears that the Sovereign has fallen, as well," she said.

"What will you do now?" Colonel Gobea asked.

Marissa approached the edge of the ridge and gazed at her troops in the canyon below.

At one thousand strong, the Red Army stood in perfect disciplined formation.

"Prepare the troops and await my command," she said. "We will show the denizens of Meridia what a real army is capable of."

"Yes, my general."

"Mayhap, I will procure some new flowers for my greenhouse. But first, I must rid the garden of weeds."